THE GIRL WITHOUT A CLUE

Ivy Bishop Mystery Thriller
Book 2

ALEX SIGMORE

Dark Woods Press

THE GIRL WITHOUT A CLUE: IVY BISHOP MYSTERY THRILLER BOOK 2

Copyright © 2024 by Alex Sigmore

1st Edition

Print ISBN 978-1-957536-91-0

Description

Secrets Have a Way of Coming Back

Detective Ivy Bishop, fresh from cracking a high-profile case, is haunted by a night she can't remember, with her family gone and her past a blur.

Oakhurst is barely back on its feet after dealing with a serial killer when a new crisis hits: two children and their caretaker have disappeared without a trace or ransom note. Despite her superiors' warnings, Ivy is drawn to the case, convinced it's linked to the night from fifteen years ago that left her wandering the streets, her clothes stained with blood.

Her investigation into the kidnappings uncovers a complex web of lies, deceit, and greed, all pointing ominously back to her. And as she gets closer to understanding the kidnapper's motives, Ivy is faced with a shocking truth that could upend everything she believes about her past.

Caught in a deadly dilemma, Ivy must choose between saving the innocent and confronting a truth that might destroy her.

"The Girl Without A Clue," the second book in the Ivy Bishop Mystery series by Alex Sigmore, is a gripping thriller that explores the shadows of the past and the complexities of uncovering the truth. In a town where secrets run deep, Ivy Bishop's quest for answers will challenge everything she knows about herself and the place she calls home.

Prologue

THE DETECTIVE SAUNTERED around the table, took one sniff of the air before bending down and getting right into the creep's face. "Come on, Iggy. You know something, and unless you want to rot for a long time, you're gonna tell us."

You're gonna tell us, Taylor mouthed along with the detective as she watched on the iPad. She'd already seen this episode five times, but it was one of her favorites and it was right at the best part: when the detective finally gets the drug dealer to flip on his friends, exposing the whole operation.

"Are you watching that show again?" Jessa asked, pulling Taylor out of her trance. She looked up at her older sister.

"Yeah." Taylor had to scrub the video back about ten seconds—Jessa had made her miss the best part.

"Why?" Jessa asked, and Taylor decided to just pause the video so she wouldn't miss it a second time.

"'Cause I like it," Taylor snapped, somewhat annoyed.

"You've been watching that show nonstop for the last week. What's so interesting about it anyway?" Jessa hopped off her bed, headed for Taylor.

"You could watch it too, it's called *Law and Order,*" Taylor replied. Jessa did this sometimes. She'd get bored with whatever she was doing and decide to needle Taylor until she found something more interesting to do. Taylor loved her older sister and they had grown closer ever since the accident, but she could still be a pain in the butt sometimes. Especially when Taylor was trying to concentrate.

"Does it have explosions?" Jessa asked, sitting directly across from Taylor on the floor of their shared bedroom. Jessa's bed bordered up against one side of the room and Taylor's was on the other, which meant they each got one window. Mrs. Baker had offered to give them each their own room when they'd arrived a few months ago, but they'd both declined. Taylor hadn't been sleeping well since the accident and didn't want to be by herself. Jessa had never said why she'd said no too, but Taylor suspected it might have been the same reason. She'd noticed, especially recently, that Jessa acted a lot tougher in public than she did when it was just the two of them. For a while Taylor thought it was because she *was* tougher, but then she'd be like the old Jessa when they were alone. The one time she'd asked Jessa about it, her sister denied it, which made even less sense.

Taylor had always been the kind of person to say and do exactly what she was feeling. When she was scared, she acted scared. And she had been scared a lot lately. Mrs. Baker had tried over and over to get them into the car, even go out for ice cream, but Taylor just couldn't do it. She wasn't sure she'd ever be able to get back into a car again.

She jumped when she looked over to find Jessa had moved to sit right beside her. When had she done that? Taylor must have gotten lost in her head again. Jessa said that's what happened when you were quiet for too long, which Taylor was a lot.

"Don't worry, it's just me," Jessa said, her voice softer.

"I know," Taylor said, trying to hide the fact she'd been startled yet again.

"Lemme see the show," Jessa said, pointing to the iPad.

"It doesn't really have explosions," Taylor admitted. "But sometimes there are car chases." She'd done research and found there were lots of different versions of this show, some as old as forty years. She hadn't gone that far back to watch them; she just liked the one with the female detective in charge. She kind of reminded Taylor of the policewoman who had come to their house last week, except older.

The girls sat side by side and watched the show for a few minutes, but it was still the interrogation scene and Taylor could tell Jessa was getting bored because she wouldn't stop fidgeting. She had always done that ever since they were little. Separated by only a year, they had always had each other, though Jessa sometimes swore she could remember the time before Taylor came along. Their mother used to say that was impossible, that people didn't keep their memories until they were at least three or four years old, but that didn't stop Jessa from insisting. She could be stubborn as an ox, as their dad used to say.

Taylor missed both of them like crazy. There were some days she missed them so much she didn't even want to get out of bed. But at least she still had Jessa. As long as the two of them were together, Taylor hoped everything would be okay. But at the same time, she was very much aware that the world could flip upside down in a second.

After all, it had already happened once.

"Let's watch something else," Taylor finally said after Jessa pulled her leg under her for the third time in under a minute.

"It just seems so…slow," Jessa said. "No huge fight scenes, no racing, no action!"

"It's a different kind of action," Taylor said, closing the video viewer and searching for something she knew would keep Jessa's attention. "You gotta watch the whole thing. You can't just see the end; it doesn't make sense."

"What's to make sense of? There's a bad guy, they catch him. Seems pretty simple to me."

Taylor just rolled her eyes before browsing for another show on the iPad. Mrs. Baker had set up parental controls, so they could only see so much. But they were almost teenagers…well, at least Jessa was, which meant they should get more privileges, right? If Jessa got more privileges, she would no doubt share them with Taylor. She hoped.

"C'mon, let's go spy on Mrs. Baker," Jessa said. "We've been in here all day."

She wasn't wrong. Ever since coming to Mrs. Baker's house, they had to change schools because they were no longer close enough to their old school to take the bus. Which meant they'd left all their friends behind too. And new girls didn't get invited to their new classmates' houses on the weekends. Fitting in since the move had been hard. Everyone at school already knew each other and just having the courage to go up and say "hi" was more than Taylor had been able to muster. Taylor thought that was probably the reason Jessa had softened towards her over the past few months. They only had each other now, and starting in a new school with only Mrs. Baker to come home to was harder than either one of them had expected.

But, Taylor surmised, that's what happened to kids who've lost their parents. She'd overheard one of the social workers say something similar when she had been sitting in the police station with Jessa.

So now they went to school five days a week, and because of Taylor's phobia, their weekends were mostly confined to the house. Strangely, Taylor didn't have a problem getting on and off the school bus. It was just cars, or anything shaped like a car. A bus was a lot bigger, a lot stronger and sturdier.

"C'mon," Jessa said, taking the iPad from Taylor.

She sighed. Maybe if she did this, Jessa would leave her alone long enough that she could finish watching her show.

When they first came to live here, they had made a game out of spying on Mrs. Baker. She was more like a grandmother than mother, because in Taylor's eyes, she was a lot older than their parents had been. But Jessa and Taylor had never had grandparents…well, technically they had them, but the state hadn't been able to locate them after the accident. And Taylor had never met them before. Her mother said they'd been there when Taylor was born but had been on vacation ever since. Taylor might have believed that before the accident, but now she knew better. They were either dead or wanted nothing to do with her and Jessa. Which was fine, she didn't want anything to do with them either.

She followed Jessa out into the hallway, both of them in socks so they walk silently across the wooden floors. The house was so large and empty it was easy to make noise when you didn't mean to, but they had already memorized which floorboards creaked.

As usual, Mrs. Baker was in the kitchen as Taylor and Jessa approached the landing to the stairs leading down into the living room. It was a wide-open space where they sometimes played, but Taylor liked the privacy of their room better. Sometimes, when she wanted some time by herself, she would hide in one of the other empty bedrooms. Mrs. Baker told them there used to be lots of kids who stayed here with her and her husband, but she could only do so much as a single parent, and two girls were "more than a handful."

"I think she's on the phone," Jessa whispered as they reached the top of the stairs. Sure enough, Taylor could hear Mrs. Baker talking to someone.

"Look, I don't know what you want me to tell you. She came by here looking for information on Kieran. That's it." Mrs. Baker sounded irritated, and she didn't get irritated very often. Usually only when one of the girls refused to go to bed.

"No, she only asked a few questions. But I don't know what you want me to tell you. I haven't seen her in years."

"Who is she talking about?" Jessa asked.

Taylor scrunched up her features. "I think maybe that

policewoman who was here a few days ago," she said. "She used to stay here when she was a kid, I think."

"How do you know that?"

"I overheard them talking the other day," Taylor whispered back.

"Shouldn't *you* know?" Mrs. Baker said, louder this time. She was getting frustrated with the person on the other end of the phone. "You're the one keeping an eye on her. I'm staying out of this arrangement."

Jessa frowned. "This is boring."

But the conversation had piqued Taylor's interest. It was like she was the female detective on TV, listening in on a suspect to gather evidence. And whoever Mrs. Baker was talking to, they wanted to know about the policewoman. Her name had been Ivy. Taylor remembered because it was like the ivy that used to grow outside her window at their old home. It hadn't been poison, which is what someone at school had told her. But her dad said it was just plain old ivy, wouldn't hurt anyone.

"Listen, do whatever you have to do. But leave me out of it. I have enough problems as it is." Taylor heard the telltale beep that went along with someone hanging up the phone.

"I wonder who that was," Taylor asked herself more than Jessa.

"Who cares?"

"Taylor, Jessa! C'mon now, the big clock on the wall is ticking. Time for dinner."

Both girls jumped at having been called, even though Mrs. Baker was still in the kitchen. They hadn't been caught, but they rushed back to their room all the same, avoiding the same creaky floorboards. Their bedroom had a bathroom attached to it, though there was only one sink and they had to take turns washing their hands. Jessa never took the full twenty seconds like you were supposed to and she often tried to hurry Taylor along. But Taylor wasn't about to eat with dirty hands.

Mom always said they should always keep their hands clean, especially before eating, to help keep them from getting sick. And sometimes Taylor wondered if Jessa even remembered that.

Once they were done, they walked across the landing normally, creaky boards and all as they headed down the stairs to the kitchen. A wonderful, savory smell was coming from the kitchen. If there was one good thing about staying here, it was that Mrs. Baker always made something delicious. She knew how to make the best foods, and rarely could Taylor eat everything on her plate.

Sometimes she felt bad about that because her parents hadn't cooked. Usually, they brought something home for dinner, or all four of them would go out to eat somewhere. Taylor still missed that, but the home cooked food couldn't be beat.

As they descended the last few steps, Taylor heard a pot hit the kitchen floor, followed by more dishes and glasses crashing. Her first thought was Mrs. Baker had fallen or had an accident, and she rushed forward at the same time as Jessa.

But when they came around the corner, all Taylor saw was a big man, dressed head to toe in black, with a mask over his face. Her mind couldn't comprehend it at first, it was like something out of her show. Mrs. Baker lay on the ground, her head bleeding as the man stood over her. Taylor noticed the back door was open.

Jessa screamed before Taylor could stop her, and the big man turned around.

"*RUN!*" Taylor yelled as the man's eyes went wide. The two of them turned in tandem and sprinted back up the stairs, headed for their room. Taylor realized, too late, that they should have gone for the front door instead. They needed to get somewhere safe. Maybe if they locked the door—

They got into their room and slammed the door behind

them. Jess threw the small lock in the handle, but they had nothing else between them and the man.

"He killed her, he killed her," Jessa was still screaming.

"Here," Taylor said, pointing to the small dresser beside the door. "Help me move this in front of the door." Her sister was stronger than her and could move things better than Taylor could. But before they could get to the dresser, something slammed against the other side of the door, splintering it at the handle. Taylor grabbed on to Jessa as the door caved in from another hit and the man in the black ski mask stood before them, breathing hard.

All the girls could do was scream.

Chapter One

"HAPPY GROUNDHOG DAY! Would you like to try the groundhog special?"

"What's the groundhog special?" Detective Ivy Bishop asked, doing her best to keep a straight face at the overly delighted man across the counter.

"It's a burger specifically made from groundhog meat! Don't worry, it's been locally sourced. We take great care to make sure all our meat is fresh."

Ivy thought she might turn green. The idea of *eating* groundhog didn't sound very appealing. Wasn't the whole point of the day to celebrate the animal? Not devour it?

"Just a regular burger, thanks."

"You sure? It's hearty. And you can't beat the marbling."

"Yeah. Just the…cow burger, I guess."

The man behind the counter got to work. "You don't know what you're missing." Ivy couldn't help but be a little perplexed. This wasn't a high-class burger joint, but it wasn't part of a chain either. Still, groundhog seemed like an odd choice to offer.

"Have you…uh, sold a lot of those today?" she asked.

"You wouldn't believe how many. We're the only place in

town who offers them. Guy came in this morning and ordered three dozen for his whole office."

"Huh." She wondered if the man's coworkers knew what they'd be eating for lunch. If the man hadn't mentioned it, she probably wouldn't have even remembered what day it was. She'd been so focused on getting back to work she hadn't been paying attention to the calendar. All she knew was it had been four days since her boss had mandated she take a "vacation," and Ivy was itching to get back to work.

She had never been the calmest person to begin with, but after the events of last week, combined with the fact that her old caretaker and two of the children under her care had gone missing five days ago, she might as well have been taking a cattle prod to her rear end every ten minutes.

"Here you go!" the man said, handing over the wrapped burger. "If you change your mind, we'll be serving it all week. Come back tomorrow and I'd be happy to give you a free sample."

"That's okay, thanks," Ivy said, and headed for the cash register while the clerk tried to sell a groundhog burger to the next person in line. She couldn't help but wonder if anyone actually wanted the things or if they were just curious.

As she was making her way to pay, someone managed to bump her from behind. Had that happened two weeks ago, Ivy might have lost it right there in the burger shop. But ever since she and her partner, Detective Jonathan White had pursued and caught a serial killer in the Oregon mountains, Ivy found she had more control over her phobia of touch than she thought. Before that night, if anyone touched or even grazed her, it had the potential to send her into a panic attack. But the serial killer, identified as Kieran Woodward, had been on the literal precipice of death, and it had taken Ivy reaching out and grabbing on to him to keep him from tumbling off a cliff, so he could face the justice system for everything he did. For a brief second, she had considered letting him fall, but she knew she never could have lived with herself if she had done that.

And while touching him had been hard, it hadn't been the end of the world. She'd made it through, and she had wanted to experiment with the phenomenon more ever since. The ironic thing was that she had managed to isolate herself from society so well she didn't have anyone to experiment on. Not even a cat. So, she'd taken to intentionally bumping into strangers in the wild. At first it had been weird, but the more she'd done it, the less anxious she felt about physical contact.

So when the guy behind her smiled apologetically and offered a "sorry," Ivy had no problem letting it roll off her back. Exploding at a guy for accidentally grazing her wouldn't make her day any better.

Instead, Ivy took a deep breath, calmly paid for her burger, and headed back out into the misty January air. This part of western Oregon didn't see snow often in the winter due to the high desert to the east and the ocean to the west, but fog was a regular sight, and today was no exception. Coming out of the strip mall, she could barely see fifty feet in front of her to the other cars parked in the lot. Her car was one row back, but as she approached, two dark forms materialized from the fog, both of them standing close to the back left side of her car. The hairs on the back of her neck immediately rose when she realized they were two middle-aged men oogling her vehicle, which might not *seem* dangerous, but didn't leave a good feeling in her gut.

Ivy steeled herself. Sometimes these encounters only went one way. But then again, maybe they were just two guys admiring a classic. She didn't *have* to assume the worst about everyone *all* the time.

"Sure could be nice," she caught one of them say. After Ivy purchased the 1977 Corvette from a police auction, she realized owning a classic car came with a couple of additional responsibilities, one of which was to talk to motorheads and engage in "the talk." Usually this just meant BS-ing about the horsepower or the fiberglass body or some random stat about the car. Contrary to what most people thought about someone who owned a car like this, Ivy was not a car person. That had been her dad. When this car had come up at auction, she'd decided she couldn't pass it up, given he had always wanted a car just like it.

But man, it was a pain in the ass to keep running. And it had already cost her a pretty penny in maintenance.

Ivy nodded to the two men standing behind the car as she approached. "Morning," she said as she put her key into the slot, unlocking the driver's side door.

"Waitasecond," one of them said. "This is *your* car?"

Ivy set her burger inside before turning to face the men. "Yep. Had it almost a year now." *Still iffy, but they might be harmless.*

"It's a damn shame," the other one said.

Her shoulders dropped. "What's that?" Ivy asked in the most neutral voice she could muster. Something in their tones told her this wouldn't go well and to just get in the car and drive off. But she'd gotten into the habit of not backing down, and where she hadn't been willing to make a big deal about someone grazing her in the burger shop, this was something entirely different. As far as Ivy was concerned, this was her *dad's* car, and she had a responsibility to confront anyone who said one bad word about it.

"Just that it could be real nice if someone who knew how to take care of it was driving it," the man said.

Ivy cocked her head. "Really?"

"I mean, no offense, but do you even know how to change the oil in this beauty?" he asked. "Plus, your exhaust is rusting; the fender looks bent and there's no way the alignment is right. This car is probably twice as old as you are."

Okay, time to wrap it up. "My age is none of your business," Ivy replied. "And neither is my car." She turned to get in.

"That's the problem with this generation," the other one said. "They just don't care about anything. Back in my day, if I had a car this nice, I sure as hell would have taken care of it."

"Yeah? Which of these is yours?" Ivy asked, unable to help herself. The fog obscured anything more than a few feet away, but she was certain there weren't any other sports cars in this parking lot. Not that her car was a particularly rare sight, but people in this area generally went for something more sensible, like trucks.

The man scowled at having been called out, and all of a sudden her heartbeat was racing and her jaw was clenched. "You some kind of smartass?"

Ivy had already sized both men up on approach. It was something she did out of pure habit, having worked on the force for a couple of years now. Neither man was in particularly good shape, and probably wouldn't be a threat to her, unless they had a weapon hidden on them somewhere. Often, Ivy found people underestimated her because of her size. And these two were no exception. All they saw was a woman about a hundred pounds lighter than either of them, someone they thought they could berate simply for not being the right age or gender.

"You gentlemen have a good day," Ivy said, proud of herself for the decision to make her exit without causing a scene. But as she turned to get back into her car, she felt a meaty hand clamp around her arm.

"Little girl like you shouldn't be so disrespectful."

In an instant, she spun and using her newfound ability to touch people without losing her shit, she grabbed his wrist, wrenched it off her and laid him out on the ground with her knee in his back in under two seconds. The man cried out as the other man yelled something unintelligible, stepping in to grab Ivy.

"Any closer and I break his arm," she growled, causing the other man to back off.

"Get her off me!" the man under her yelled.

"I—I'm calling the cops," the other one said, pulling out his phone.

"Don't bother," Ivy replied, revealing her shield with her free hand. "Now do I have to arrest you two for assault, or can I go about my day in peace?"

"You can go, you can go!" the man under her squealed, his voice pitched an octave higher than before. Ivy thought he might be on the verge of tears. Given how much pressure she was putting on his arm, she wouldn't be surprised. She couldn't help but smile as she let him go, standing back up. She liked this new-found ability. Who knew touching people could be so fun?

"As I said, you gentlemen have a good day." Ivy got back into her car as the other man helped his friend up. With one twist of the key, she turned the engine over and revved it a few times before shifting it in gear and speeding off, leaving the men in the parking lot.

Why did people always feel the need to insert themselves into her business? Did *she* go around commenting on people's cars and what they should be doing with them? She was willing to bet if she was *Ivan* Bishop instead, she wouldn't get nearly so much blowback. All she had wanted to do was get her lunch and go back home in peace.

Ivy sighed as she pulled up to the next stoplight, glowing red in the late morning fog. It was one of those days when the fog probably wouldn't burn off, and instead it would just sit on the town of Oakhurst like a troll with a grudge. Generally, she enjoyed days like this, but not when three people were out there missing. One of which she knew personally. And despite her insistence to work the case, she'd been given "extended vacation" following her ordeal with Kieran Woodward.

As the light turned green, Ivy's phone rang, and she put it

up to her ear as she gingerly made her way through the inter-section. "Bishop."

"Where are you?" Her boss's tone was unmistakable. Lieutenant Natasha Buckley was rarely in what anyone would call a good mood, but from the dark tone of her voice, Ivy could tell this would be a particularly difficult call.

"I'm doing great, how are you?"

"Cut the shit. We just received a call at the station complaining about a quote *real piece of work bitch driving a seventy-seven stingray* unquote. Sound familiar?"

"I have no idea what you're talking about," Ivy replied, glancing down at her burger. Suddenly she wasn't even hungry anymore.

"The man said you assaulted him," Nat replied.

"Did he happen to mention he grabbed me first? And that he and his friend were distinctly out to cause trouble?" Ivy said. "It's a good thing it was me and not some random civilian or someone might have gotten hurt."

"He's claiming you dislocated his shoulder."

"Then he's either exaggerating or he did it himself," Ivy said. "When I left those two, they were in the peak of health. Minus the beer guts of course."

"Ivy, this is serious. He wants to press charges."

"Okay, bring them in and I'll talk to them personally," she said. "They had no problem throwing their weight around before they knew I was a cop."

She could hear her boss sigh on the other side. "Fine. I'll take care of it."

"While I have you," Ivy said. "What's the latest on the Baker case?" She and Nat had been at odds lately, something that only seemed to have been exacerbated by Ivy's most recent case, but Nat was still her direct supervisor and the person primarily responsible for case assignments. Ivy had been gunning to take the Baker case as soon as she'd found out about the woman's disappearance that night at the diner, but Nat had refused, saying Ivy needed time off after her ordeal.

It had already been five days. How much time did Ivy need?

"We're working on it," Nat said. "Nothing you need to worry about."

"But—"

"I'll keep you updated if anything changes," Nat said, and hung up before Ivy could get another word in.

That did it. She didn't care if she was on "vacation" or not. Ivy spun the wheel, skidding on the wet road a completing a one-hundred-eighty-degree turn and drove back in the other direction. Something about the encounter with the two men had lit a fire under her ass. She was tired of waiting. And she'd tried asking nicely, but if Nat was going to stonewall her, then Ivy was just going to have to take things into her own hands.

Chapter Two

DETECTIVE JONATHAN WHITE sat at his desk scowling over the stack of cases that seemed to have tripled while he'd been away. He'd only been out of the office for a few days following the ordeal with Kieran Woodward, but it seemed his workload had grown a life of its own and sprouted offspring. Given how short-staffed they seemed lately, he guessed he shouldn't be surprised.

Everything from domestic disturbance reports to public lewdness and even some reports of gang violence. But curiously, the biggest case in town *wasn't* among them. He had a proven record with difficult cases during his time working up in Portland, so it seemed like a no-brainer that he'd be roped in on the case. But going over all the updates both in his email and on his desk showed no mention of Baker or the two children.

Then again, they had just tracked down a serial killer. Maybe his boss wanted him working easier cases for a while, considering how gruesome that one had been. But he was dead sure the lieutenant had assigned Ivy to the case, considering her personal connection with the victim. And if she had been assigned to it, shouldn't he have been as well? One glance at his partner's desk told him she either hadn't been back into the office or was working remotely. He wished someone would have kept him in the loop. Sure, he'd been dealing with some personal stuff lately, but that didn't mean he was out of the country.

Then again, there was a process to these things, and Jonathan wasn't one to shake the apple cart. Their boss was a lieutenant for a reason, and he trusted she knew what she was doing.

Just as Jonathan resigned himself to start working through his pile, his personal cell phone rang. He took one look at the caller ID and rolled his eyes. He wasn't in the mood for this, not today. But if he didn't answer it would lead to an even bigger mess.

"Hello?"

"I'm surprised you picked up this time," the woman on the other end said.

"Hi, Mom," he replied, taking the first case file off the top of the stack and opening it up. It was a report about a series of graffiti tags all over the city, seemingly perpetrated by the same person or group of persons. A nothing case with no witnesses. There wouldn't be much to investigate on this one. He closed the folder and set it aside.

"How can you just *hi Mom* me?" she asked. "Don't you even want to know how I'm doing?"

He wouldn't call his mother a completely cold person, but she could be bitter and harsh when she wanted to. And when she was hurting, she lashed out at those around her. Which was one of the main reasons Jonathan was here instead of Portland. "I know how you're doing. You're having a difficult time. We all are."

"No, I'm dying inside, Jonathan. I'm losing a part of my soul, and you're down there twiddling your thumbs instead of staying up here where you belong."

It took all of Jonathan's willpower not to say something he

knew he would regret. Instead, he sat silent on the other end of the phone, his own passive aggressive way of dealing with his mother when she got like this.

"Are you still there?"

"I'm still here, Mom."

"Did you hear what I said?"

He took a deep breath. "I've already told you; I'm not leaving Oakhurst. We just opened a major case, and I'm neck deep in work. Maybe I can come visit in a few weeks."

"A few *weeks*?" his mother reiterated, using such a high-pitched tone it sounded like she'd been stabbed. He was sure that, in her mind, that's what had happened. "You need to come home now. Stop this foolishness. You've had your time down there, but you need to be with family."

"No, *you* need to be with family," he replied. "I came up, I did what I needed to do. And now my life is here. I need to focusing on something else for a while."

She adopted a sterner tone. "Jonathan, I will only put up with your insubordination for so long. You're coming home."

"Mom, I have to go," he replied. "My boss is calling me. I will talk to you later." He hung up before she could get another word in, then closed his eyes and slipped his phone back in his pocket. It began vibrating again immediately. He let it vibrate until it went to voicemail, knowing it wouldn't hold her off for long. His mother was a headstrong, stubborn person. And if he wasn't careful, she'd show up at the precinct's front door one day.

He tried sifting through the rest of the cases on his desk for the next thirty minutes, hoping to find something to distract him from the call, but they were all run-of-the-mill incidents, nothing noteworthy enough to spend his time on.

Frustrated, he stood and headed for Lieutenant Buckley's office. Her door was open, and he poked his head inside, knocking on her door first.

She was behind her desk as usual, staring at her laptop

when Jonathan walked in. He'd never seen the lieutenant smile, and today was no exception. She wore a scowl as large as the back end of a semi, and heavy bags hung deep under her eyes. She always had what Jonathan would have described as an angular face, but today it seemed exaggerated under the computer's harsh light. Paired with the large stacks of boxes on either side of her desk, the lieutenant reminded him of those monuments in ancient Rome and Greece. A god framed by epic proportions.

"Yes?" she asked before he made it all the way inside.

"I wanted to ask about the Baker case," he said. "If Detective Bishop needs some assistance, I'm happy to help. I didn't see any updates regarding the progress."

"That's intentional," she replied without looking up. Though she didn't elaborate.

"It's a big case," he replied. "I could—"

She let out an exasperated sigh and looked up. "What is it with everyone and this case today? Don't you have enough work to do without adding something else to your plate?"

"That's just it, ma'am," he replied. "Detective Bishop and I work better as a team. Wasn't that the point of bringing her in to work with me?"

"It's being taken care of," she replied. "Trust me, plenty of people are already looking into it."

"Lieutenant, I don't want to be difficult, but if Ivy is interviewing suspects, I should be there to assist—"

"Detective Bishop isn't working the case. She's still on leave," Buckley replied.

"*Still?*" He hadn't seen Ivy since she'd been put on leave, though they had spoken the night news broke that Mrs. Baker and the two children under her care were missing. He'd assumed she'd come right back in and had been plowing forward ever since. But because of his own family issues and his request for some personal time, he hadn't been back in to check on her. Part of that had been on purpose. He liked Ivy, maybe a little too much. And the rule of thumb was you didn't let things get personal. He'd made that mistake before.

Still, his own hangups shouldn't have prevented her from being assigned to the case. Had the lieutenant kept her off the assignment because he hadn't been here to assist?

"But Mrs. Baker was Ivy's caretaker before she was adopted, shouldn't Ivy—"

The lieutenant looked up again, the scowl on her face deeper than before. "Do you have a hard time hearing?"

"No, ma'am. I just don't understand why. She's our best chance at finding who took them. She might have inside information that could be useful, something she learned while she was staying with the Bakers."

"The detective is on leave until further notice," she replied. "She can't work the case while she's not here. We've been shorthanded since the two of you have been absent, so I need you working the cases on your desk. Given what the two of you went through, you're lucky to be back here at all." She glared at him under hooded eyes. "I considered extending your time away as well. But because you've been in the chair longer, I didn't feel like you needed as much recovery time. Was that a correct assessment?"

While it had been a harrowing couple of days leading up to the capture and interrogation of Kieran Woodward, Jonathan had weathered it. Much like he weathered everything in life. He was just glad they'd arrived in time to save Alice's life. Had they been any later, she would have been his next victim, for sure.

And had he not absolutely needed the personal time off, he would have been back in the office the very next day, ready to go.

Okay, maybe that was an exaggeration, because the ordeal *had* taken a toll on him. But he would rather be here, working cases, than back home trying to avoid calls from his mother.

"Heard loud and clear, boss." He turned to head back to

his desk. "Honestly, I'm surprised Bishop has stayed away for this long. She's not one to take something like this lightly. Especially seeing how she reacted to being in that house."

His boss perked up. "What do you mean?"

"Nothing, just that being there had a visible effect on her. I think it was hard for her, going back to her childhood. It would be for anyone, don't you think?"

Her eyes lingered on him a moment too long, but then she turned back to her computer. "I suppose. Regardless, she is too close to this investigation to have any impartiality. Trust me, I've known her a long time. Keeping her off this one is better for everyone in the long run. We have plenty of other cases to solve." She motioned with one hand to the desks that surrounded the bullpen in their department.

"Yes, ma'am," he replied and returned to his desk. Jonathan had always been a stickler for the rule of law and the chain of command, something that had earned him a reputation in the office. But he didn't care that some people thought of him as too much of a rule-follower. If everyone operated on their own set of rules all the time, it would be constant chaos. Nothing would ever get done. Even though he wasn't sure it was the right call, the lieutenant knew Ivy a lot better than he did. They'd only been working together for a few weeks, and despite her eccentricities, she was still mostly an enigma to him.

Preferring not to linger on thoughts about his partner, Jonathan sat back down and removed the first case from the stack, diving in headfirst.

Chapter Three

As Ivy PULLED into the parking lot, the back wheels of her car spun on the wet pavement before catching, jerking the car forward before they launched her up the small incline into the lot itself. It was a reckless move, and one that probably would have ended up with her rear fender in the back of someone else's squad car if not for the fact Ivy managed to straighten out in time. She was pissed, and her carelessness was coming out as a result. But it was fine, she'd managed to save it.

No harm done.

Ivy hopped out of her car, the burger forgotten on her passenger seat as she made her way for the side door to the precinct. This bullshit with Nat had gone on long enough, and it was time for Ivy to get some answers. After brooding on what could have happened to Mrs. Baker for almost five days while simultaneously trying to convince herself she was doing the right thing, she'd built up enough steam to pressure cook the entire Oakhurst police force if she had to.

But as soon as she walked through the door, someone called out her name. She turned to see officer Wright approaching, a big smile on his face.

"Hey there, hero. Congratulations," he said, holding out his hand for Ivy to shake.

She knew she probably looked like a deer in the headlights because she didn't move, even as he continued to smile and beam at her, his smile almost as big as his face. "What?"

"The Woodward case," he said, taking her arm and pressing her hand into his by force. "That was one hell of a job. Everyone's talking about it."

Ivy pulled her hand from his, probably too forcefully. A gut reaction. Despite her recent foray into physical contact, if she wasn't prepared for it, she could still fall back into her old cycle. Especially palm to palm contact. She willed herself to calm down, to look at it as just another experiment.

If Wright caught on, he didn't show it, just continued to smile at her. Which was weird. She'd never even spoken to the man before.

"Uh, thanks," she said.

"Hell, I don't know how you did it," he continued. "If it were me, I woulda let the somfabitch fall."

"Yeah…well, it was just instinct, I guess," Ivy replied. She didn't want to stand here talking to someone who couldn't have been bothered to give her the time two weeks ago. She wanted to confront Nat, and Wright was throwing her off her game, dissipating some of her frustration. "I've got to get upstairs."

"Sure, but let me take you out for a beer sometime. I'd love to hear the whole story from your perspective."

Ivy shied away from him and headed for the stairs. "Yeah, sounds great." But as she started making her way up the stairs, there was another shout from the top landing.

"Ivy Bishop! Hey girl!"

Ivy stared, perplexed at the officer bounding down the stairs towards her. She had to step back off the steps to ensure the woman didn't barrel right into her. "Officer Portnoy?"

"What is this, the academy?" Portnoy asked, smiling as

well. "It's Missy, you know that. I just can't believe what you had to go through. Are you okay being back at work?"

What the hell was going on here? Sure, Ivy and Portnoy had been in the same class during training, but they'd barely said two words to each other after graduation. In fact, she didn't think they'd even exchanged two words *before* graduation. Portnoy was one of those outgoing types, the kind of woman who always had to be involved in some activity or event. And since Ivy actively avoided those types of things, their paths didn't cross often. Ivy hadn't even given it a second thought when they were assigned to the same precinct.

"I'm…uh, fine," Ivy said. "It was no big deal."

"No big deal? You caught a serial killer. With your bare hands! Do you have time for a coffee? I'm getting together with a couple of the guys coming off patrol. Our treat."

Was this always what it was like when you solved a big case? The Woodward case had been Ivy's first big assignment as a detective, and as such, she hadn't expected it to turn so personal. But once she'd learned that she had a potential connection to the killer, she couldn't ignore the consequences. Those had been some of the hardest days of her entire life, but she'd made it through, and solved the case in the process.

"I…" She just wasn't used to all this attention; usually people just ignored her, and she was happy to ignore them right back. "…can't right now. I have to talk to Nat."

"Okay, we'll rain check then," she replied, her voice bubbly. "Let's get something on the calendar. And I'm serious. I'm not just saying that."

"Yeah, okay," Ivy replied. "Just…I guess email me?"

"Sounds great," Portnoy replied. "Catch you later." She headed off as Ivy resumed climbing the stairs. She thought that might be the end of it, but it was like every person she passed had something to say about the Woodward case. She hadn't been back into the office since the night she'd "interviewed" Kieran, so the consequences of her actions hadn't really sunk in. She couldn't help but soak in the attention. She was *not* the kind of person who sought out accolades or the spotlight, and frankly it made her uncomfortable, but at the same time, the validation felt good.

By the time she reached Nat's office, a lot of her anger had mutated into bewilderment. Yet she was determined to find out what was going on with the Baker case and find her way on it before she left this building. She could only wait around for so long.

Ivy didn't even bother knocking, instead strode into Nat's office and closed the door behind her. Her boss looked up, her eyes going wide. "What are you doing here?"

Ivy fanned her hand in front of her face. "Whew. Did you start smoking again?"

"I asked you a question," Nat replied, glaring at Ivy. Still, after all this time, they were both going to ignore the elephant in the room. So be it.

"You hung up before we could finish our conversation," Ivy replied. "So, I decided to come down here where you couldn't avoid me. I want to know what's going on with the Baker case."

Nat flared her nostrils. Her dark red hair was pulled back as usual, though a few strands had come loose. In the light, Ivy could tell it was somewhat frazzled, like it hadn't been washed in a while. There was also a definite odor beyond the smokey smell, though that could have just been something lost in the piles and piles of boxes and files Nat had stacked everywhere. "I've already told you; it's being handled. If you're looking for something to do, there's plenty of filing to be done."

"I'm not here to do your busywork," Ivy said, and it was amazing how quickly her frustration could return in full, especially in the presence of her boss. She'd thought when she first began working here that she and Nat would only grow closer as time went on. Because Nat had been the person to find Ivy the night her family went missing, she was also the person who helped set her up at the Baker home. The person who stayed in contact with her all those years, even after she'd been adopted. And Nat had been the one to sponsor her application to the academy.

But ever since Ivy had begun working here, and especially after she was promoted to detective, Nat had only grown more and more distant. It was like they didn't even know each other anymore.

"It's not your case," Nat said. "You need to leave it alone."

"How can you even say that?" Ivy asked, advancing on the desk. "I stayed at her home. I *was* one of those little girls. I already know more about this case than anyone else in this building, and you know it. Why are you blocking me out?"

Nat sighed and closed her laptop to stare at Ivy. "I know you don't believe this, but there are other competent detectives here. And they have the case perfectly well in hand. We're getting closer to finding Mrs. Baker and those little girls every day. There have already been some significant developments in the case."

"Really?" Ivy asked. "Like what? Do you have a suspect?"

"We're close," Nat replied. "I know you want to help, but trust me, you've been through a traumatic experience and have done enough. Let someone else take the wheel for a while. You go too hard too quickly, and you'll burn out. Trust me, I've seen it."

"So that's it? You've benched me because you're afraid I might burn out?"

"Believe it or not, I'm trying to help you," Nat replied. "You have this habit of running too hot for too long and yeah, I've seen what happens to you when you do that. You need some time off, away from all this."

"What about Jonathan?" Ivy asked. "I saw him on the way in. He's back at work."

"Just today," she replied. "But Jonathan has been doing this longer than you have. He can recover faster."

"Recover from what?" Ivy demanded. "You're acting like I was in an accident. Nothing even happened to me!"

Nat stood and reached out, grabbing Ivy by the wrist. A sudden coldness hit Ivy's core and she wrenched it back, shocked by Nat's brazenness. Her breath hitched, but she managed to keep herself under control. Nat's move had been worse than Officer Wright's, because Nat *knew* better.

"Not bad. The Ivy I knew would have been in convulsions over something that simple," she said. "But look at you, doing everything you can not to fall apart and almost succeeding."

"What's your point?" Ivy asked, the anger returning as she let go of her wrist. She'd found she could mask the phobia with her anger. It's what had allowed her to be so unabashed with the man in the parking lot.

"You've undergone a transformational change, and I don't think even you realize just how big of a deal this is. You can't just come back to work like nothing happened."

Some of the anger dissipated. This was the first time Nat had acknowledged their shared past in a long time. But she was still livid at Nat for having grabbed her. "Glad to see your memory still works."

"My point is, you need time. Time away from this place and time to reconcile what's happened to you. I'm trying to help you out here. Do you think any other boss would let you have this much time off with such a big case looming over our heads?"

"No, they wouldn't. So don't. I feel *fine*," Ivy insisted. "I can come back to work immediately. What are you going to do, keep me on leave until I'm cleared by a psychiatrist?"

"I've considered it," Nat replied, surprising Ivy. "But I don't think we need to resort to something that drastic, do you?"

"No," Ivy said. She'd been boxed in, and she knew it. She

couldn't lash out without risking a psychological evaluation, which was the *last* thing she wanted to do. Nat knew how she felt about any kind of head doctor, and because she was Ivy's boss, she could use it against her. And it wasn't like Ivy could go to Captain Armstrong. He already didn't like her very much. Unlike apparently everyone else in the precinct. But there was no way he'd side with Ivy over Lieutenant Natasha Buckley.

Nat pressed her lips into a line. "Go back home, get some rest. Try not to think about work for a few more days. Let's talk at the end of the week. If everything looks good then, you can come back to work. Look at it this way, you're getting a paid vacation."

"Doesn't feel like one," Ivy replied. "Feels more like exile."

Nat returned to her seat and opened her computer again. "View it however you choose to. Now, if you'll excuse me, I have a lot of work to do."

Ivy huffed, frustrated that she'd been outmaneuvered. This was the problem with her boss knowing her so well. It was like working with someone who not only knew all your greatest fears, but all your weaknesses as well. There had been a time Ivy would have bet her life that Nat never would have manipulated her like this. But apparently those days were in the past.

Ivy flung the door open, letting it slam hard enough against the wall that she was surprised the glass didn't break. She stormed out, headed for Jonathan's desk. He looked up before she could reach him, his eyes lighting up as soon as he saw her.

"Ivy, hey, sorry I've been out of touch for a few days. I've had—"

"Are you working the case?" she asked.

"What?"

"The Baker case. Are you working on it?"

"No, I was told it's being handled by someone else in the office."

"Who?" Ivy demanded.

He pulled his eyebrows together. "I don't know. Are you all right?"

"Nat has shut me out," she said. "Insists I need time off after my traumatic experience. Have you ever heard anything so ludicrous?"

"I dunno," he said, turning back to his pile. "I just got back in myself this morning."

"Got back in? From where?" Ivy asked.

"Doesn't matter. I've got a ton of work to do." He motioned to the large pile of files on his desk. Ivy glanced at her desk that sat across from his. It was empty of everything except her computer and phone. Almost like she didn't even have a desk here. Nat had done everything she could to wipe her from this place.

"Does she want me to quit? Is that it?" she mumbled.

"She's probably just worried about you," Jonathan replied, though she could hear the pained resignation in his voice. She was obsessing, and it was just making things worse. But wasn't he supposed to have her back? Wasn't that what he'd said, that they were partners and could count on each other? Because right now, she didn't feel like she could count on anyone.

Ivy turned and stormed out without a word. Jonathan did nothing to stop her.

Chapter Four

As she suspected, the fog hadn't moved nor had it burned off as the day progressed, which made driving over to Aunt Carol's house more treacherous than normal. Ivy couldn't believe she had been so naïve to think she could just walk into Nat's office and demand to take the case. Nat wasn't an idiot, and she knew Ivy better than most anyone. She should have pushed back, should have insisted that Nat clear her for duty. But Ivy knew Nat well too, and the woman did not respond well to threats. Nat was like one of those exotic flowers that closed as soon as you got near it. And once she closed up, she was a fortress, dead set in her ways. The harder you shoved the harder she retaliated.

But there was something else too. Ever since Ivy had begun working in the Violent Crimes division under Nat, the woman had been cagy and distant, but now it was almost like she was hiding something from Ivy, though there was no telling what that could be. Ivy just wasn't buying the line about her "health." She was *fine*. Sure, there had been a lot of changes lately, but she'd managed to handle them on her own. In fact, she had been proud of how far she'd come in such a short amount of time. She probably wasn't ready to start hugging strangers, but she could at least survive short bouts of contact unscathed. Today had proven that more than anything.

There had to be another way to get on the case.

As she pulled up to Aunt Carol's house, Ivy promised herself she would find a way to break through Nat's wall and get the woman to listen to reason. Maybe all she needed was a few more days to cool down. At least other officers were making progress with the Baker case. And even though Ivy wanted nothing more than to help, it was better to wait and prove Nat wrong. Show her that Ivy was perfectly fine to come back to work. And *then* she would pounce.

Ivy shut off the engine, the car shuddering the same way it did every time she turned it off. As much as she hated to admit it, she would probably need to bring it into the shop again soon. The car was almost too powerful for its size and would sometimes feel like it was going to shake itself apart. She'd managed to teach herself some rudimentary mechanic skills, but she only had so much time and equipment. If she really wanted to keep it running, it would need more maintenance than she was capable of.

She grabbed the now cold burger on her seat and headed up the walk to Aunt Carol's house, letting herself in without knocking. Unsurprisingly, the front door was unlocked, despite Ivy insisting otherwise.

"Hello?" she called out.

"In here," a lithe voice responded. Ivy rounded the corner to the living room where Aunt Carol sat, her legs pulled up on the couch as she read a book. Ivy's adoptive mother was one of those women who just didn't seem to age. She had lines on her face, of course, but they only enhanced her natural beauty. And her gray hair remained long, though she kept it pinned up most of the time. She wore simple dresses or house clothes, though she would have looked at home in a Chanel suit if she'd so wanted. On more than one occasion, Ivy lamented the fact they didn't actually share any genes. What-ever fountain of youth Aunt Carol had dipped her toe into would have been worth more than all the beauty products in the world ten times over.

"You were gone a while. Did you find something for lunch?" the older woman asked, setting her book down. Ivy caught the title. *The House in the Cerulean Sea.*

Ivy glanced down at the burger in her hand. "I…uhh, got sidetracked. Here, you can have it if you want. I'm not hungry anymore."

Carol pursed her lips and gave Ivy *the look*. The one that said she was being silly and that she needed to eat something if she didn't want to waste away to nothing. Ivy had heard the same spiel from the woman for nearly a decade now. "Here, let me fix you something like I offered the first time." She gingerly removed her legs out from under her and slipped on a pair of warm slippers before getting up and heading for the kitchen.

"No, I'm fine, really," Ivy said. "I'll just heat this up."

Aunt Carol stopped, studying Ivy for a moment. Ivy hated when she did that; it was like she was a walking x-ray machine when it came to Ivy. She didn't know how she did it. "Something's wrong."

"It's nothing," Ivy said, heading for the kitchen herself. She opened the microwave and tossed the burger, wrapper and all, inside. It bounced off the back and landed upside down. Ever since she'd learned that her dreams hadn't been dreams at all and were actually memories—memories of being covered in blood—she'd been staying at her adoptive mother's home. It had been the first time she'd been back since moving out six years ago.

But she hadn't come back to stay with Aunt Carol out of sentimentality, but rather her obsession with finding out what her memories meant. Her time off had given her the opportu-nity to start sifting through everything in the house for some connection that might explain her past. In fact, it was the only thing keeping Ivy from going crazy thinking about Mrs. Baker and those kids. But so far, her search hadn't yielded anything useful. And the only person who might be able to tell her more—other than Nat—was now missing.

"What happened?" Carol asked, following her into the kitchen.

"Nothing. I just ran by work real quick," Ivy replied. "Just…checking on things."

"Did you talk to Nat?" Carol asked.

"Yeah, but just about the case. She…wasn't happy to see me."

Carol reached for Ivy, but instinctively pulled back. Ivy hadn't told Aunt Carol about her newfound ability yet. Besides, she wasn't sure she was ready for physical contact between people she knew. Somehow it felt easier if it was a stranger. Her encounter with Nat only confirmed that. Once she let Carol in, there would be no going back. And she still feared that kind of contact. Not that she would ever admit it aloud.

"I still think you should just ask her about it," Carol said. "She was there that night. She could give you all the answers you need."

Ivy shook her head. "You don't understand. Nat has known about this for over ten years and never said a word. Don't you think that's strange? That she couldn't be bothered to tell me? And now she wants me to take *more* time off because she's worried about my psychological health."

"She means how you grabbed that man to save him," Carol said.

"I guess she thinks I need more time to deal with what's happening. And she doesn't want me back in the office until she can be sure I'll be okay."

Carol's gaze lingered on Ivy for a moment and Ivy thought she saw something in the older woman's eyes before she turned away, heading for the kitchen's small pantry. "I'm sure she has her reasons. But you never know, she might just be waiting for you to ask."

"You don't know her like I do," Ivy replied. "She's…what are you doing?"

Carol stuck her head out of the pantry. "Fixing you a proper meal. There's no telling what's in that." She motioned to the burger still in the microwave.

Ivy couldn't argue with the woman's logic. She still wasn't sure the clerk hadn't slipped a little groundhog into her order. "Really, Aunt Carol, I'm fine. I'm not hungry."

"Well, I am," she replied, coming back out of the pantry with an armful of supplies. "And I'm going to make myself a light lunch. You can have the leftovers if you feel like it later."

Ivy couldn't help but smile. Despite her best efforts, Carol had been doting on her ever since she'd started staying in her old room. She suspected it was because, despite her social schedule, her adoptive mother was still living in this house all alone. It was something that occasionally worried Ivy, though living with her again, she'd been astounded at how well Carol got around and took care of herself. She was less like a sixty-year-old and more like someone in her thirties.

As the woman got to work on the stove, Ivy took a seat at the kitchen table, her thoughts swallowing her whole. With Mrs. Baker missing, Nat really was the only person who might be able to give her any information about what Kieran Woodward had told her.

…THEY'D FOUND YOU COVERED IN BLOOD…

BUT THE PROBLEM WAS, NAT *KNEW* WHAT KIERAN HAD SAID— she'd reviewed the interview of course—and she *still* hadn't broached the subject with Ivy. Which bothered her more than anything. One night, Ivy had become so frustrated with the radio silence she'd almost called Nat at home in the middle of the night and demanded answers. But if today had taught her anything, it was that it would never have worked. And probably would have backfired.

"Can I help?" Ivy asked, though she knew it was a useless question. She did it out of politeness anyway.

"Not at all. Just keep me company," Carol said, placing a glass of iced tea in front of Ivy. If nothing else, the woman knew how to make a place feel homey. Ivy drank as they talked back and forth about nothing significant, but it was important all the same. Ivy hadn't realized how much she'd missed this while living on her own. Her self-imposed exile from humanity had rendered her numb to socialization. And it hadn't been until recently that she'd begun to rediscover the benefits.

Not that she was ready to deal with people full-time. Even with her newfound "freedom," she'd discovered people were still a disappointment, no matter how close you got to them.

"Where are you?" Carol asked.

"Huh?"

"You've gone glassy-eyed," she replied. "Thinking about the case again?"

"Not exactly," Ivy said. She'd been thinking about how Jonathan had almost dismissed her back at work like she was blowing things out of proportion. She thought they had made a connection, that she could count on him. "I don't want to talk about it."

"Fair enough. I thought maybe you were thinking about Oliver." Ivy snapped up, her eyes flaring, causing Aunt Carol to chuckle. "There's a reaction if ever I've seen one."

"What are you talking about?" Ivy demanded, though she had an idea she already knew.

"Nothing." Aunt Carol gave her a sly smile. "Just

wondering how it's been going since you reconnected. You're not exactly the kind of person to volunteer information."

"It's going fine," she replied. "But he's got his own work to do. He doesn't have time to deal with my stuff."

"I bet he'd beg to differ," she replied. "He seemed willing enough to help that night in the diner."

Ivy thought back to the night she first heard about Mrs. Baker and the children on the news. It had been when she'd confessed what she'd learned about her "memories" to Aunt Carol. And while it was true Oliver offered to help, he wasn't bound by the same oath she'd taken when she'd joined the force. Not to mention he had something of an ambiguous moral code that seemed to ebb and flow with how he felt on a particular day. He'd promised he would stay within the confines of the law, but Ivy had told him that she and Jonathan could handle it. That was before Jonathan went on full radio silence for three days and Nat benched Ivy semi-permanently.

"Maybe if you're feeling stuck, it might be an avenue worth exploring."

"I just don't know if I want to go down that road," she replied. "Especially if I ever want to get anything out of Nat. I think it's best if I just keep looking into stuff here."

"If you insist," Carol said before setting a plate of grilled salmon in front of Ivy, complete with roasted vegetables and bread. She brought her own plate over and sat across the table.

"*This* is a light lunch?" Ivy asked, arching her eyebrow.

Carol shrugged. "Can you blame me? I haven't been able to cook for you in almost six years."

She was right. Up until a few weeks ago, the most Ivy would see her adoptive mother was once every few weeks, when they would meet somewhere for a quick meal before Ivy would retreat back into work or the safety of her own home.

Going out had been a chore, but, strangely, didn't feel like as much of one anymore.

"Well, if you won't talk to Oliver or Nat, I guess all I can do is keep cooking for you," she said. "Taking this on all by yourself is going to require a lot of energy. I need to keep you fed with more than just fast food."

Ivy shot her a deadpan glance. "Very funny."

Carol plucked off a piece of her bread and popped it into her mouth. "Tell me I'm wrong."

Ivy huffed and dug into her lunch, deciding not to dignify that with a response. Besides, any response was lost as soon as she took a bite of the delectable fish.

Chapter Five

THE SECOND TAYLOR opened her eyes, she panicked. Because even though she could feel her eyes were open, she couldn't see anything. She never had liked the dark, but this was worse. Because even in the dark, she could usually at least see *something*. She could make out the outline of her dresser or the line of light under the door to their room. But here, she couldn't see a thing. She tried holding up her hand in front of her, but it was no use.

She cried out, which at first came out like a gasp, then more of a wail.

"Taylor?" a familiar voice asked.

"Jessa? What's going on? I can't see."

"Neither can I," Jessa said. "Where are you?"

"I don't know, everything is dark," Taylor replied. Her sister's voice was close, but she wasn't sure how close. It felt like she'd been lying on hard carpet, the kind of carpet they used in office buildings. Not hard like the driveway, but not exactly soft either.

"Can you move?" Jessa asked.

"I think so," Taylor said, holding her hands out in front of her. "What happened? What's going on?" She hated how scared she sounded, but she couldn't help it. She didn't want to be blind.

"I'm not sure," Jessa said. "But stay there. Keep talking."

"What? Keep—" Before she could say anything else, she felt something cold move across her hand, and she screamed.

"It's okay, it's just me," Jessa said. "Sorry, I'm freezing."

Taylor reached out until she felt the edges of Jessa's clothes. She pulled herself up until she could wrap herself around her sister. Jessa's arms wrapped around her back. "What happened?"

"I don't know," Jessa said. "I don't feel right. My head hurts a lot."

"Yeah," Taylor said, noticing the pounding in her head now that she knew she wasn't alone wherever they were. She hadn't realized it at first because she'd been so scared about not being able to see. "Mine too."

"What's the last thing you remember?" Jessa asked.

Taylor thought hard. "Running up the stairs. Hiding in our room."

Jessa sighed. "That's all I remember too. You don't know what happened after that?"

"No," Taylor admitted. Now that she thought about it, that was very strange. She'd never been missing memories before. "Jessa, I'm scared. Do you think we're blind?"

"No," her sister said, relaxing her grip. "I just think this is a very dark room. We should try to find a light switch." She began to pull away, but Taylor held fast.

"Don't leave me."

"Okay, here, just take my hand. We'll go together, okay?"

Taylor nodded, even though Jessa couldn't see her, and took her older sister's hand. They stood together, and Taylor felt Jessa pull her along. The floor was hard under her shoes. Not like the carpet at all. And not like the wood floors either. More like a sidewalk. Taylor was unsure about walking in the dark at first, thinking she might trip over something, but there didn't seem to be anything to trip over. Thankfully, Jessa went slow. Taylor stuck her free hand out, hoping to feel…something. But there was nothing there. It was like they'd been dropped in the middle of endless nowhere.

"Hey, I found a wall…I think," Jessa said, letting go of Taylor's hand.

"Jessa——" Taylor said, panicked, but her sister's hand found hers again and led her forward, placing her hand against what felt like a wall. She was right, they must have been in a room of some kind. "Feel anything?"

"Not yet," Jessa replied. "Here, come with me, we'll keep going." Taylor kept one hand on Jessa's back as they walked, running their hands alongside the wall so they wouldn't lose track of it. She was afraid if she took her hand away it might disappear, and then she'd be back in the middle of nowhere.

"Hang on a second, I think I found something," Jessa said. A second later the room was bathed in white light which made Taylor shut her eyes quickly. She took a couple seconds to open them back up, allowing them to adjust.

"Oh," Taylor said. They were in a room not much bigger than their own bedroom. It even had a bed large enough for the two of them. But it wasn't very nice. The frame was metal, and it looked hard and uncomfortable. And it didn't have any sheets. There was also a toilet in the far end of the room without a door or anything separating it from the main space. "Ew," Taylor said.

Jessa took a few steps back into the middle of the room. "It's like a jail cell."

"We're in *jail?*" Taylor asked.

"You tell me. Didn't you watch all those shows that tell you what jail is like?"

She was right. Taylor took in the rest of the room. There were no windows, and only one door with a slot in the middle. From what she could tell, it was made of metal and didn't look like it could move. There wasn't even a handle anywhere.

Other than the light switch, there didn't seem to be anything else in the room other than the bed and the toilet. Nothing on the walls, no other furniture. And the floor *was* just hard concrete. Taylor recalled seeing a room a lot like this from one of her shows. "Yeah, I guess it is." She was trying to remember the episode. It hadn't been a regular jail cell, but she was having difficulty remembering. Her head felt all scrambled. All she knew was regular jail cells had bars on them. And this room didn't have any bars.

"What are those?" Jessa asked, pointing to the floor. Closer to the toilet were some dark stains on the floor, but Taylor couldn't tell what they were. All she knew was she wanted out of this place. It was scary, and it smelled bad. She ran over to the door and started pushing on it before pounding on it with both her hands, crying out. She didn't care what it took, they needed to get out of here. This place was all wrong and they didn't belong here.

"Hey, hey," Jessa said, taking Taylors arms and pulling her away from the door. "Don't."

"Why not?" Taylor asked, tears running down her face.

"Remember that time Mrs. Caruthers found us in her classroom when we were supposed to be out at recess? You wanted to stay so we could play on one of the computers, but she heard us yelling at the game, and then they had to call Mom to tell her."

"Yeah," Taylor said, sniffing and wiping her nose with her sleeve.

"Well, it's probably the same, right? We need to be quiet. We don't want things to get worse."

She was right. Maybe before the accident Taylor wouldn't have thought things could get worse. But now she knew better. "So what do we do?"

"We need to hope Mrs. Baker finds us," Jessa said. "She's probably already looking for us."

"Wait a second," Taylor said. "I do remember something.

Mrs. Baker was on the floor. That big man was standing over her."

Jessa squeezed her eyes together, almost like it hurt her to do it. "Oh yeah. My head hurts really bad."

Taylor's did too. Sometimes Mrs. Baker would complain about headaches in the mornings. They were usually after she had some wine the night before, almost to the point where Jessa and Taylor would expect her to feel bad if they saw an empty bottle in the trash. Was this the kind of pain she was talking about? Taylor's head was pounding, like a rhinoceros was running circles in there.

"I think I remember something else," Taylor said. "I felt a pinch…after he came into our room. I tried hiding under the bed, but he…he pulled me back out. And I felt a pinch… here." She pointed to her arm. Pulling up her sleeve she didn't see a red mark or anything. But when she rubbed the spot, it was sore.

"Oh yeah," Jessa replied. "I think I remember that too. But that's the last thing I remember. I'm sure of it."

"Me too," Taylor replied. She looked around again, feeling like everything had gone wrong in the world. She shouldn't be here. She should be back home with her sister and her parents. But it seemed like everything that happened only made things worse. And now she was stuck in this little room with no way out. She began to cry again. Jessa came over and led her to the bed, which was low enough that they could both sit on it and their feet still touched the ground. Taylor had never been on a bed this short before. It was as hard as a rock. And that only made her cry harder. Jessa continued to hold onto her, rubbing her back and soothing her much like their mother used to do. She hadn't done that since their parents had died. Taylor thought she'd forgotten that Mom used to do it for them. But it seemed she hadn't. And it was helping. Taylor was already starting to feel better.

"It'll be okay," Jessa said. "We'll find a way out of here. We're still together, right?"

"Right," Taylor said. *For now,* a voice deep in the back of her mind added. It was a voice she'd never heard before and she tried not to listen to it. "I'm hungry." Actually, now that she thought about it, she was *famished*. Her dad used to say he was hungry enough to eat a horse when he would come home from work. She'd never wanted to eat a horse, but she thought she might be able to eat a horse-sized waffle and not get sick of it. And she was definitely sure she could consume a horse's weight in ice cream.

"Yeah, me too," Jessa replied.

In fact, Taylor felt like this one time when she was sick and didn't eat for three days because she had been throwing up so much. Her parents had been so worried, but when her fever finally broke, she was hungrier than she ever had been in her whole life. Now that she thought about it, this was almost worse. Was whoever brought them here going to feed them?

As if she'd asked the question aloud, the little slot in the middle of the door opened, startling them both. They rushed forward as a tray appeared in the opening, but before they could get to it, it fell to the floor, scattering the contents all over the ground.

Taylor and Jessa scrambled to grab what food they could, which consisted of mostly rolls and bread and not much else. Taylor didn't care, she loved bread. But she didn't want it touching the disgusting floor.

"Is that it? Did we get it all?" Jessa asked, holding a few different types of breads. One looked like a croissant.

"I think so, but it's all dirty," Taylor replied.

"I don't think I care," Jessa said, taking a bite of one of the rolls.

Taylor had to admit, they looked pretty good, and her mouth was already watering. She wiped a biscuit on her shirt, trying to get as much dirt off as she could before taking a bite.

But as she ate, she found she only got hungrier and quickly devoured everything in her arms.

"Here," Jessa said, heading for the sink beside the toilet. She turned on the tap and made a cup with her hands, drinking the water from them. Taylor copied her and the cool water felt good after all the bread. But she was still hungry. There wasn't anything left other than the tray which had fallen to the ground.

She walked back over to the door, looking for any they might have missed, realizing something was different. "Hey!" she whisper-yelled to her sister. Jessa was still by the sink, getting water. She looked up as Taylor pointed at the slot in the middle of the door. It was still open.

Jessa's eyes went wide, and she ran back over as they approached the slot carefully. If they could see out, they might be able to figure out where they were. They peered through the slot together, but Jessa couldn't make out anything other than another concrete wall. She bent this way and that, but every view was obscured by that wall.

That's when they heard it. A horrific scream from somewhere beyond the wall.

They retreated from the door together, Taylor thinking that somehow they caused the scream. Only it came again. And again. So many times that Taylor had to cover her ears.

"Oh no," Jessa finally said.

"What?" Taylor asked, pulling one hand away.

"Don't you recognize it? When we found that mouse in the kitchen, remember what Mrs. Baker sounded like when she saw it?"

Taylor's hands fell from her ears. "You're saying…"

"That's…Mrs. Baker screaming."

Chapter Six

Ivy pulled the next box down off the stack and took a seat, setting the box before her. After lunch she had returned to her mission, finding anything in Aunt Carol's stuff that might give her a clue to what could have happened the night she was brought into the Bakers' home.

It was unlikely she would find anything, but her time was better spent looking here than sitting and doing nothing while she fumed over Nat's pigheadedness or Jonathan's apparent lack of sympathy. There had to be an answer somewhere, and she needed to do a thorough dive through all Aunt Carol's records just to make sure. There was always the chance they'd forgotten something, or that some seemingly insignificant fact could maybe shed light on the situation.

For what it was worth, Ivy was doing her best not to think too hard about the ramifications of what the memories meant. What she'd always assumed to be bad dreams from a cheesy horror movie she'd caught too late one night were actually her real memories of when Nat found her. As far as she could tell, she didn't have any scars or deep cuts to explain the blood as her own. Which could only mean she was covered in someone else's blood.

Not only was that a terrifying thought, but it opened up so many more questions. Because the only time she'd been back in the office since she'd learned the truth had been to confront Nat, she hadn't had a chance to look back through the system for any additional details on her original case. Not that it would have mattered much, she'd already investigated the reports when she first began working for the department, finding nothing out of the ordinary. Fifteen years ago, she had been found wandering the streets of Oakhurst by *Officer* Buckley, then was brought in and eventually released to social services when her family couldn't be located. It was as simple as that.

Except, the report never mentioned that Ivy had been covered in blood.

She was missing a good chunk of her memory from that time. She recalled going to bed one normal night, then nothing but a bloody arm until she was walking up the steps to the Baker home. She'd been told she fell into a coma for days after she was found. Her recollections were a little scattered after that but had started to come into focus more and more. She recalled meeting Oliver and some of the other kids, recalled the bullying and the fights and then of course when she met Aunt Carol for the first time. And the further she moved away from those events, the more her memories remained intact.

She knew that people who endured highly traumatic events often blocked them out of their conscious minds, even though they remained in their subconscious. Often, they could only be recovered through intense therapy, which was a path Ivy wasn't ready to take yet. Things were hard enough already; she didn't need to add trying to placate a therapist to the mix.

Ivy removed the top of the box and started sifting through the contents. Much of it was from her time at school while she'd been with Aunt Carol. Old papers, projects, reports, and the like. Not many pictures as Aunt Carol was the digital camera type. But it seemed like she's saved almost everything else. Ivy shifted through the box, flipping through its contents until she reached the bottom, finding nothing noteworthy. This had all been after her time at the Baker home.

Sighing, she stuffed everything back inside before placing the top back on and adding it to the stack of boxes she'd already been through. There wasn't much left. She'd been up in the attic most of the afternoon and the cold was beginning to get to her. Not to mention there wasn't much ventilation up here, and at least once she thought she heard something scurrying around.

"Any luck?" Carol asked as Ivy emerged into the kitchen again. Despite just having eaten a large meal, the woman was back at it, fixing something else.

"I think I need to go for a drive," Ivy said. "Clear my head."

Carol turned around, wiping her hands on a nearby towel. "If that's what you think you need."

"Yeah," Ivy said, not looking her mother in the eye. "Just for a few hours. I'll be back."

"Be careful. The weather's supposed to turn in the next few days. Cold front coming in."

Ivy nodded; she'd seen the same report. "I will." With that, she grabbed her keys and her jacket and headed back out. It was almost seven and the sun had set long ago. Ivy didn't mind driving at night, in fact she enjoyed it. But really what she wanted right now was some mental solitude. She could go home, but ever since her encounter on the cliff, home had seemed so…empty. She had a desire to be around people, though she wasn't sure why. She didn't really want to interact with them, just observe. Maybe her subconscious mind was looking for examples of ways that people interacted with each other. Something she had ignored for the past couple of years. Attempting to re-integrate herself back into society had proved challenging, and she felt like maybe if she could turn her mind off and just watch people, maybe she'd figure out how to fit in better.

That and she really needed a drink. After everything, Ivy was feeling the weight of the day. Aunt Carol kept some gin and schnapps up in one of the top cabinets, something Ivy had taken advantage of more than once when she'd been a rebellious teen. In fact, Aunt Carol never touched those bottles and Ivy was dead sure they were probably still filled with water from when she'd replaced their contents years ago.

She headed out from Carol's house to an old haunt of hers, one where she was sure *not* to run into any members of the Black Pistons—the motorbike gang she had a history with. It was because of that history she'd been able to count on them for information in a pinch on tough cases up until her promotion to detective. But they'd made it very clear during their last encounter they wanted nothing to do with Ivy now that she was a "certified dick." And for the first time, she actually felt threatened by them.

Even though she knew the Pistons never came on this side of town, she was relieved when she pulled into the gravel parking lot of *Lucky Bernie's Bar* and didn't see any bikes in the lot.

Inside the place was dim, as always. A row of booths lined the wall beside the door, each with its own window and most of them with patrons. A bar ran the length of the room with only a dozen or so stools. Despite being one of the oldest establishments in Oakhurst, the place had a warm, homey feel. Maybe some would have considered it a dive bar, but to Ivy, it was just a place where locals hung out. She'd been here a few times to interview witnesses or get someone's statement, but it had always struck her as a safe place to be a patron too.

"Just one?" the bartender asked. Ivy nodded. "Take any seat you can find."

Ivy headed down and perched herself on a stool near the

end of the bar. Only two other patrons shared any stools and they kept to themselves as Ivy passed. It was a far cry from the attention she'd received earlier at the precinct.

"Menu?" the bartender asked, walking over. He had on a striped button-down shirt and was probably in his fifties, his hair mostly gray. His face was full and clean shaven, though it didn't look to Ivy like the man was the smiling type. He didn't have the telltale wrinkles around the eyes.

"Just a beer. Whatever's on tap."

"Coming up," he replied. Ivy wasn't a big beer drinker, but then again she hadn't been a big anything until the events of the past few weeks. She figured now was as good a time as any to start acclimating herself to her fellow humans.

The other two patrons at the bar seemed to know each other, at least by their body language, though they weren't speaking. Occasionally one would make a motion to one of the two television screens behind the bar, replaying some sports program while an announcer made commentary on the highlights. The other would just grunt in either agreement or dispute, Ivy wasn't sure which.

"Want to start a tab?" the bartender asked, bringing over the pint of amber liquid.

"No thanks," Ivy said, and slid a ten in the man's direction. She glanced over her shoulder at a couple sitting in one of the booths. They looked young, like they might even still be in high school. They were deep in conversation, leaning in close over the table. The girl's face was pinched with worry, while the boy was trying to soothe her.

Ivy winced, trying not to read too much into it. Maybe coming here to observe hadn't been such a good idea after all. Because when you started looking deep into people's lives, you generally uncovered something dark, private—something no one else should ever see.

She shuddered. If anyone started digging into her past, they'd find nothing but a lot of pain—pain Ivy wasn't willing to share. And she definitely didn't want strangers pitying her when they didn't know the whole story. She wasn't about to do that to someone else.

She turned back to watch one of the TVs but decided instead to focus on her beer. Maybe what she really needed was a distraction, something to keep her mind off Mrs. Baker, or Nat, or the fact she still wasn't any closer to discovering the truth about what had happened to her family. Some people would probably say she needed a hobby, but hobbies were for normal people. She needed to *do* something, not just sit around all day crocheting.

Why had she thought coming here was a good idea? She didn't feel any better about not finding anything at Aunt Carol's house, and it turned out she didn't want to know as much about strangers' lives as she thought she had.

"Thanks, have a good night," Ivy said, getting up, having barely touched the beer.

The bartender didn't even look up, though Ivy thought she caught one of the barflies eye her drink. She was about to dismiss the entire exercise as nothing but a bad idea when something caught her eye.

"Hey, can you turn that up?" she asked, motioning to one of the televisions. It was tuned to the local news, and a familiar face caused Ivy to stop cold.

The bartender grabbed one of the remotes and turned up the TV's volume, which now came through loud and clear.

"—neighbors they never heard anything. And while an investigation is still ongoing, Police say they're still no closer to finding out what happened to the three victims."

On the screen was a woman Ivy had become intimately familiar with, considering she had helped save her life not more than a week ago. It was Alice Blair, a local reporter with Oakhurst's only local television station: KTLV. But Alice wasn't what had caught Ivy's attention. It was the Baker home she stood in front of as she made her report.

"We reached out to Captain Armstrong with Oakhurst PD, but he was unwilling to give an update to the case. However, sources from within the Police Department itself say that progress on the case has been slow. If you have any information regarding the disappearance of these three individuals, you're encouraged to call the Oakhurst PD hotline."

Alice's face was replaced with a graphic and the number for the hotline, though Ivy didn't think it stayed up long enough for anyone to copy it down or dial it. When Alice came back on, she made a few more remarks before tossing the coverage back to the woman in the studio.

Nat had lied to her *again*. There hadn't been any progress on the case at all. Alice might be nosy, but she was a good reporter, and she wouldn't throw accusations around like that unless she had confirmation no progress had been made on the case. Ivy couldn't believe it. *This* was why she couldn't trust Nat to tell her the truth about that night fifteen years ago. If she could convincingly lie to Ivy's face about this, she could lie about virtually anything.

And to find out the case she *could* have spent the last week working had made zero progress? Ivy couldn't stand around any longer. She was tired of getting jerked around. It was time to take matters into her own hands.

"Hey, you okay?" the bartender asked Ivy. The two barflies turned to look over their shoulders at her.

"Yeah," she replied. "Just dandy."

Chapter Seven

As Ivy PULLED onto the block, she was surprised to see the news van was still parked across the street from the Baker house. The news report had been made almost twenty minutes ago, and Ivy had figured Alice wouldn't linger at the site any longer than she needed to. In fact, she'd been counting on the scene being deserted. The woman was full of surprises.

Well, she would just have to deal with it. It was too late to hide or turn back as there was no way the occupants of that news van hadn't seen her turn the corner. Kilkenny Road wasn't a very long street by any means and Ivy's car stood out like a sore thumb. Still, she might be able to turn this to her advantage, or at the very least get confirmation of the story. Ivy would really have to sell this if she didn't want to cause herself any headaches down the road.

Ivy pulled up and parked on the curb just as the sliding door of the van opened, revealing Alice Blair wearing the same outfit she'd had on for the report. This was the first time Ivy had seen the woman in person since that night on the cliff when Kieran had held her at knifepoint and Alice had suffered a significant injury to her neck. Thankfully the ambulance had been nearby and had managed to save her life with Jonathan's help.

Still, Ivy wasn't fond of Alice. The woman had used Ivy's computer to gain access to information about Kieran and pursue him on her own, putting her own life in danger. Not only that, but she'd ambushed Ivy outside the precinct, almost giving Ivy a panic attack out in the open. Thankfully, Jonathan had been there to cover for her. Alice had apologized later, but that made little difference to Ivy. She saw the reporter as someone who would do anything for a scoop, even if that meant violating the personal rights of others. No doubt the information she shared on the news report was *not* meant to be shared with the public. And while Ivy could respect that Alice was determined and passionate, she thought she went about it in the wrong way.

"Detective," Alice said as Ivy got out of the car. "Fancy seeing you here."

Five days with no progress—if Alice was to be believed— meant Mrs. Baker and those kids were probably already dead. But Ivy wasn't going to leave it up to anyone else to find them, not anymore. She guessed in that way, she and Alice were somewhat alike.

"Just making the rounds," Ivy said. "Who was your source on the force? Was it Jonathan?"

"At least buy me a drink first if you're going to come in that hard and fast," Alice quipped. A man stuck his head out of the back of the van, causing Ivy to look over the other woman's shoulder as they came face to face. Alice turned. "It's okay, Jim. Just talking to an old friend."

"I need to know," Ivy replied. "Who was it?"

"Did Armstrong send you down here to shake me down, is that it? Wasn't man enough to do it himself?"

Ivy didn't reply, only stared the woman down. Alice didn't need to know Ivy wasn't sanctioned to be here. In fact, the less Alice knew, the better.

She huffed. "Fine. It was Leo Bruneau. Happy? There goes another perfectly good source."

Damn. Bruneau must be one of the officers Nat said was working the case. So the information *was* legit. "Maybe if you don't want to lose your sources you shouldn't broadcast confidential information," Ivy said.

"No one told *me* it was confidential," Alice said, her voice dropping an octave, like she was trying to make herself sound both sultry and innocent at the same time. Ivy narrowed her gaze at the woman, trying to figure out exactly what she was trying to accomplish. "Ugh. You're impossible. Maybe it was insinuated. But never spoken aloud."

Ivy pursed her lips. Well, that was partially Bruneau's fault too. He knew better than to talk to reporters. Especially Alice, whose reputation preceded her around the department. She and Jonathan had been an item for a while, and Ivy had learned she'd developed a rep as someone who wouldn't take no for an answer once a big case broke. Bruneau should have known better.

Ivy motioned to Alice's neck, which was still covered by a stylish scarf. "How's your neck?"

The other woman's face softened. "Getting better, thanks."

"I wouldn't come around the station for a few days. Armstrong won't be happy after seeing your report this evening."

"That was kind of the point," she said, tucking her blonde hair over one ear. "It's been five days since we learned about this story. And zero progress. Doesn't that infuriate you?"

"Of course it does," Ivy replied. She considered telling Alice then and there that she was now heading up the investigation, but she didn't need to perpetuate the lie. Let Alice think what she wanted; Ivy just wanted to get into the Baker house to start looking for clues. More than likely, Bruneau and his partner had already been through the house the night of the disappearance, and CSI had followed closely behind.

Which meant Ivy was unlikely to contaminate any evidence already found. Given they hadn't made much progress, Ivy suspected there hadn't been much evidence collected initially.

But she knew the house like the back of her hand. She might be able to find something the others missed.

"Is that it then?" Alice asked. "Am I clear to leave?"

"You were never being held," Ivy replied with a smirk then turned and headed for the house. She crossed the dark street and skipped a few steps heading up to the front door. Pulling on a latex glove from her pocket, she tried the door but wasn't surprised to find it locked. As she turned to head back down the steps, she practically jumped back, finding Alice only a few steps behind her.

"Whatcha doin?"

"What does it look like I'm doing? I'm investigating the house again." Ivy pushed past Alice, barely brushing the other woman's shoulder, but making contact nonetheless.

"Starting from scratch, huh?" Alice said, following her down the stairs.

"Don't you have somewhere you need to be?" Ivy asked.

"Not until the eleven o'clock," Alice replied. "And I fully plan to do my report from here. Jim and I were going to get some dinner, but I think I'm much more interested in what you're doing."

Ivy leveled her gaze with Alice. "Go to dinner. This is police business."

"Right, about that," Alice said, following Ivy around the side of the house, tracing the small concrete walkway that wound to the side door. "When I spoke to Bruneau, I asked about you. Because you were the one to originally interview Mrs. Baker, I figured you would be working the case, but he said you're on leave after what happened last week."

"My lieutenant wanted me to take some time off, but I'm back now," Ivy replied.

"Ah. Right. *Natasha*," Alice said, following Ivy up the steps to the side door. "The enigma."

"What does that mean?" Ivy asked.

Alice flashed her an innocent smile. "Nothing. Just that she's a hard egg to crack. Never could get a good read on her, despite how much time I spent at the station."

"Great," Ivy replied. "Well, if you don't mind, I have work to do here." She tried the side door, finding it too, was locked. Not surprising, but she had to at least try.

"Didn't you bring the key from the precinct?" Alice asked, her voice was back in that almost teasing cadence. Like Alice already guessed Ivy wasn't here "officially."

"Must have forgotten it," Ivy replied. She bent down, feeling under the concrete edge of the small porch. It stuck out a little from the brick, giving the porch a lip that overhung slightly on all sides. There had once been a metal railing that ran up the stairs as well, but that had long since broken off, probably from some kid trying to slide down it or use it as a makeshift skate rail. Only the postholes remained, mostly filled in with black dirt.

But Ivy was more interested in the top row of bricks under the lip. She felt along their rough clay until one moved slightly. Smiling, Ivy pushed one side of the brick. At first, it didn't feel like it would move, until it did. Ivy pulled the brick out and shook it until a small key tumbled into her hand.

"The old key in the brick trick," Alice said. "Clever. How'd you know about that?" She gave Ivy a suspicious look.

"Trade secret," Ivy replied. "Now please. I have work to do."

"You know what, there's something different about you," Alice said, crossing her arms. "I'm not sure what it is."

"Is that a bad thing?" Ivy asked.

"I don't know," she admitted.

Ivy huffed. "Can you please leave me alone now?"

"I don't think so," Alice replied. "You're proving to be more interesting than I gave you credit for."

"I could have you removed," Ivy said, her frustration getting the better of her. Since she wasn't sanctioned to be here, calling in for assistance would not only raise some red flags, but it would alert Nat to what Ivy was up to. And if she had it her way, she was going to wait until the last possible moment before getting her boss involved.

"Yeah?" Alice taunted and began tapping her foot, daring Ivy to make a move. She'd called Ivy's bluff and there was nothing she could do about it. Ivy either had to commit and arrest Alice herself or let her stick around. And since Ivy had no cause for which to issue an arrest warrant, she had little choice. She wasn't about to delay this investigation any longer because of Alice Blair.

"Just…stay out of my way," Ivy grumbled as she inserted the key into the deadbolt and unlocked the door.

It swung open with a creak, and something sparked in Ivy's distant memory. She recalled hearing that creak anytime a person went in or out of that door. No matter how many times the kids tried to shoot it with some WD-40 in a vain attempt to stop the door from revealing their nightly attempts at escape, it never worked. The door was the Baker's own personal guard dog, alerting the entire house to the illicit activities of its younger members, and something Ivy now vividly recalled.

It was amazing how she could have forgotten something so simple.

"So, are you going to tell me the real reason you're here?" Alice asked from behind her.

"Not unless I want it to end up on the front page tomorrow morning," Ivy replied, taking a few ginger steps inside the kitchen. The lights were off, but she knew exactly where the switches were and flipped them on, bathing the room in florescent light.

"Ouch," Alice said. "But you know, it would end up on Good Morning Oakhurst. I work for the news station, not the paper."

"Knowing you, you'd sell it to any outlet you could find," Ivy muttered.

"That hurts, Detective," Alice said, though her tone suggested anything but. "Who knows, maybe I can help."

"No," Ivy said, turning around to face the woman. "Don't touch anything. I don't need you contaminating the scene."

"I tell you what," Alice said. "You allow me to assist and give me an exclusive if you find anything that leads to the missing woman and those girls."

"And why would I do that?" Ivy asked.

"Because if you don't, I might find myself making a trip down to the police department. You know, just to check on things. I have to find a new source now, thanks to you. And you never know what might slip from a reporter's lips when she's within earshot of *certain* captains or lieutenants. I mean, we as a unit are pretty much the devil incarnate, right?"

This was what Ivy had hoped to avoid the second she saw Alice's news truck still sitting across from the Baker house when she arrived. The woman was too damn wily for her own good. And right now, Ivy was out of options. It was either work with Alice Blair or continue to delay any chance of finding Mrs. Baker and the girls.

"Just stay out of my way," Ivy said.

Alice held up her right hand, her middle three fingers in a line. "Scout's honor."

Chapter Eight

THE FIRST THING she noticed as they walked through the kitchen was the mess. The whole kitchen had been ransacked, like a tornado had come through and left only the walls and ceiling intact. But as Ivy looked closer, she noticed a method to the madness. The kitchen table had been flipped, and upon further inspection had suffered a broken leg. Silverware was scattered all over the floor, and the knife block on the counter had been turned over. But all the knives were missing. More than likely taken by Bruneau for testing, or maybe even by the kidnapper. The door to the oven was open, though it was empty inside.

As Ivy followed the path of destruction around the room, she could almost replay it in her mind. Mrs. Baker had probably been in the kitchen, maybe even fixing a meal. The perp came in through the same door she and Alice had just used, surprising Mrs. Baker. He may have struck her immediately, or she might have gone for the knife block, scattering silverware all over as she grabbed for something to wield. He must have knocked her back, and she fell into the table, probably breaking the leg.

Of course that was only one possible sequence of events.

It could have happened another way entirely, but Ivy knew Mrs. Baker.

"What time did the neighbor notice them missing?" Ivy asked Alice.

"Oh, don't you know? I thought you were working the case now," the woman replied.

Ivy turned to her. "I think we can drop the pretense, considering you're already blackmailing me."

Alice nodded in acknowledgement. "The person to report it was her next-door neighbor, a Mrs.—"

"Willoughby," Ivy said, nodding.

"Yeah," Alice replied with a frown. "She said Baker didn't show up for her bridge club meeting. Something the woman never missed, even when she was sick."

Mrs. Baker had practically lived for that bridge club back when Ivy stayed here. She suspected it was the only time the woman ever got away from the kids, leaving them with Mr. Baker. She wondered what she did with the two children under her care now when she went to the meetings. Did she let them tag along? Or did she allow them to stay here alone? Given her financial situation, Ivy didn't think she'd be out hiring a sitter.

"Nighttime bridge club?" Ivy asked.

"Yeah. Seven thirty."

"Who saw her or the kids last?" Ivy asked.

"Wow, you weren't kidding," Alice said. "You haven't even read the case file."

"Hey," Ivy said. "I'm helping you. So you help me."

Alice relented. "I saw something about someone seeing them at the grocery store earlier in the day."

Ivy furrowed her brow. That was a close timeline. Only a few hours between the last sighting and when they were reported missing. She glanced at the oven. Mrs. Baker was making dinner when she was interrupted. She continued to scan the kitchen, taking in all the details. There was a small yellow marker on the floor with a *6* printed on it. Ivy bent down and pulled out her phone to shine the flashlight on the marker. Just beside it was a dark mark on the linoleum floor.

"Blood," Ivy said. More than likely from a blow to Mrs. Baker.

"Oh wow, really?" Alice asked. Ivy shot her a nasty look, and the other woman took a step back. "Sorry."

Ivy stood, tucking her phone into her pocket as she made her way into the rest of the house. She flipped on the lights in each room as they went, inspecting the contents. For the most part, everything else looked like it did when she and Jonathan had been here last week. In fact, not a lot had changed since Ivy stayed here as a kid. It had been strange coming back here for the first time. This was even stranger.

Ivy glanced up the stairs. The bedrooms were up there. She pulled out another pair of gloves and tossed them at Alice. "Don't touch the handrail."

"Afraid someone might find out you were here?" she asked, pulling on the gloves.

"Sure, go ahead and leave your DNA around for anyone to find. I'm sure that won't bite either of us in the ass."

Alice grimaced and followed Ivy as she climbed the stairs. She'd managed not to come up here the first time because there had been no reason to. Her interest had been in Mrs. Baker's records. But she knew the kids' rooms would be up here. She needed to see them for herself.

As Ivy reached the top of the stairs, she was hit with a wave of nostalgia, of times sitting up here with Oliver, listening to the Bakers squabble down below. Or watching the other kids bicker in the living room while they stayed apart and separate from it all. There had been times when she thought she would never leave this place, not until she aged out. And yet, she'd only been here a year. But so many of her formative memories were made in that time, it was like she was stepping back into her past.

She checked a few of the doors at the top of the stairs, very much aware Alice was right behind her the whole time, watching for secrets Ivy was unwilling to give. She was a reporter, observant by nature. But Ivy was *aware* by nature, and she wasn't going to show any more of her hand than she already had.

The first few rooms were empty, their carpets stained long ago by residents who had grown up and moved on into their lives. There was almost a ghostly quality about the empty rooms, which didn't even have furniture in them anymore.

Finally, Ivy came to the room she had occupied as a child, along with three other girls. It was obvious this had been the missing girls' room as well, since it was marked with yellow tape. It was also clear from this side that a large boot print had been embedded in the particleboard itself, almost having broken the door in two. Whoever wanted to get in here wasn't going to let a flimsy door get in their way. They'd probably kicked the door enough to break it open.

She pulled the tape away and pushed open the door to find the dark room full of possessions. Instead of two bunk beds on either side of the room, single twin beds now occupied their spaces. A dim glow poured in from the single window, the moon trying it's best to break through the day's fog. Ivy flipped on the light and was immediately surprised at the amount of color in the room. The walls had been painted a light blue, and a rainbow ran all the way around the ceiling. Toys filled the cubbies and remained strewn all over the floor. But what interested Ivy the most was the lack of covers on the beds. Both beds had been stripped, probably by Burneau looking for any evidence of assault.

"Wow, this is sickeningly cheery," Alice said from behind her.

Ivy bent down, looking at distinctive grooves in the carpet. There were two, side by side. She put one hand out, trying to gauge their size. "What are you doing?" Alice asked.

"I think they might have been pulled out from under the bed," Ivy replied, standing back up. "Look. Two identical patterns side by side. They may have tried to hide under the bed but didn't quite make it."

"Delightful," Alice replied.

Ivy tried to replay it in her mind. He broke in—for it was most likely a large man at this point— attacked Mrs. Baker first. Then went for the kids. And he took all three of them. Who was he really after? Mrs. Baker or the kids? She had a hard time believing it was both. More than likely, he had a target and took the other party or parties so no one could identify him. Better not to leave any witnesses. Which didn't make their chances of still being alive look very good.

"No blood up here, I hope," Alice said, breaking Ivy from her thoughts.

"None that I see, and none that anyone else found. Otherwise, there would be a marker." She pointed to the marker beside the door, identical to the ones downstairs in the kitchen, except this one had a *9* on it.

"Right."

Ivy continued inspecting the room, though after a good ten minutes, she didn't find anything of note. Whatever happened in here, it had been quick. The kidnapper hadn't lingered, which made sense. But she wondered how he got three people out of the house and into a vehicle without anyone seeing him. They probably hadn't been conscious, so he either used blunt force to subdue them, or was carrying some kind of chemical. Based on the blood downstairs, Ivy's bet was on the former.

Without anything else to find up here, Ivy headed out and back down the stairs.

"Hey, don't you have to replace the tape up here?" Alice asked even though Ivy was halfway down the stairs already.

"It'll just look like it came loose," she called back. "Don't touch anything."

"I heard you the first fifty times, *Mom*," Alice called back.

Ivy just rolled her eyes and headed into the living room. Around the other side of the stairs was a smaller room tucked in the back of the house. When Ivy had stayed here as a kid, the space served as Mr. Baker's office where he did all the paperwork for the adoptees. But when she and Jonathan had come to see Mrs. Baker last week, they'd realized she'd taken over and not done a very good job at keeping the place organized. There weren't any evidence markers in the office like there had been in the kitchen and upstairs, leading Ivy to believe the kidnapper never even came in here. But the computer was missing, of course. Bruneau had taken it to get the hard drive cloned.

But it didn't appear he had even attempted to sift through the stacks and stacks of paper documents filling the room.

"Holy shit," Alice said, entering behind Ivy. "And I thought *I* was messy."

The room had originally been designed as a library of sorts, as it had shelves on every wall that didn't already have a window. But now they were all crammed full of papers and folders. *This* was what Ivy wanted. She knew Bruneau had already taken everything he deemed important, but she'd been hoping he'd be too lazy to deal with all the overflowing paperwork.

But any detective worth their salt knew this was a gold mine. The answer to who took Mrs. Baker and the girls was in here somewhere, buried in all these documents. She just needed to find it.

She picked up the nearest stack of papers and began to flip through them.

"Wait, you're not going through *all* these, are you?" Alice asked.

"Feel free to grab a stack and help," Ivy said.

"Are you kidding? You'll never find anything in this mess." Alice put her hands on her hips, looking around the room.

"You're the one who wanted to tag along," Ivy said, flipping through the folder.

"I didn't say I wanted to get stuck doing paperwork."

Ivy grabbed another folder and shoved it in Alice's face. "You want the glory; do the grunt work."

Alice grumbled as she opened the folder. "And what is it I'm looking for, exactly?"

"Anything that might look suspicious. Baker was deep in gambling debt. I'm wondering if someone came to collect."

"And took the kids too?" Alice said.

"That's the part I can't figure out, which is why I want to figure out who she owed money to. It's the most logical place to start. So that's what we do."

"You really think there's going to be a piece of paper in here that says, 'Big John's Loan Sharking Operation'?"

"You never know," Ivy replied. "You'd be amazed what some people will leave lying around."

Alice huffed and sat in the nearest chair, flipping through the file. "Your job sucks, you know that, right?"

"Versus selling my soul on TV every night? I think I'll take it." The file had nothing but a bunch of old receipts in it. Ivy put it to the side and grabbed another.

"Hey, I provide a vital public service. Where would we be without freedom of the press?" Alice asked.

Ivy glanced up. "That's not what you do, though. You prey on people's misfortune for ratings."

"Hey, newsflash. People *want* to hear the bad news. And they have a right to know. You want me to just pretend like everything is sunny and cheery all the time? The world doesn't work that way."

"Yeah, I'm aware," Ivy said, glaring at her.

"Anyway, what do you care? You're not responsible for other people's misfortunes."

Ivy winced. Maybe that was true, but sometimes it felt like it. That had been one of the reasons she left organizations like the Black Pistons and instead joined the force. She didn't want to inflict pain on people. She'd had enough of that in her own life and didn't want it for anyone else. She had originally thought rebelling and joining local criminal organizations would provide her a sense of family. A place of belonging because she was...untethered. A woman without a pack.

But they had turned out to be full of nothing more than selfish, hurtful people, and Ivy wanted nothing to do with them. She thought she could walk the line for a while, to be the rebel and have a positive impact at the same time, but that proved to be impossible. It had left such a rotten taste in her mouth, in fact, she'd swung in the complete opposite direction, appealing to Nat to sponsor her to join the force.

Though, now that she looked back on it, why had Nat even bothered? Her attitude towards Ivy had only grown colder as time drew on, and they'd lost what little bond they'd created between them. It was like Ivy's effort to find a connection in the force had backfired, cutting off the only person other than Aunt Carol who seemed to care about her.

"Hey," Alice said, waving a piece of paper above her head. "Earth to Ivy."

Ivy blinked a few times, realizing the folder in her lap was slipping off. "What?" she asked, grabbing it before it could fall.

"Are you sure we should be going through this stuff? These are all adoption records for kids she kept. Isn't this stuff supposed to be protected?"

Ivy's heart skipped a beat as she jumped up, the folder in her lap spilling on the floor. She went to grab the other folder from Alice, but the woman was too quick and snatched it back. "Hey, what's the big deal?"

"Nothing," Ivy said, trying to reach around Alice for the folder. "You're right, those aren't for public eyes. They should be sealed somewhere."

"Now wait a second," Alice said, having stood in an effort

to avoid Ivy. She had a couple of inches on her and was able to keep the folder out of reach. Ivy would have to tackle the woman if she wanted it back. And while she wasn't above brushing past someone or even grabbing an arm or two, a full-on bear hug wasn't quite in her arsenal yet. "There's no harm in just flipping through, it's not like—" She trailed off as her eyes went wide, looking at another file in the folder. "Wait a second. Ivy…*Stanford?* This is you. *You're* an orphan?"

Something overcame Ivy and for a brief second, she didn't care how much skin she'd need to contact to get that file. She practically scrambled up Alice, grabbing her arm and tearing the file from her hands.

"Ow!" Alice said as Ivy stepped back, having successfully grabbed the file. She didn't wanted Alice to know about her situation here at the house, of course. But more than that, she thought maybe her own file might contain some missing information from those few weeks. Information she *definitely* didn't want anyone else seeing.

Ivy flipped through the file, scanning the information contained within. There was nothing on her condition when she arrived. Just a handwritten note that said, *Keep an eye on her.*

And it looked like Mrs. Baker's handwriting.

Chapter Nine

"You need to learn how to be more considerate," Alice said, pulling her glove off. Beneath it, the palm of her hand was streaked in crimson from a deep paper cut.

Ivy's eyes went wide as she closed the folder, setting it to the side. "I'm…I'm sorry," she said. "I didn't mean—"

"Damn," Alice replied. "I need to wash this. May I use the sink, Your Highness?"

There was no sense hiding it anymore. Alice had already found out about Ivy. She nodded. "There's a bathroom right around that corner." She pointed to the library's other entrance, which led to the back of the house.

Alice made her way into the bathroom, and Ivy could hear the water running. She cursed herself. Of course Alice would pull the one file with incriminating information about Ivy. She wasn't used to people knowing things about her, especially people she didn't trust.

Alice returned a moment later, her hand wrapped in a paper towel. "I think I'll leave you to your business," she said.

"I'm sorry about your hand," Ivy said. "I shouldn't have been so…rough."

"I kind of figured it out anyway," the other woman

replied. "You knew where the hidden key was, you were already familiar with the house. It didn't take a genius to put two and two together. Why do you care so much?"

Ivy took a deep breath, then sunk into one of the nearby chairs. "Everyone always pretends like having a family is the end-all and be-all of being a…whole person, I guess. I used to have a family. Now I don't. Other than my Aunt Carol. I just don't want people to think there's anything more wrong with me than they already do." She'd kept so many people at an arm's length that she'd forgotten what it was like to be vulnerable. But somehow, it was easier admitting this to a stranger like Alice than it would have been to Aunt Carol or even Oliver. Alice barely knew who she was; she didn't care about Ivy or her past. Maybe that made her the perfect person to open up to.

Alice sighed and perched herself back on her original chair, holding her palm tight. "Family is complicated. Even when you have one it's…well, it's not always sunshine and roses."

Ivy looked up, surprised. She hadn't really thought much about Alice's situation or her family. On TV, she always appeared as the polished, perfect reporter, never a hair out of place, never bothered. So it was something of a shock to learn she had her own family issues. Though, as much as Ivy wanted to learn more, she didn't want to pry.

"Well, I think I'll leave you to it. You obviously have a handle on things here and I just don't think I'm going to get the story I'm after," Alice said, standing back up. "Plus, I need to get this under control before the eleven o'clock. And I need to eat."

"Do you need any bandages?" Ivy asked. "I have a first aid kit in my car."

Alice shook her head. "We have one in the van. Poor Jimmy is probably trying to figure out how to cut the segments all on his own out there." She paused a moment.

"Do you…do you want me to bring you back anything to eat?"

Ivy smiled, despite herself. "No. But thanks anyway."

Alice nodded as if she knew that would be the answer. "Well, best of luck finding something useful in all this. And thanks for letting me tag along." She left Ivy alone in the library, feeling like she'd sorely misjudged Alice Blair. She had to admit, they hadn't met under the best of circumstances. Alice had come into the bullpen full of confidence and bravado, all which Ivy now suspected was nothing more than an act. Maybe she wasn't so bad after all.

Then again, all of this could have been nothing but a seasoned reporter's attempt to soften a source. Ivy wouldn't let her guard down completely, but she also planned on being more open in future interactions with the woman. And really, what had Alice learned that could hurt her? That Ivy had once resided here? Ivy doubted that would be enough for the eleven o'clock.

She turned back to the stacks of folders and files. It was a lot to go through by herself, but she wasn't about to call Jonathan, not after how he'd dismissed her today. She did consider Oliver, but bringing him into an active crime scene would be a step too far, even for her. Alice she could explain away. But a civilian with no ties to the case at all? And a former resident who could have contaminated the scene? Nat would fire her for sure.

Which meant it was her job alone to make some headway. She started with the closest files, skimming through them quickly but thoroughly to make sure nothing was missed. A lot of it was old records, stuff Mrs. Baker had no need to keep but had apparently decided wasn't worth throwing out either. Things like reports from the social security office, change of address forms for children who had once stayed with her, correspondences from colleagues of Mr. Baker from the seventies and eighties, and everything else in-between.

Finally, after what seemed like an eternity, Ivy found a box of bank records.

"About time," she muttered under her breath, pulling out stacks and stacks of receipts. They were in no particular order and had been haphazardly thrown in the box itself. Ivy removed the box and brought it into the living room where she was able to sit on the floor and sort out the receipts by type. Ivy couldn't even imagine how Mrs. Baker made it through tax season. As she dug deeper, Ivy started to find bank statements from Oakhurst Federal Credit Union. And the very first one showed a negative account balance.

"Not looking good," Ivy said, pulling out more statements. Some of the statements hadn't even been opened, just tossed in the box without another thought. How someone could be so careless, Ivy didn't know. But she took the liberty of ripping them open and laying them all in order by month. When she reached the bottom of the box, she had almost two years' worth of statements from the account. And now that they were all in order, Ivy was able to see the story they told.

Apparently, Mrs. Baker had taken out a rather large loan eighteen months ago, almost fifteen thousand dollars. And little by little, she had whittled it away, using cash withdrawals every week or so until there was nothing left. The account had gone into the negative because of the interest owed on the loan, none of which had been paid back.

It wasn't much, but it was at least a start. She folded up all the statements and shoved them in her jacket pocket before returning to the library.

She spent another two hours going through the paperwork, finding little else of note. As Alice had predicted, there was no receipt from a loan sharking operation anywhere that Ivy could find. But at the very least, she had something to start with. The credit union would be open tomorrow, even if it was only for half a day considering it was Saturday. But Ivy only needed a few minutes to speak to them about the loan.

As she walked around the house, turning off all the lights, she wondered if she should even reach out to Bruneau. Had he already found the same evidence Ivy had? Or was the tech department still trying to crack Mrs. Baker's passwords on her computer?

Ivy closed the door and locked it, hiding the key back in the piece of brick and replacing it under the porch. She'd been the one to sit here and pour through hundreds, if not thousands, of Baker's documents. Why would she hand all that over to Bruneau? And as far as she was concerned, this was *her* case now. She'd wake up early and head over to the bank first thing. After that, maybe she'd re-evaluate.

Ivy trotted back over to her car, past the news van still parked outside the Baker home. Ivy glanced over as she passed, but the front cab was dark. Alice and her cameraman were probably in the back, preparing for the next broadcast.

Still, she hesitated.

And immediately brushed it off. Why was she being so wishy-washy? She didn't owe a local TV reporter anything, nor did she need to "check out" with her. Ivy wanted to strangle herself for being so irrational.

She returned to her car and gunned it, pulling away from the curb before she could spend one more ounce of brain-power on Alice Blair.

~

Ivy was parked in front of Oakhurst Federal Credit Union a full hour before they opened. She'd returned to Aunt Carol's the night before, late enough that the other woman had already gone to bed. She hadn't slept well.

Thankfully, she'd awoken to the smell of coffee and waffles, both of which she consumed at Aunt Carol's kitchen table. Sitting there, she'd been struck at just how similar Aunt Carol's kitchen was to Mrs. Baker's, which only led to thoughts of what it would look like should someone break into Aunt Carol's house, which sent Ivy into something of a mental tailspin.

Thankfully, she'd left early with the excuse she was working a new lead and had been able to clear her head during the drive over, her coffee from Aunt Carol still warm in the travel mug beside her. Ivy had learned early on that sometimes her mind liked to spiral into dark places, and the easiest way to get out of that was to get up and start moving. And the fastest way to move was to hop in her car and gun it. Maybe the car wasn't in the best shape, but it could outrun just about any other car she came up against and did it with the roar of a hundred and eighty horses. It was in those rare moments when it was as if she could get away from everything.

The fog from yesterday had finally burned off, and the sky was an uncharacteristic blue for February in Oakhurst. But a cold front had moved in off the Pacific and temperatures had dropped overnight. That, combined with the fact the Corvette didn't have the most reliable or efficient heating system, meant Ivy was in her heavy jacket, complete with gloves, watching her breath as she waited for someone to come open the building next door.

OFCU was neither a large nor impressive building. It had once been a restaurant chain that had been repurposed into a branch of the bank about twenty years ago, and it was showing its age. The stucco on the sides of the building was cracked and worn, and the sign out front was yellowed from too many UV rays over the years.

"There you are," Ivy whispered as she saw a woman headed for the front door. She looked to be in her late fifties, carrying a modest bag, and was dressed for the weather with a long coat and hat. She took a minute to fumble with her keys before finding the one she needed and opening the door.

Some part of Ivy's mind couldn't help but case the situation. She'd learned early on to spot vulnerabilities and exploit them where she could. That had been the de facto motto of the Black Pistons, but Ivy had found it came in handy when she was evaluating crime scenes.

Due to this, she couldn't help but think about how long it had taken the woman to open the door. Any criminal would have seen that as an opportunity. Thankfully, there was no one else around except for Ivy.

She gave it about ten minutes, watching two more employees enter before she cut the engine and got out, headed for the front door. It was still about ten minutes before they officially opened, but Ivy figured it would be better to do this before any customers came along.

Reaching the door, she found it locked from the inside. She knocked a few times, and the same woman who had first opened this morning looked up from her desk, consternation painted all over her face, and pointed to her watch. Ivy pulled out her badge and held it up so the woman could easily see.

The consternation turned to confusion as she got up and headed for the doors, unlocking them for Ivy.

"Good morning," she said. "Is everything all right?"

"I need to speak to someone about one of your customers," Ivy replied.

"Alright. I'm Beverley Waddle, the manager here. What can I help you with?"

"Detective Bishop, Violent Crimes," Ivy said as Mrs. Waddle closed and locked the door behind her. "I need information on Jillian Baker."

"The missing woman from the TV?" Mrs. Waddle asked, her eyes wide.

"Yes. She has an account here."

Mrs. Waddle furrowed her brow. "I'm not sure. I'll have to check."

Ivy winced. That wasn't meant as a question, but the bank manager had heard it as such. Ivy had hoped her tone would have indicated the potential urgency of the situation, but the teller moved with the slow speed of her age.

Mrs. Waddle used her passkey to get around the partition to one of the stations at the bank. She hauled herself up into the chair and began typing away on the keyboard. "Baker? With a B, right?"

"Right," Ivy said, beginning to lose her patience.

"Here we go. Yes, she has accounts here with us." The woman looked closer at the screen and Ivy saw something pass over her features. She thought it might have been alarm, but couldn't be sure.

"She has more than one?" Ivy asked.

"I…uh, I'm not allowed to give out customer information without a warrant or writ. Do you have one with you?"

"You saw the news report," Ivy said. "She's missing and we believe what is in her bank records may have something to do with her disappearance. I already know one of her accounts is in the negative, the one with the loan. I'm going to need all the details about that loan and anything else that might be pertinent to her activity here."

"I'm sorry, Detective, but without a warrant, there's nothing I can do. I can't break the law, no matter what the situation. But I'll be happy to release everything we have as soon as I see the official order."

Ivy huffed. Getting a warrant would mean going to Nat. "Look, it's already been five days. Getting a warrant will take another day, at least. Maybe more because of the weekend. Can you just…help me out here?" Ivy asked.

"I wish I could," Mrs. Waddle replied.

"Will you at least give me the reason she took out the loan?"

Mrs. Waddle pursed her lips, though her eyes were down-turned in sympathy. Ivy took a deep sigh, realizing this had been a waste of time. Again, she'd assumed she could barrel her way into a situation and get what she wanted. She was still learning the limits of what the badge could and couldn't do. Maybe if she'd spoken to one of the younger employees, she might have been able to make some headway.

"Thanks for your help anyway," Ivy said, turning back to the door.

"Sorry again," the woman replied, walking back out into the lobby so she could unlock the door for Ivy. "Like I said, I'll be happy to help with the proper documentation." Ivy didn't think that was very likely. Not unless she wanted Nat to stop her dead in her tracks before she barely got off her ass. Ivy pulled her coat tighter as she walked back to her car, trying to keep the cold wind from seeping into her bones. As soon as she was inside the car, she hit her palm on the steering wheel.

Stupid. Should've known that wouldn't work.

But she wasn't done yet. She still had a few cards up her sleeve. She pulled out her phone and dialed.

"Hello," a familiar voice on the other end said. "I wondered when you'd be calling."

"Can I come over?" Ivy asked, hating the desperation in her voice.

"Feel free. I'm not going anywhere."

Chapter Ten

It was nearing ten in the morning by the time Ivy arrived at Oliver's house, and despite the cold, it looked like the residents of Oakhurst were trying to take advantage of the clear weather. In his neighborhood alone, she passed more than three groups of walkers and many people out trying to clear debris from their driveways and gutters. She guessed that's what normal people did on the weekends, they took care of household chores or went for leisurely strolls or spent the day with their families.

Ivy hadn't had a day like that in years—no need to go out beyond work unless she was out of groceries. And thanks to the modern convenience of DoorDash, she didn't even need to do that if she didn't want to. Her apartment required no maintenance on her part, and no one other than Aunt Carol ever bugged her to spend time with them, so she'd often find herself reading on a Saturday afternoon. But ever since her promotion, she'd found she had less and less time to spend on leisure activities as so much of her focus was on the job. Maybe it was better that way; it kept her busy and her mind off other things. Things that had become…intense.

Ivy got out of the car, taking stock of Oliver's house. It

was the only one on the block with a metal fence around the front yard, which itself was full of overgrown weeds and plants. A concrete pathway led up to the front door, but there were KEEP OUT signs posted everywhere, and Ivy noticed the mailman hadn't even ventured up to the front porch. He'd just dropped Oliver's mail over the fence so it was lying on the ground as she opened the gate. Ivy smiled, picking up the mail and walked confidently up to the front door to knock. It hadn't been too long ago that she and Oliver had been estranged. But after his help with the Kieran case, they'd done a lot to repair the rift Ivy had intentionally set between them.

Ivy looked up at the camera mounted above the door, waiting for Oliver to come let her in, but it was taking him an inordinately long amount of time. She tapped on an imaginary watch on her wrist as she glared at the camera some more. What was taking him so long?

After a full two minutes, she finally heard the bolt on the other side of the door slide. Ivy smiled as Oliver opened the door, but he put one finger up before she could say anything.

"Don't make any sudden movements. And don't freak out. I'm trying to train him."

"What are you—" But as he stepped aside, she saw what he was talking about. At the end of the hallway was a small dog, probably no more than twenty or twenty-five pounds, sitting on the carpet and panting heavily. It looked as though the dog might launch itself from the carpet and barrel itself into Ivy from the way he was nervously vibrating.

"When did you get a dog?"

"Three days ago," Oliver admitted, not taking his eyes off the animal. He held up one hand, palm out, which caused the dog's eyes to flash, though he remained rooted to the spot. "Give me a second. He's not used to anyone else coming into the house. I've been trying to prepare him for this."

"For what? Me?" Ivy asked.

"For anyone. They told me down at the shelter he was a

little skittish. But he calmed down after being here a day. I just need to—" Before he could continue, the dog jumped up began trotting in their direction.

"Hero," Oliver said sternly, and the dog froze. "Rug." Amazingly, the dog backed up until he was on the rug again and sat back down, though a few whines escaped his throat.

"You can let him go," Ivy said. "I don't mind dogs."

"That's not the point," Oliver said. "If he doesn't learn now, he'll be running this house, I know it."

"What on Earth possessed you to get a dog?" Ivy asked. "I didn't even know you liked animals."

"We had that rabbit at the Baker's house, remember?" Oliver said, leading her into the hallway. "Here, come into the kitchen."

"What about him?"

"He'll get there, he just needs to calm down for a second," Oliver said. "I took care of that rabbit more than anyone else. Don't you remember?"

"I guess," Ivy said, walking past the vibrating dog into the kitchen.

"Hero," Oliver called once both he and Ivy were out of the dog's sight. "Come." Hero trotted into the kitchen, though his focus never left Ivy. "I think he likes new people. I guess that's better than the other way around," Oliver said. He reached into a jar on the counter and produced a dog biscuit. "Hero, sit."

The dog looked at Oliver and tentatively sat on the floor. Oliver broke the biscuit in two and fed half to the dog before giving the other half to Ivy. "Here, try a command. Tell him to come."

Ivy wasn't sure about this. She'd never had a pet—not because she hadn't wanted one, but because it had never been practical. She'd asked for one when she was young, but it hadn't happened by the time her family disappeared, and Aunt Carol was allergic to most types of pet dander. When she moved into her apartment, she thought about getting one, but realized it probably wouldn't be fair as she'd be gone most of the days with her job, and the pet damage fee at her apartment was astronomical.

"Hero, come," Ivy said, holding out the biscuit. The dog approached her, practically drooling. "Sit." His butt plopped down on the ground with a thud, and Ivy couldn't help but smile. "Good boy." She fed him the biscuit, petting his head as he ate. "What kind of dog is he?"

"The shelter said he's a mix. But there's some French Bulldog in there somewhere."

The little dog continued to try wagging his non-existent tail for Ivy as she scratched behind his ears. "He's cute. Where'd the name come from?"

"It came with him," he replied.

She cocked her head at her friend. "And tell me again what possessed you to get him?"

Oliver sighed. "*You* did, remember?"

"Me?"

"You said I'd shut myself off, that I needed to get out more. Make some connections. Well, I didn't want to do that. Then at the diner, you said I needed a dog for company. I figured that was as good of an idea as any."

She was surprised he'd put so much stock in what she'd said. She barely even remembered saying anything at all. It wasn't like she had a lot of room to talk. "Well, I'm glad you have him. This house is too big for you to be here alone."

"He's keeping me on my toes," Oliver said. Thankfully after the head rub, the nervous energy of meeting Ivy seemed to have seeped out of the dog, and he went over to the water dish that hadn't been in the kitchen the last time Ivy had been here and began lapping up water. "So, what's wrong?"

She turned to him. "Why does something have to be wrong?"

"Because you wouldn't be here otherwise," he said,

leading her down the hall and back into his office. However, it was less like an office and more like a cave. Oliver had covered the windows with blackout curtains and had filled the room with monitors and computer equipment. All of it was beyond Ivy. Then again, this was what he did for a living. She supposed everything in the room had a purpose. Though she did notice a small dog bed at the foot of Oliver's desk.

"Aww, that's just the cutest."

"Uh-huh, whatever. Are you going to stop dancing around it or admit that you need my help?"

"Fine," she said. "I've run into a roadblock on the Baker case."

"I didn't think you were *working* the Baker case," he said, sitting in his chair. A second later, Hero trotted into the office and took up residence in his little bed, making circles until he was laying down.

"I wasn't. Until yesterday. Did you see Alice's news report?"

"I don't have a TV, you know that," he replied.

"All of these screens and none of them can pull in a TV signal?" she asked. He just stared at her, his face like a block of stone. "Nat's been lying to me. She said the case was making progress, that the detectives working on it were close to nailing a suspect. But I found out from Alice last night that isn't even close to being true. They've gotten nowhere. And it's already been five days."

"So you decided to take on the case by yourself?" he asked. "Where's Jonathan?" The way he said *Jonathan* made her think he might be a little jealous, but she dismissed the thought as soon as it crossed her mind. She didn't need any more drama.

"He's busy," she said.

"What happened? I thought he was all gung-ho to take on this case."

"I don't know," Ivy admitted. "I didn't ask. He's been out on leave or something."

"Both of you on leave at the same time?"

"Yeah, doesn't stand to reason, does it?" She looked for another seat somewhere else in the room, but there were only consoles. Ivy ended up leaning against one of the towers holding equipment. "Regardless, Nat doesn't know I'm on the case. Not yet anyway."

"And you'd like to keep it that way."

Ivy sighed. There was no way she'd be able to keep her boss in the dark forever. She might be new, but she wasn't *that* naïve. "I need to have some hard evidence before I go to her. Something that will show her she's wrong for keeping me away from this one."

Oliver drew his brows together. "I don't get what her deal is. Why keep you off this at all?"

"That's the million-dollar question."

He smiled. "I'd like to take this opportunity to remind you I already offered to help you on this case. And you refused me. Flat out rejected me. It was heartbreaking."

"Very funny," she said drawing her features in. "You know, every time I think I can trust Nat again, something else comes up and shatters what little belief I have in her."

"Please," Oliver said, exasperated. "Enough about your boss. Tell me what you need."

"Bank records. Specifically, information on a loan Jillian Baker took out. I have the original bank statements, but I couldn't get the bank to release the information. Not without a warrant."

Oliver smiled even bigger. He knew how much Ivy didn't like the thought of him using unscrupulous means to get into places he shouldn't be. But at the same time, she was out of options. "Wait, I want to hear you say it. Say, 'Oliver, please break into the bank records for me.'"

Ivy worked her jaw, glaring at him.

He just smiled and folded his arms. "Say it or no deal."

She was making a lot of concessions for this case. Concessions she hadn't seen herself making before. And maybe if she hadn't been connected to Mrs. Baker, she wouldn't be so determined. But not only might Mrs. Baker have information about Ivy's past, but those girls were technically Ivy's responsibility. If she had just reported Mrs. Baker to social services like she had threatened to do, none of this would have happened. They would have made a visit, taken one look at Mrs. Baker's finances, and removed the girls for their own safety. Instead, Ivy decided to do nothing, because catching Kieran Woodward was more important.

Ivy's delay may have cost those two little girls their lives.

"Oliver, break into the bank records for me."

"You didn't say please," he said. "Hero, don't you think Miss Ivy should say please?" Hero looked up from his bed at Oliver, then at Ivy.

"That's all you're getting," Ivy growled.

Oliver scoffed, leaned over and opened a drawer on his desk. He pulled out a stack of papers and handed them over to Ivy.

"What are these?"

"Jillian Baker's bank records," he replied. "I pulled them as soon as I got home from the diner that night. Figured you might come looking for them. Oh, I also have her credit card statements, her police record, her credit history, and her mortgage information. I can even tell you when she last checked out a book from the library. It was 1998 if you're curious."

"Holy shit," Ivy said, looking at the stack of papers in her hands. "You did all this without being asked?"

He shrugged. "I figured if you ever needed it, it would be urgent, so I thought it was better to collate it all at once. By the way, she's never going to be approved to buy a house or get a credit card ever again. I've never seen a rating worse than hers. Which is weird, because just a few years ago, it was stellar."

Ivy began flipping through the pages, reading the information Oliver had found. "How much of this have you examined?" she asked.

"All of it," he replied.

"Okay," she said. "Walk me through it."

Chapter Eleven

THEY SPENT the rest of the morning pouring through everything Oliver had collected. He'd not only broken into different agencies to gather the information, but he had collated it so it told a timeline story of Mrs. Baker's life over the past fifteen years. It was almost a complete picture from the entire time Ivy had known the woman. Ivy couldn't believe it; he'd done the work of an entire police department all on his own and kept it in his drawer *just in case*. She really wished Oliver would put his skills to better use. But he didn't need her commenting on his chosen lifestyle, so instead she decided to focus on everything he'd gathered.

Back when he and Ivy were staying with the Bakers, their finances had been the picture of health. They hadn't been well-off by any means, but they'd been solvent. Mr. Baker had been with the military in his youth and had a good military pension that provided a base income. Then, of course they had the income provided by the state to help take care of the children. But beyond that, they had savings and some investments that provided additional security. They didn't spend in excess and stretched the money they received from the government. While Ivy had only been with them for a year, she hadn't felt like things were tight at any time.

Then again, she hadn't been focusing much on money back then either.

But after Mr. Baker got sick, things began going downhill. Medical bills began pouring in, wiping out a lot of the couple's savings. Mrs. Baker did the best she could to keep them afloat, but because of his illness, she couldn't afford to take care of as many children. Oliver could almost point out the very moment things began passing the point of no return.

"Right here," he said, pointing to a graph that showed the full length of the Baker's financial lives. "Almost two years ago and about six months before Mr. Baker died. You can see they're outspending themselves. That's when Mrs. Baker went to the credit union for the loan."

"So then where does the gambling come in?" Ivy asked. "So far all this looks like nothing but medical bills."

"He dies here, on September 9, 2021," Oliver said. "Funeral costs and medical bills are overwhelming her. I think maybe she was looking for a way to pay for it all."

"So the loan wasn't for gambling at all, but bills?" Ivy asked.

"Looks to be that way." He turned to his computer and pulled up a new screen. "You can see here how many children were under her care over the past ten years. Up until Mr. Baker got sick, they always maintained at least ten kids in their house. But then it drops dramatically, down to nothing in early 2021. She was caring for him full time."

"And burning through everything they had with nothing else coming in. She was getting desperate."

He nodded. "And that's where this comes in." He pulled up another screen showing an account with VirtualVegas.com. The username was *BakerLady*.

"Wait, is that her account? How did you get in there?" Ivy asked.

He kept his eyes on the screen. "Don't worry about that. The website keeps a log of all the user's transactions. You can see the registration date, along with every bet and win or loss they've made under this account."

"How did she pay for it all?" Ivy asked, looking at the rows and rows of losses.

"Simple. Credit card," Oliver replied, bringing up another screen. This one was logged into a credit card account, which had been maxed out.

"You broke into her credit card account as well?" Ivy asked, deadpan.

"Hey, do you want to find out what's going on or not?" he said. "Keep in mind I usually charge a premium for this kind of service."

She huffed. Since he was already in, she might as well take a look.

It was just as he said. Lines and lines of charges on VirtualVegas.com. There were a few unrelated items that looked like grocery runs. But that was about it. "How many cards does she have?"

"At least four that I've found. She was using the credit from some to pay the others. Not a very smart decision. And the interest rates were piling up."

"She was spiraling," Ivy said. Personally, she never bought anything unless she could afford it in cash. Which meant she rarely bought anything. But she'd never faced a large medical expense like Mr. Baker either. Who knew what she might resort to, given the huge financial constraints of watching someone she loved suffer? "And trying to use gambling winnings to cover her debts."

"Honestly, she wasn't doing bad," Oliver said, switching back to the online gambling site. "You can see she was winning more than she was losing in the beginning. But I think that's probably on purpose. No doubt these things are fixed to keep you coming back. And then when they have their tenterhooks into you—"

"—you're too deep in to get back out," Ivy finished. She and Jonathan had discovered Mrs. Baker's affiliation with VirtualVegas.com on their last visit here, where Ivy had assumed the woman just had a gambling problem. She didn't realize there had been much more to the story. "Look at all these withdrawals. I've seen the ones from this account here, but she was pulling money from a second account on alternating weeks. That's at least two hundred dollars in cash every week. Where was it all going?"

"That part I don't know," he said. "What I do know is the bank wouldn't approve any more loans, her credit is shot."

Ivy sat back in her chair. She was thankful Oliver had pulled in a second one from the kitchen so they could both go over the documents, because after pouring through financial documents for two straight hours, her mind felt like mush. She rubbed her eyes. "So the question is, do online casinos employ muscle to kidnap people and make them pay their debts?"

"I highly doubt it," Oliver replied.

"Yeah, me too. Even though she owes them, what, about forty grand?"

He nodded. "And the bank loan. And the medical bills. She's in the hole almost a hundred and seventy thousand total."

That was a lot of debt for a sixty-something widow. "So, she brings in a couple of kids to try and help the finances, but it only makes things worse."

"What are you thinking?" Oliver asked.

"I don't know. But I'm not willing to discount the possibility this all might have been an inside job."

"What, like she just took the kids and ran?" Oliver said.

"Think about it. She's over a hundred thousand dollars in debt. Creditors are knocking on her doors; she gets a visit from me and Jonathan exposing her online gambling 'addiction,' and she panics. She packs up the girls, doesn't tell anyone where they're going and just gets out of town."

"You're saying she staged all this?"

Ivy shrugged. "Maybe not staged. But ran away from the problem, yeah. I mean, why not? Maybe she figured if they disappeared, the creditors would too."

"But didn't you say you found blood at her house?"

"We did. But I wouldn't put it above someone to stage a scene."

"Wait a second, *we*? I didn't think Jonathan was working with you." Oliver's voice had a concerned tone underlying it.

"Don't get sidetracked," Ivy said. "I need to start looking into her next of kin. Or anyone who might know where she went. Even if she did leave on her own accord, it's still kidnapping."

"But there would be activity on her credit cards. Or her bank accounts," Oliver said, turning his attention back to the stack of papers.

"I would agree, except for all those cash withdrawals she was making," Ivy replied. "She might have been hoarding money in case something happened." She furrowed her brow. That didn't quite make sense though. Because she would have been stocking cash away long before things got out of hand, and way before Ivy and Jonathan showed up.

"If you say so," Oliver said, though he didn't sound convinced.

"It's just a working theory," Ivy admitted. "Hang on a second. Let me work through this." She closed her eyes, trying to imagine herself as Mrs. Baker. She's just lost her husband, facing a mountain of bills. But she's not an idiot. She knows she can't just rely on online gambling to get her out of this. That's a longshot. So, she starts pulling out cash. First from one account, then from another. Why? What was she doing?

"I hate to ask this," Ivy said, sitting back up and opening her eyes. "But I need your computer for a minute."

"What for?" he asked, suddenly defensive.

"I need to log into the Oakhurst system. I want to check to see if she has a record."

"I can do that," he said, preparing to type.

"*No*, I'll do it," Ivy insisted, elbowing her way into his space. "You get so weird about your computer."

"Wait a second," he said, causing Ivy to pause. "You just touched me. On purpose."

"Yeah," she replied flatly, opening up a new window and navigating to the station's site. "I do that now."

"*What?* Since when?" Hero's eyes snapped open at the intensity of Oliver's voice. He'd fallen asleep at their feet hours ago.

"Just…something I'm working on," she said, trying to keep her focus on logging into the system. She knew if anyone looked, the Oakhurst Police records system would show Ivy had been researching Mrs. Baker. She'd just have to hope no one would be bored enough to investigate.

"Ivy, that's incredible," Oliver said. "So you can actually touch people now without—"

"It's not a big deal," she said.

"Are you kidding? It's a *huge* deal." He was practically jumping up and down on the balls of his feet. "Can I try?"

"Try what?" She froze as he reached his hand out, moving it closer to her shoulder. All of a sudden, her heart was slamming against her ribcage at the same time it was being squeezed in a vice grip. Ivy took a few short breaths, unsure how to respond. She hadn't let anyone she knew initiate contact yet, just strangers. People that weren't close to her. What if she freaked out again like she had with Nat? What if she went right back to the way things were? She didn't think she could do that.

"Just…wait," she said as his hand was inches from her shoulder. "Not yet."

"Oh," Oliver said, pulling his hand back. "I'm sorry, do you—"

"I just…" She squeezed her eyes shut trying not to let her emotions overwhelm her. "I'm not ready yet. It's a work in progress."

"Okay," he replied, though it was impossible not to hear the disappointment in his voice. Dammit, she wasn't responsible for making him feel better. It was her body and if she wasn't ready for people to touch her yet, she had every right to make that a hard boundary.

"When did all this start?" he asked. "I didn't even know you were trying to…well, I mean you never seemed to have a problem with your haphephobia before."

"Maybe I just got tired of living that way," she said, finishing her log in and going through Oakhurst's records. She typed in Mrs. Baker's full name and date of birth, waiting for the system to process. Unfortunately, Oakhurst's servers weren't the quickest to respond.

"I didn't mean…I just wanted to say that I'm really glad you're working on it. It has to have been hard, all these years."

"You get used to it," she replied. She still wasn't ready to talk about it yet, but if she was, Oliver would probably be her most logical choice for someone to open up to. He'd known her the longest, other than Nat. And while Aunt Carol was great, Oliver had been through the same stuff Ivy had. They shared a kinship over their time with the Bakers. A kinship they'd been able to easily rekindle, even after a long time.

"Here, look, she's got speeding tickets," Ivy said, looking at the data populating.

"Is that what you were looking for?" Oliver asked.

"I'm not sure what I was looking for," she replied. "But maybe…wait a second. Look at these. They're all in Coos County. And all of them over the past six months. But that's two hours away."

"So, she was going to Coos a lot?" Oliver asked.

"Yeah, must have been. Assuming these tickets only represent a small slice of the times she went, which is what I would expect. A lot of that road is empty highway. Nothing out there." She sat back, thinking. Finally it struck her. "Except."

"What?" Oliver asked.

"Three Rivers," she said, getting up and startling Hero again. He hopped up to follow her.

"Three Rivers?" Oliver called after her, but she was already halfway to the door, the folder Oliver had prepped tucked under her arm.

"Don't you watch TV?" She stopped, turning to him. "Right, I forgot. Then I guess you never see the commercials. There are two tribal casinos in Three Rivers. The perfect place to spend some cash on the weekend. Cash you've pulled from the ATM."

"And a real casino is much more likely to employ a collection agency than an online casino."

"Exactly," Ivy said. She still wasn't sure if the staging angle was viable, but this was too much of a connection to ignore. If Mrs. Baker got in trouble with one of the tribal casinos, then it might start to explain some things.

"You're not driving out there right now, are you?" he asked, as he and Hero followed her to the door.

"Why not?" she asked. "I'm investigating this case, after all."

"But by yourself?"

She grinned at him. "I'd ask you to come, but you have someone here to take care of." She shot Hero a wink then headed out to her car.

Finally, she thought. *Progress.*

Chapter Twelve

It took her just over two and a half hours to get to Three Rivers from Oakhurst. As Ivy drove, she made sure to take note of the stretches of road where Mrs. Baker had been pulled over for her speeding tickets. Because her record had been clean before the tickets, Ivy had the sneaking suspicion they hadn't been the first times she was pulled over. She'd probably been stopped at least once and issued a verbal warning before anything was entered into the system. Perhaps even twice.

But something had kept Mrs. Baker coming back and back again, each time in enough of a hurry to warrant being stopped by the county patrol officers. She had three tickets in a six-month period in the system, which meant if she was stopped one more time, the officer would have taken her license. If she was willing to risk it, there was definitely something in Three Rivers that had caught Mrs. Baker's attention. In her research with Oliver, it seemed the gambling had just been a solution to a problem. But this suggested it might have become a problem all its own, just as she and Jonathan had first suspected when they met the woman.

Ivy should have realized it sooner. She could recall the

look of shame on Mrs. Baker's face when they confronted her about it. She'd given them some lame story about one of the girls "accidentally" signing her up to that online casino, but Ivy had already known that was nothing but bullshit. She'd allowed her pity to get the best of her looking back through the woman's history. Yes, it was terrible how her husband had died, and Ivy could understand she'd been desperate. But if Mrs. Baker was taking out cash and driving down to Three Rivers every weekend to gamble it away, even in an attempt to cover all her bills, she had taken things too far.

She might have even reached the point where someone thought a more extreme type of debt collection was warranted.

Ivy wasn't familiar with Three Rivers, but as she drove into the town, she was surprised by just how large it was. The town itself sat on a sound where the relentless Pacific Ocean met the rolling hills of Western Oregon, wrapping the town in scenery that was breathtakingly beautiful. The first thing she noticed as she approached were the towering emerald forests that cloaked the surrounding hills, their lush foliage providing a striking contrast to the expanse of the ocean. The town hugged the shores of Coos Bay, a large sound where the Coos River, the Ross Slough, and Brainard Creek all met, giving the town it's iconic name.

As she crossed over the Bay Bridge, Ivy took stock of the town. It didn't strike her as the kind of seedy place typically associated with a casino. Instead, what she found were quaint historic buildings, and plenty of shops and restaurants for locals and tourists alike. As she drove by, people walked around bundled up with smiles on their faces, and she even received a few waves despite not knowing a soul here.

It certainly didn't seem like the kind of place that would harbor the type of people who would kidnap a woman and two children for a gambling debt. But then again, it was always the innocent-looking towns that held the deepest secrets.

Ivy made her way through the downtown area, slowing down on some of the more historical streets which were lined with old brick. She saw signs for local golf courses and country clubs, but as she made her way to the far side of the town—following the GPS on her phone—the luster of the quaint village slipped away. Gone were the brick streets and cute shops and restaurants. What replaced it was a stretch of highway lined with power lines running beside what looked to be abandoned railroad tracks, which filled the small plot of land between the road and the sound itself. Tall trees bordered the other side of the street, and Ivy felt like she'd left Three Rivers behind entirely, having missed her destination.

Only as she came around the slow bend did she see the tower of the first casino on her list: Bear Paw Casino and Hotel. The place looked like a compound. A large neon sign stood outside the property, which sat right up against the sound, replacing the dilapidated railroad tracks. Ivy surmised they must have at one time supplied lumber or coal to the town but had long since been abandoned.

Beyond the sign was a high-rise, probably ten or fifteen stories tall, connected to a larger building to the side which held the casino, meeting space, and event center along with a special theater for shows. The sign out front advertised "Legend of the Firehawk," accompanied by a giant LED screen showing a bare-chested man with wings on his back as he soared through the air. She assumed it was probably like those "Cirque" shows she'd seen advertisements for.

But she wasn't here for any of that. She pulled in and avoided the valet parking option, instead parking her car in the far part of the lot and walked back to the casino. It was only slightly warmer here than in Oakhurst and Ivy had to pull her coat tight to buffet against the wind coming off the sound. But the air was fresh and despite the overcast sky, it felt like this was probably the best weather Three Rivers received.

The place was packed, and given that it was late Saturday afternoon, that wasn't a surprise. She didn't know how long she'd be staying in Three Rivers, but figured it was probably better to keep a low profile. She would only be in the casino as long as necessary and planned on finding a local motel if she needed to stay the night. She wasn't a flashy kind of person, and given what she'd been through, she'd found she could sleep most anywhere as long as it had some semblance of a mattress.

The automatic doors parted, revealing a large, gilded lobby accented with carved wood undertones. The place screamed opulent, as casinos were wont to do, but it also had an earthy feel, like it had tried to remain connected to the surrounding environment. A large atrium filled the middle of the casino, surrounded by eight beams, each of which had been carved or shaped to look like a tree trunk. A different animal was carved into the base of each of the massive structures, all of which surrounded a large fountain formed by rocks laid in an irregular pattern. It reminded Ivy of the natural beauty of the woods but if humans had a hand in shaping them, which she supposed was the idea.

Off to the left was the main casino, where she could hear the machines blaring their unending currency harmonies. The lobby itself was full of patrons, and there was a large bar on the other side of the fountain. The bar was raised about half a floor, giving patrons a fantastic view of the entire place.

Ivy looked around for anyone who might be able to help and decided her best bet was to just speak with someone at the check-in desk. However, there was a significant line of people waiting to check in. Some had two or three suitcases while others carried nothing more than an overnight bag. She figured the casino attracted all types from locals to tourists alike. It was probably responsible for a lot of Three Rivers' appeal *and* revenue.

Bypassing the line, she walked up to one of the clerks busy checking someone in. The man looked annoyed as Ivy sidled up beside him, but she didn't pay him any attention, instead showing her badge to the young clerk. "I need to speak with someone on your security detail," Ivy said.

The man at the desk took a quick glance at her badge. "Regarding?"

"A missing person's case," Ivy replied. She purposely kept the details scarce and would continue to do so until it was absolutely necessary to reveal more. It was better she get as much as she could without giving anything up. Less likely word would get back to Nat that way.

"One moment, please," he said, picking up the phone and speaking into it a moment. He hung back up. "Someone will be with you shortly."

Ivy nodded and left the man to finish checking in the customer.

While she waited, she wandered over to the large fountain, from which four different spouts shot water high into the air. They were precise enough that the water didn't fly everywhere on the way back down, instead staying in a nice, contained column. The patterns it made were more mesmerizing than she'd expected.

"You wanted to speak with someone in security?"

She turned to find herself standing next to a tall man in a pressed black suit, his sharp, dark hair pulled back in a neat ponytail at the base of his neck. He had a kind face, though it was lined with years of hardship, that much was plain to see. He held himself in a way that suggested nothing but professionalism, like he'd been doing this job a long time.

Ivy pulled out her badge again. "Detective Bishop, Oakhurst PD. I wanted to ask you some questions about a missing persons case."

"I'm Reese Alquema. Head of Security," the man replied, extending his hand for Ivy. She didn't want to be rude, but at the same time, recalled her experience with Oliver. She didn't know Mr. Alquema personally, but she hadn't done a full handshake before. First time for everything.

She tried to keep her face neutral and stuck her hand into his. When his large fingers wrapped around hers, for a second it felt like a bear had taken up residence on her chest, and suddenly Ivy thought this might not have been a good idea. She was going to lose it right here in the middle of this casino, and everyone would know she wasn't fit to wear the badge. That she had been nothing but a phony this whole time.

But thankfully, Mr. Alquema's grip was brief, if strong. He let go, giving her a grim smile. "I noticed you watching our fountain."

"It's quite the show," she replied.

"It is. The whole lobby was designed to mimic nature in every way imaginable. We have the water, the trees, the animals," he indicated the carvings on the posts, "and yet, none of it is real. It's all a fantasy."

"You sound like you don't like it very much," Ivy said.

"Let's just say I'd rather be out in the real thing. But we're not here to talk about me," he replied. "What is your case?"

"A missing woman and two children," she said, pulling out her phone to show him a picture of Mrs. Baker. "They've been gone for five days, missing from Oakhurst."

"And you think they may be here?"

"Not exactly," Ivy said. "I believe the woman, Jillian Baker, was coming here to gamble on a regular basis. I also believe she may have gotten herself in a little too deep."

His face darkened. "What are you suggesting?"

"Nothing. I'm just here looking for answers. Do you happen to know if she visited your establishment during the last six to eight months?"

"I don't recognize the face, but a thousand people come

through here every day," he said, his posture having tightened. "Let me go see if we have a flag on her account. You say she's running a deficit?" He turned and headed in the other direction, not waiting for Ivy to follow.

"I don't know that for sure, but that's part of the reason I'm here," she replied.

Alquema led them past another security guard standing beside a locked door, which required a keycard to enter. Once through, Ivy found herself in a brightly lit hallway, completely different from the moody and ornate lobby.

They passed another man headed the opposite way as Alquema led her into a large command-center looking room. He had to use his keycard again to reach this room, which was large, expansive, and full of monitors focused on tables, slot machines, poker tournaments, cashier payouts, and more. The number of people in the room scanning each image was immense.

"Wow," Ivy said as Alquema led her up a short series of steps to an upper level.

"We use the most advanced security techniques here," he said. "Our AI-trained system watches for anything that might be suspicious, which then routes it to one of our human controllers. From there, any incident is examined from as many angles as possible as our security team on the floor sorts out any problems." Alquema sat down at a large terminal and typed in Mrs. Baker's name.

Less than a second later her image, name and account number popped up. Below all her general information was her ledger balance. "She was in the red all right," he said. "Eleven large."

"How come it wasn't collected?" Ivy asked.

He pointed to the screen. Below the amount were the initials IA. "In arrears," he said. "We approve people based on the amounts they have in their bank accounts or their credit ratings. She was approved as good to excellent when she first opened an account with us nine months ago. And she paid her losses promptly, though she never lost more than a couple hundred at a time." He tapped the screen, scrolling back through her history. "But this last visit was the big one. That's where she lost it all. And because we don't update ratings until someone defaults on payment, we weren't aware her credit had become…undesirable."

"Do you employ collection agencies?" Ivy asked.

"No, we employ the local district attorney," he replied, his voice growing gruffer. "He files a motion demanding payment within ten days. If the money isn't received, which in this case it wasn't, he files a motion for wage garnishing. It was approved by a local judge and should have begun by now." He stared at the screen a moment.

"It hasn't because she doesn't have a penny to her name," Ivy said. "All her accounts are in the negative. She's completely broke."

Alquema sat back in his chair. "That's unfortunate. But it happens. We'll keep the account open in the event she ever does earn income we can garnish."

"That's kind of a cruel stance, don't you think? Especially for a woman who has gone missing?" Ivy asked.

"Or skipped town to avoid paying her debts," he said, turning in his chair to face her. "Did you consider that?"

"I did," Ivy replied. "But the blood at the scene suggests otherwise."

If the notion that someone had been harmed rattled Mr. Alquema, he didn't show it. "Was there anything else I could help you with?"

"Your company never employs collection or repo agencies?"

"I already told you, no. And I don't like the insinuation," he said.

"Right," Ivy replied. "I guess I'll just see myself out, then."

He got up. "I'll walk you. You can't get through any door without a card around here." They walked in silence all the way back to the lobby where Alquema left Ivy without another word. She thought maybe he might have something else to say outside of the security center, but she was wrong.

As she made her way back to her car, Ivy couldn't help but wonder if he'd been telling the truth. A casino didn't get rich by letting people default on their payments. She suspected she wasn't getting the whole story, or at the very least, she was getting a scrubbed-down version of it.

She was so deep in thought that as she approached her car, she realized someone had come up behind her. The sun had already set, and she was parked so far away that the lot lights were few and far between. She spun, ready for a fight, only to find a young woman in a suit standing behind her.

"Don't!" she yelled, holding up her hands and cowering.

Ivy dropped her fists. "Who are you? What do you want?"

"I want to help, if I can," she replied.

Chapter Thirteen

JONATHAN LOOKED UP, noticed the time on his computer, sighed, and returned his attention to the case in front of him. It was Saturday, and he'd been at it all day, trying to catch up on the mountain of work the lieutenant had seen fit to drop on his desk. He'd cut through a good chunk of it yesterday, only to come in this morning and find even more cases clogging up his email.

As before, none of them were urgent by any means, and in fact they looked like cases that hadn't been touched in a while. Things that had come across the desk that no one else had wanted to work. Jonathan, by nature, was the kind of person who thought everyone deserved a fair shot, so when a case came in, no matter how big or small, it was part of their responsibility as the police to at least take a look.

But even he was reaching the limit of his patience. All of these cases were nothing but busy work. A complaint about a lost smartphone, a fender bender follow-up that didn't even warrant examination by an insurance company in Jonathan's opinion, and a noise complaint from one neighbor about another, complaining about wailing cats. Nothing urgent and nothing dire. And yet, what was he supposed to do, tell his boss he just wasn't going to do the work assigned to him? Jonathan was well aware of his reputation as a boy scout around the precinct. And with that reputation came a stigma—that people could walk all over him and he wouldn't put up a fight. And until now, that had been true. His boss was purposely keeping him busy and away from the Baker case, he just couldn't understand why.

"Hey there." Jonathan looked up with surprise to see Alice Blair sauntering into the bullpen like she owned the joint. She still had the scarf around her neck, covering the wound made by Kieran Woodward, but otherwise looked as polished as a runway model. For a brief second, he forgot himself and realized he was staring before he turned back to his work.

"What are you doing here?" he asked, trying to keep his attention on his computer.

She pushed a couple of his files aside and took a seat on the edge of his desk, which had become something of a signature move for her. She liked to get under his skin, ever since they'd broken up. Where any other reporter would have called or emailed, Alice saw it necessary to weasel her way into the police station to accost the officers directly.

"Not very friendly this afternoon, are we?" she asked in that sing-song voice she sometimes employed. They hadn't gone out for more than six or seven months, but in that time, Jonathan had learned Alice used many different techniques for getting what she wanted. Sometimes that meant acting demure, and other times it meant pretending she owned whatever operation she was investigating. Either way, it had been too much for Jonathan. He could never tell when the woman was being honest with him, or if her affections were just an act.

"You better get out of here before Armstrong sees you," Jonathan replied. "He might find a reason to put you in handcuffs this time."

"Nice try," she said. "I happen to know Captain

Armstrong is enjoying a very nice steak dinner at Allegro's at this very moment. I don't think I'm in any danger." She paused a moment. "The question is what are you still doing here on a Saturday night?"

He checked the clock again. "It's still technically afternoon."

"Stop avoiding the question," she said.

"I'm trying to work," he replied.

Her voice trilled. "Oh Jonathan, you never did know how to let go and have a little fun, did you?"

Resigned to the fact she wasn't going to leave him alone until she got what he wanted, he finally turned his attention to her, sitting back in his chair. "So then what are you doing here?"

"Just my own little investigation," she replied. "I was hoping Bruneau might still be around. I've hit something of a wall."

"Bruneau?" he asked. "You're looking into the Baker case?"

"Don't worry," she said, reaching over and patting his hand. "I know you don't have anything to do with it. So I won't bother you any longer. I'll just have a look around, and then I'll be out of your hair."

"Trying to illegally access police records again?" he snapped.

For a brief second, Alice's veneer of confidence broke, but it was back in an instant. "That was just a little slip-up," she said.

"You spied on Ivy's computer and it almost got you killed," he replied.

Her face fell again, and this time he could tell he'd struck a nerve. "I'll…let you get back to work," she said, slipping off his desk and heading for the exit.

"Wait," he called out, hating how he'd just come across.

He wasn't that guy, nor did he want to be that guy. "I'm sorry, I didn't mean to be so harsh."

Alice returned to the desk, but she didn't sit down again. "What's going on? Is there something wrong?"

"It's nothing to worry about," he said. "I'm just under a lot of pressure."

"It's your family, isn't it?" she asked. "Your mother?"

Dammit. No one could say Alice Blair wasn't good at her job. In the months they had dated, she'd been privy to many of his conversations with his overbearing mother and the situation back home. They'd discussed it on many occasions. She was probably the only person in Oakhurst who knew the full story, and consequently, was the only person he could really open up to. He'd considered telling Ivy, but they didn't know each other well enough yet. They'd only had one major case together after all.

"It is, isn't it?" she asked again, taking one of the chairs from a nearby desk and taking a seat so they were both sitting at the same height.

He figured if he was going to get this off his chest, this was his one opportunity. No one else would understand. "She's just being more dramatic than usual," he said. "About Marie."

Alice nodded. "No improvements?"

He shook his head. "I even went up there for a few days to try to calm her down. But she won't listen to reason. She wants me to quit and come back to Portland full-time."

"And what do you want?"

"To stay down here, stay busy and not think about it," he admitted.

She held his gaze for a moment, looking like she was performing a serious interview on television. Alice had an uncanny ability to get others to share their pain with her and consequently, the world at large. Jonathan had made it clear in the beginning of their relationship that his personal business was never to be a subject of any exposé or deep dive into the police department. It was his business and his business alone. As a reporter, she had told him she could respect the need for confidentiality and could be the perfect sounding board for him.

In that respect, she had been right. And that had been one of the best parts of their relationship: their shared bond over the grief their families poured on them.

"But I guess that's not very realistic, not in the long run."

"Would you going up there change anything?" she asked. "Would it make anything better?"

He considered the question. "It would probably make things worse because she and I would be butting heads all the time. And that wouldn't be good for Marie either."

"Then it sounds like you're doing exactly what you're supposed to be doing," she replied. She'd been leaning forward, listening, but now she straightened to depart again.

"Thanks, Alice. If nothing else, at least you get it."

She gave him a sardonic smile. "I think we've both been on that particular merry-go-round, and I have no desire to keep getting yanked in circles" She sighed. "To be honest, I wasn't here to see Bruneau. I wanted to see if Ivy had made any progress."

"Ivy?" he asked. "Progress on what?"

Her eyes went wide for a split second. "Oh, just…a story she was assisting me with."

"What kind of story?" he asked. As far as he knew, Ivy and Alice went together like water and vinegar. Ivy wasn't the kind of person to warm to others easily, and they'd formed a contentious at best relationship during their last case. What had she been doing with all that time off?

"It's not important," Alice said, getting up. "I should get going. I have some deadlines to meet."

"Alice," Jonathan said, following her to the door. "What's going on with Ivy?"

"Nothing," she said. "Don't worry about it." But he held

her gaze with her same intense stare until she broke. It was enough to convince him she was hiding something, potentially something big.

"I was honest with you," he said. "Just tell me what's going on."

"I think if I did that, I'd be breaking someone's confidentiality," she said. "And I may be a lot of things, but I'm not willing to give up my journalistic integrity. You have a phone, why don't you call her and find out?"

She was right. Jonathan could have picked up the phone and called Ivy at any point, but he hadn't done it. He hadn't called to let her know he was going out of town, nor had he asked her how she felt about their boss sidetracking both of them from this case.

But it was a two-way street. She had a phone too. Did she even know he'd gone back home? That he was dealing with what his mother called "a crisis in the making," even though, in reality, it was nothing of the sort? No, because he hadn't *wanted* anyone to know. He'd left without a word to anyone except Lieutenant Buckley and returned in much the same way.

"I'll see you around, Jonathan," Alice said, pushing through the door. "Remember what I said."

"Yeah," he called after her, watching as she stopped to talk to a duty officer she'd somehow snuck past to get into the department. She left him with a smile on his face and made her way to the door, disappearing from view.

Jonathan returned to his desk and stared at the pile of cases he had yet to go through. Maybe it wasn't what *the boy scout* would have done, but he was tired of being pushed around.

He grabbed his phone and dialed.

Chapter Fourteen

"IDENTIFY YOURSELF," Ivy demanded, her heart racing.

The woman shuffled forward. She couldn't have been more than five foot one or two. From what Ivy could see, she was probably in her early forties, and her black hair was graying at the temples. Even though her suit matched the others she'd seen in the casino, it was somewhat wrinkled and looked to be in need of a good press.

"I overheard you speaking with Mr. Alquema," the woman said. She pulled out a pack of cigarettes from her pocket. "Decided now was a good time for a smoke break." Singling one from the pack, she removed it deftly and lit it with a lighter from her other pocket. The wind brushed the flame but didn't put it out.

"You were in the command center," Ivy said. "What's your name?"

"Andrea. But that's not important," the lady replied. "Just know you're never going to get a straight answer out of Alquema or anyone else who works here. Or at the other casino in town, for that matter."

"Why's that?" Ivy asked.

The woman glanced over her shoulder. "We should be good out here. Cameras can't see this far. But it's cold. Could we get in your car?"

"I don't want my car smelling like smoke," Ivy replied.

The woman took a long drag, then dropped the fresh cigarette and stomped it out under her heel as she let the smoke from her lungs go. Ivy unlocked her door and got into the car, reaching over to unlock the other side for the woman. Once inside, she turned on the engine and cranked what little heat the car could produce, though she could still smell the stench of the cigarette.

"I started working at Bear Paw almost four years ago," the woman said. "It's a good job. The Casino helps with tourism, keeps the town on the map. We've even got a small airport where people can fly in for a night or two. You know the types."

"But," Ivy prompted.

"But this town also has a lot of demons. It's strictly off the books, but I know for a fact people in the casino are in touch with criminals. There's nothing official of course, but I've overheard enough conversations. And growing up here, you're aware of things."

"What kinds of things?" Ivy asked.

"People who go missing. Corrupt cops. Businesses making money hand over fist. It's all connected."

"Why are you telling me this?" Ivy asked. It was suspicious for someone to just appear and start telling her everything she wanted to hear. This woman admitted to working for the casino; she could be nothing more than a plant from Alquema.

She pulled out the pack of cigarettes again, then seemed to remember and put them away. "You know, they advertise casinos as places where you can have some fun for a few hours and go home. Like it's all harmless. But they never talk about the addiction side of it."

"I'm assuming you know someone who has a gambling addiction?"

She nodded.

"But you work for the casino," Ivy said.

The woman dropped her eyes, sighing. "I figured if I worked there, I could maybe figure out a way to help him, or at least keep him from getting into so much trouble."

"Who is he?" Ivy asked.

"My husband. Or…he was. I haven't seen him in almost two years." She gave Ivy a sad smile. "Sometimes I think I'll see him on the security cameras, but it's never him." She paused a moment. "I don't think he's ever coming back."

Now was not the time to press the woman for information about Mrs. Baker. Ivy knew better than that. She needed to listen and let the woman get there in her own time. "What happened?"

"Gregory's friends got him addicted. After working at the sawmill, they'd all go down to have some laughs and throw some money away. But when they went home, he stayed. And it just got worse. Eventually he started funneling his whole paycheck there. He always said he had it under control, meanwhile we were having trouble covering the grocery bill, and the interest just kept piling up. I thought maybe if I worked at the casino I could act as a buffer, stop him before it got too bad. I had to lie on my application to say I didn't know anyone with a gambling addiction before they'd hire me. But I didn't realize just how much he owed them. He'd kept it all from me." Her breathing was becoming more irregular. "I told him I didn't care about the money; I just wanted him to get better. For the kids and for our future."

"People hide their shame well," Ivy said. "There are some secrets people will take to the grave, no matter how much support is offered up."

She nodded. "Greg might not have been the smartest man, but he was loving. And he was a good father when he was around. But living here, I think the temptation was too great. I think he got into some seedy stuff and lost money to the wrong people."

"You think someone did something to him?" Ivy asked.

She nodded. "I'm almost certain of it. The last time I saw him, Greg had lost an obscene amount of money. Money that I knew for a fact we didn't have. He'd snuck out there in the middle of the night, and when I got there for work that morning, they were hauling him out. I tried calling him, but he never picked up. I thought maybe he went home to sleep it off. But when I got off work, he wasn't there. I ended up filing a police report, and no one has seen him since."

"What about the security cameras around the building?" Ivy asked. "They must have picked up something."

She nodded. "They show Alquema and another man helping Greg into a black van. When I asked Alquema about it later, he said they'd just helped him into an uber to take him home. I'm sure you've probably guessed it wasn't an uber."

She swallowed hard and continued. "There's a man around town named Cole Cook. But the locals know him as *Ironfist*. He's a big-time businessman, owns a lot of property. But that's just what all the legal stuff says. He also runs a couple of side businesses, one of which is loan sharking."

Ivy arched an eyebrow. "You know this for a fact?"

She nodded. "Growing up here you learn to know and fear the name Ironfist. It's not something people talk about, but everyone knows. He makes sure of that."

"Did the police talk to Mr. Cook about your husband?" she asked.

"It wouldn't matter if they did," she replied. "He never would have told them anything. I'm sure some of the police are on his payroll anyway. Otherwise, how would he still be able to operate in town?"

Ivy sat thinking for a moment while Andrea's leg bounced with nervousness. "You think Mr. Cook has your husband?"

She shook her head. "No. I think Greg is dead. I think he *had* my husband. Hopefully for a short time. But knowing the man's reputation, I'm not sure that's the case." She turned to look Ivy in the eye. "But if the casino delivered my husband to Ironfist, I wouldn't be surprised if they did the same to the woman you're looking for."

"Where can I find this *Ironfist*?" Ivy asked.

"You have to promise me something first," the woman replied, grabbing hold of Ivy's arm. Her grip was tight, and Ivy felt an immediate shock at the sudden contact. She began to tremble at the intensity of it. "Find out what they did with Greg's remains. Just so I can at least give him a proper good-bye." Tears had formed in the woman's eyes, and Ivy was doing everything she could to focus on those, not the five fingers pressing lines into her arm.

"I'll do what I can," Ivy replied, her voice shaky.

Andrea let go, leaning her head back against the headrest. She wiped her eyes. "He'll be at one of his businesses around town. He likes for people to see him. Makes us remember who is in charge." She listed off a series of businesses he was known to run, which Ivy jotted down on her phone.

While it wasn't a silver bullet, it was at least a start. If Cook was in charge of all the loan sharking in town, there was a good chance he knew something about Jillian Baker. Even if the Casino hadn't turned her over to him, he might have heard of her. She was the kind of person someone like Cook might be interested in dealing with.

Then again, it could be nothing but a dead end.

"Thanks for your help," Ivy said. "And I'm sorry for your loss. I'll…do what I can to find your husband."

The woman opened the door to the car, an unlit cigarette already back in hand. "Thank you. And be careful. I wouldn't put it past Ironfist to make a cop disappear too. That shield might not get you very far."

Ivy nodded, ignoring the slight as Andrea closed the door

and made her way back to the casino, a new cigarette glowing in the darkness.

Ivy turned on the radio and sat in the car, thinking as she watched the light patterns dance on the casino's large signs. So much money passed through this place, and it had the potential to ruin so many lives.

She felt bad for Andrea, but at the same time she remained suspicious. The woman had been passionate, that much was for sure. But Ivy couldn't be certain she hadn't been Alquema's or someone else's plant. Maybe she worked for Ironfist personally and was just trying to get Ivy into his clutches.

This was where she faltered. She needed someone else to help her evaluate witnesses and suspects, to make sure the emotions she was seeing on their faces were real. As much as she hated to admit it, she needed Jonathan's help. He was better at reading people, at figuring out what was going on in their heads. And if she was going to confront this Ironfist, she'd much rather do it with some backup. Because if Andrea was to be believed, the man could make her disappear, and no one would even know. In fact, other than Oliver, no one *did* know she was here. She'd be serving herself up on a silver platter.

Ivy sighed, supposing she needed to swallow her pride and just ask for help for once. Her arm still felt like someone had shocked her with an electric cattle prod. Maybe she hadn't made as much progress as she thought she had. Between Andrea, Nat, and Oliver, she was beginning to doubt things had changed at all.

But just as she was trying to come up with an excuse not to call Jonathan at six o'clock on a Saturday night, her phone vibrated in her hand, his name showing up on the screen.

She chuckled. He was calling *her*?

"Bishop," she answered, all business.

"Ivy, where are you?" Jonathan asked. He sounded out of breath, like he'd been running.

"Why, what's going on?" she asked.

"Are you working with Alice on a story?"

She screwed up her features. "What?"

"Yeah, that's what I thought," he said. "She came into the office looking for you. Said you were helping her with a story, and she wanted to follow up."

"Was that all she said?"

"Yeah, why? What's going on?"

Ivy had to hand it to Alice, at least she hadn't ratted her out. "I'm not helping her with a story, so you can relax," Ivy said. "She just thinks that's what's happening."

"What's *really* happening?" he asked.

She could try to play it off, act like she wasn't about to call him too. But that wasn't the kind of relationship she wanted with her partner. She'd already blown him off once; she didn't want to do it again. "I'm investigating the Baker case. On my own."

He was quiet on the other side for a moment. "Have you made any progress?"

Ivy could barely contain her surprise. "What, you're not going to chide me for taking a case I've been told to stay away from?"

"That we've *both* been told to stay away from," he said. "I think you might be right. Something is going on here and I don't know what. But I want to help. I'm leaving the office now, where are you?"

She winced. "I'm in Three Rivers."

"What are you doing down there? Wait, never mind, you can tell me when I get there. I'm getting in the car now. See you in a few hours." He hung up.

Ivy sat stunned, looking at her phone. She hadn't expected Jonathan to actually drop everything to come help her. In fact, she'd been preparing herself for a verbal battle about why she was doing what she was doing. It was actually refreshing not to have to fight about it. And with the two of them, they'd be in a much better position to confront this Ironfist.

Chapter Fifteen

It was closing in on midnight, and Jonathan still hadn't showed up.

When Ivy had made the drive from Oakhurst, it hadn't taken her more than two and a half hours to get down to the hamlet. At first she wasn't worried, but as time crept on, she became more and more anxious. Had he decided he'd been too impulsive and decided to leave her to her quest on her own? Or had there been an accident of some sort?

She was just about to call him when a pair of headlights illuminated the parking lot of the restaurant where Ivy had texted she'd meet him. Ivy had waited until eight, gotten hungry, and popped in for a bite and a drink before closing the place down. It was only a few blocks away from the casino, its lights shimmering in the night and lighting up the town.

Ivy got out of the car as Jonathan pulled up. He looked somewhat disheveled, like he hadn't had a shower in a few days. Had he looked like that at the precinct yesterday? She couldn't recall; she'd been so angry at Nat she'd blocked out almost everything else.

"What happened?" Ivy asked.

"I had to run by my house first," he admitted. "And then

there was a big wreck on the 101. I tried calling but the service out here sucks." He glanced at the restaurant. "I guess dinner is out."

"I'm sorry I brushed you off yesterday," Ivy said. "I've been so focused on this Baker thing that I haven't really looked up."

"I shouldn't have been so dismissive," he replied. "I've been dealing with some…personal stuff lately and it's been taking up a lot of my headspace." He looked around, glancing back at the casino in the distance. "Glad to see you haven't fallen back into your old habits."

She glared at him. "Not entirely. Oliver has been helping."

He nodded. "Care to catch me up?"

She hugged her coat around her. The temperature had dropped another ten degrees since her conversation with Andrea. "Yeah, but not out here. I'm sure we can find somewhere that's open in this town."

"What about that?" Jonathan asked, pointing to the Bear Paw Casino.

"No. Definitely not that."

THEY MANAGED TO FIND A LITTLE HOLE-IN-THE-WALL DINER that advertised it was open twenty-four hours. The place wasn't big enough to hold more than thirty people, and that would have been pushing it. They grabbed a table in the back, a couple of coffees, and Ivy began explaining everything she'd found starting with investigating Mrs. Baker's house with Alice up to what she'd learned from Andrea only a few hours before. Jonathan listened without interrupting, doing nothing but occasionally sipping his coffee.

"She seemed to insinuate that this *Ironfist* wouldn't be above disappearing a cop or two," Ivy said, draining her mug. "I don't know if there's any reality to that or if she was just trying to impress me with how dangerous this guy is."

"He's definitely worth looking into," Jonathan said. "But I'm also interested in this other angle you're playing with. That maybe Mrs. Baker took those kids and ran."

"Yeah, but the blood—"

"As you told Oliver, could have been staged."

"And the drag marks on the carpet?" Ivy asked. "And the kicked-in door?"

He tilted his head towards her. "Okay, yes that's a little extreme. But someone who was really committed might go to those lengths to make it look genuine. She could be halfway to New York by now on a Greyhound."

"When I pulled the case file at Oliver's house, I looked over everything Bruneau had done so far. He's got a BOLO out for all three of them. That would cover the airports, bus stations, and taxi services. There hadn't been any developments last time I checked."

"Still, we can't discount the possibility she managed to slip past them or set up fake identities," he said. "Personally, I don't like the idea of going up against a loan shark, but we can't ignore that connection either. Especially since you have evidence she was coming here to gamble."

Ivy leaned forward, dropping her voice. "Do you really think a loan shark would send someone two hours away to take an old lady and a couple of kids?"

"For money, anything is possible," he replied.

"If what Andrea told me was true, then I don't think it's a good idea to go in there as cops. We might do better undercover." She could practically see the discomfort in his bones. "What?"

"We're not sanctioned to work on this case, Ivy. That means no backup if something goes wrong. And we can't use department resources, not unless you want to explain yourself to our boss."

She gave him a dismissive wave. "We can handle it. I know you're not great at lying, but the good news is I'm an expert at it. We can pretend to be people who are down on our luck, just needing a quick loan until the next payday. We could throw in a couple jitters here and there, make them think we're on something."

"Or we could just go in and demand information regarding Mrs. Baker," Jonathan said.

"Without a warrant," Ivy replied. "I've already run into that problem once. If the bank wasn't willing to give up anything, I doubt this Ironfist will."

"We still need to find him first," Jonathan said.

"I've been thinking about that. I'd say we should coordinate with the local PD here, but I'm afraid if any of them are in his pocket they'll blow our cover before we have a chance to use it. Let me get in contact with Oliver and he can get started on the fake IDs. Meanwhile, you and I can case a couple of the businesses, see if we can't get a bead on Mr. Cole Cook."

"You want to use Oliver in this?" he asked. "No way. That would be a clear violation—"

"Hey, you said it yourself. We can't use department resources. Plus, Oliver is quick. And he already knows the case."

Jonathan took a deep breath. "You're playing with fire here. I still say we should go back to the lieutenant with everything you've found so far. You've done great detective work; she might be swayed to put you on the case with Bruneau."

Ivy shook her head. "No, something is going on with Nat. I don't know what, but if I take this to her, she'll find a way to get me suspended to force me off this case, I know it. She's been acting weird ever since this one came up, and she isn't being honest with me. We can't trust her to do the right thing. Either we find Baker and the kids our way, or we don't find them at all." She took a breath. "I don't have a lot of faith in Bruneau, do you?"

"I guess not," he admitted.

"Right." She pulled out a couple of bills and left them on the table. "We need to find somewhere to sleep tonight. I'll call Oliver on the way; I'm sure he's still up."

"It's almost one thirty," Jonathan said, following her out. "Surely he's asleep by now."

"Doubt it," Ivy replied. "Oliver has always been a night owl, ever since we were kids."

As they reached their respective cars, Jonathan stopped, looking over the top of his at Ivy. "You know this is crazy, right?"

She smiled. "I know. What's even crazier is you're going along with it."

THEY FOUND A MOTEL ON THE EDGE OF TOWN THAT STILL took cash. Though between the two of them, they only had enough for one room. At least it had two beds. Ivy didn't give a second thought to sharing a room at first; after all, she'd done it enough as a kid. But as they both got in each other's way trying to get ready for bed, she realized she hadn't slept in the same room with anyone since her time at the Baker's house, almost fifteen years ago. She'd become used to her own routine, her own way of doing things, and having someone in her space all the time was both frustrating and inconvenient.

Thankfully, Jonathan didn't seem to be faring much better. He kept going into the bathroom anytime he needed to do something, enough that Ivy realized his routine might be more involved than her own. She definitely caught the smell of eucalyptus and chamomile at least once, which was funny, considering there was an old stain in the corner of the room that she couldn't say *wasn't* blood.

At least they had their own beds. The motel hadn't been busy, and they had their pick of rooms. The clerk had tried to offer them a king bed at first. Had that been the only room available, Ivy would have slept in her car. But thankfully, it hadn't been the case and she had taken the bed closest to the door. She checked her phone and saw no word from Oliver, which made her think maybe Jonathan had been right— maybe Oliver had changed over the years and no longer kept hours like he was on third shift all the time. She figured if you worked for yourself, you could pick and choose which hours you wanted to sleep pretty freely. Though now that he had Hero, that might change some. She still couldn't get over Oliver adopting a dog. His house was not what she would have called dog-friendly, but he was working on making it that way. Maybe he'd gotten tired of being lonely. Still, it seemed like a quick decision.

Finally, Jonathan shut off the light and got into his bed. Ivy had been laying on her side, trying to ignore the noise from the bathroom while he got ready, hoping that she'd be exhausted enough from the day to fall asleep immediately. But whether it was Jonathan's routine or the case itself, she was wide awake.

"Finish everything you need in there?" she asked without turning over.

"Skincare is important," he said. "I can't just brush my teeth and go to bed."

She halfway turned over. "What, like I do?"

"Did you even wash your face?" he asked.

"Of course I washed my face," she said, flipping all the way on her other side and sitting up. "I'm not a heathen."

He held up both hands. "Okay, okay, it's been a long day. Let's just get some rest and pick this back up in the morning."

"Maybe we should get up early to give you enough preening time."

"Very funny," he replied. "But when you get liver spots, don't come crying to me."

"Everyone gets liver spots," she replied, falling back down on the bed. "Whether or not you can see them."

"That's the point. I'd be happy to take you through my routine," he said.

"I think I'd rather gag myself," she replied.

"Must be nice, having naturally clear skin," he said after a moment's silence. "You're lucky."

Ivy didn't know what to say to that, so she just left it. It felt like a compliment, but she couldn't be sure. Regardless, she tried not to think about it and focused on recounting the case details.

If she wasn't going to sleep, she could at least get some thinking done.

Chapter Sixteen

"Yep, nothing fancy. Just enough to get past some low-level criminals. Fake credentials, and most important, fake financial histories," Ivy said before shoving a forkful of scrambled eggs in her mouth.

"And you need all of it today?" Oliver asked.

"Well, as soon as you can do it," she admitted, her mouth still half full.

She heard him exhale on the other side of the phone. "How detailed does this need to be? Because if you want iron-clad, it's gonna take a few days. Systems take time to populate, there are certain safeguards I have to go through to make sure it doesn't look like someone is doing exactly what I am trying to do."

"Don't go overboard," she said. "It just needs to pass a general test. We're not dealing with *Anonymous* here. It's just an insurance policy anyway."

"The IDs won't take long," he said. "I can just use your pictures from your DMV files. But you won't have physical copies. If anyone checks, though, you'll be in the system. It's the other stuff that will take a little longer."

Ivy went for another bite of eggs but had to stifle a yawn

instead. "That's fine. Get started with what you can and keep me updated. We'll stay in town and do some reconnaissance." She heard a bark in the background. "And tell Hero hi from me."

"He's getting the royal treatment over here," Oliver said. "Be in touch soon." He hung up and Ivy shoveled another forkful of eggs into her mouth.

"Did I hear him say it would take a few days to get these fake identities together?" Jonathan asked, sitting across the table. As she'd assumed, he'd been up early to shower and go through his routine. Though she had to admit, he came out of the bathroom without one hair out of place. In fact, the only time she'd *really* seen him flustered and out of sorts had been that night they were chasing down Kieran. She, on the other hand, had showered, dried her hair and been ready in under fifteen minutes. But she hadn't slept well. Her mind had been running, and it took forever for her to get to sleep.

"I know, it's too long," she said. "I told him to focus on the essentials only. He's going to set up digital IDs, but we won't have physical ones. We just have to remember to leave our real ones at the motel. Everything else he can do from there."

"We could forgo the IDs. Pretend like we're transients," Jonathan offered before taking a sip of his coffee. He'd ordered waffles, which Ivy couldn't help but eye with envy.

"No offense, but no one in the world is going to believe you're a transient," she said, stifling another yawn. "We'll go in as middle-class people, down on our luck. I think we're more likely to get something out of them that way."

"And how does us going in there get us closer to Baker and the kids?"

She snapped her fingers. "Shoot. I meant to tell Oliver. He needs to make us related to her somehow. So when we start asking questions, it's not suspicious." She pulled out her phone and shot him a quick text.

"Ivy, this is very off-the-cuff. I don't know if it's going to work. I still say we just question them, then leave. It will be quicker, cleaner and—"

"—won't get us anywhere," she replied. "It might even put targets on our backs."

"Is that worth waiting a whole additional day, or days to speak to them? We could go find this Ironfist right now, interrogate him, and be done with it. By waiting, we're delaying finding out where Mrs. Baker and the kids are."

She took a bite of her bacon. "He's not going to be straight with a couple of cops. What do you think he's going to say? 'Yeah, I took her. She's over in my other warehouse'? He's going to tell us to fuck off and then he'll know we're onto him. At least this way, he won't suspect the police are close."

"*If* he even has them," Jonathan said. "All we have is the supposition from one casino worker to go on. No hard evidence. This isn't how we do things, Ivy."

"Maybe not, but it's what we have to work with," she replied. "Nat has cut us off at the knees. But I'm not about to let it stop me from finding them. Not only will we be saving three lives, but Mrs. Baker will be able to tell me more about the night I was dropped off."

He pulled his features together. "I know you're anxious to know what happened. But that doesn't mean we should be reckless. We should at least coordinate with Bruneau. That way we have some backup if—"

"He'll just go to Nat," she said, cutting him off. "And we'll be sunk."

Jonathan sat back, apparently not wanting to argue. He took another sip of his coffee before starting in on his waffles.

Ivy felt the need to explain. She knew how she sounded— like an obsessed maniac. And that's how she felt sometimes. They were way off-book here, and she knew it. But at the same time, she'd been boxed into a corner of Nat's making. The woman had underestimated her. And Ivy wasn't going to be shut out of this one.

"You have to understand. I don't remember anything about the night my parents disappeared," she said. "I remember going to bed, then the next clear memory I have is walking up the steps to Mrs. Baker's house. And even that is a little fuzzy. Nat was there, by my side the whole way. She was the one to rescue me. But to learn that I was covered in blood, *someone else's blood*, and that I needed 'special watching'? Something about all this isn't right."

He regarded her. "You're going to have to confront the lieutenant. At some point, you won't have another choice."

"And she'll just keep lying to me, like she's lied up until now," Ivy replied. "You don't understand. You don't have someone in your life who is keeping the truth from you. Someone you thought loved you."

He was quiet for a moment, his waffles forgotten in front of him. "No. But I do have a little sister who is slowly wasting away and dying from a disease no one seems to be able to diagnose."

"What?" Ivy said, looking up.

He nodded. "My younger sister, Marie. She's probably a year or so younger than you. But she's developed this rare type of blood poisoning which is slowly killing her. And my mother is driving me mad, telling me I need to be there, by her side. Not down in Oakhurst, wasting my life away on a dead-end detective job."

"I…had no idea. I'm sorry," Ivy said. "Is that where you went when you were off?"

He nodded. "I went to see her. It had been a few months and Mom said she was getting worse. Honestly, she looked about the same to me. But to hear my mother tell it, Marie was on her deathbed."

"Don't you want to be by your sister's side when she passes?" Ivy asked. She immediately thought of her younger brother, Daniel, who had disappeared with her parents. She would give anything to see him again, even if just for a few seconds.

"That's just the thing. The doctors don't think she's going to die in the next few weeks, or even months. It could be another year. They just don't know. And Marie—she's so strong. She wants to live life to the fullest. She still has her job at the library, much to my mother's consternation, who would much rather she sit around the house all day with *her*, keeping *her* company." He blew out a frustrated breath. "That's the problem with people with money. They think that everyone should bend to their will, all of the time."

Ivy arched an eyebrow. "Money? Really? Like, how much?"

He met her gaze. "Plenty."

"So why are you working at all? Let alone in Oakhurst." She asked.

"Because I enjoy the work. I enjoy solving a puzzle, and I enjoy helping people. I enjoyed it in Portland too, but things… things got too heavy up there. Body count was getting too high, it was just another gruesome murder every week. I needed to move somewhere I could get away from all that."

Ivy smiled. "And then you get stuck with me and the headless corpse case."

He chuckled. "Seems I can't escape it no matter where I go. But at least down here I have some distance from my mother. And distance from her right now is a good thing. She always imposed her will on people, but it's gotten so much worse since Marie became ill."

"How long has she been sick?" Ivy asked.

"Noticeably? Only about a year. But the doctors say that whatever is in her blood has been there much longer. She might have even been born with it. Mom has taken her to doctors all over the country, looking for someone who knows something about this. Haven't found one yet." He took another bite of his waffle. "But on the bright side, she's already the subject in some prominent scientific papers. I'm sure that will make mother very happy when she's gone."

"Jonathan," Ivy said, feeling the strange pull to reach out for him, and had to work to resist the sensation. It was as if she had been turned into a human magnet and was drawn in to him in a way she had never felt with anyone before. The severity with which she had to exercise restraint almost frightened her with how severe and strong the initial sensation was. It was like fighting back against gravity itself. "I'm really sorry."

"It's okay," he said. "Just know that you're not alone. We all have issues with those that we love."

"Yeah, I guess we do." She willed herself to think about anything else, to distract herself from these unfamiliar stirs. When she focused, something he said sparked a lightbulb in her brain. "Hey, I think I might have a way to make us both feel better about this little subterfuge plan."

"What's that?"

"I think you need to conduct an interview."

IVY PRESSED THE SMALL BUTTON BESIDE THE DOOR. THE HOUSE was a one-story ranch with blue siding and a small porch that covered the front half. The cracked driveway held an unattached garage and two old vehicles, a red pickup truck and a maroon SUV. A large satellite dish sat on the roof, and tall evergreens surrounded the property.

"You sure this is the place?" Jonathan asked.

Ivy shrugged. "If Oliver is good at his job, it is. Otherwise, he's going to get an earful from me." She reached out and rang the bell again. A moment later the door opened to reveal the same woman who had slipped into Ivy's car the night before. An aura of cigarette smoke hung heavy in the air. As soon as she saw Ivy, her eyes went wide and she tried to slam the door.

Thankfully, Ivy had some practice and stuck her foot inside the jamb just enough to prevent the door from closing. "Andrea Dunwhitte," Ivy said.

"W-what are you doing here?" she asked. "You're gonna get me killed."

"Why is that?" Ivy asked.

"Here, just come in already," she hissed, standing close to the door as Jonathan and Ivy entered the home. She closed the door behind them, deadbolting it.

"Andrea, this is my partner, Detective Jonathan White," Ivy said. "We'd like to ask you some follow up questions."

"How did you even find me?" the woman asked, walking past Ivy into the home's kitchen. It was a modest house, though the stench of cigarettes hung heavy. The carpet was a shade browner than it probably should have been, and Ivy examined a nearby picture of Andrea and whom she assumed was her husband hanging on the wall. He was handsome enough, though the picture looked like it had been taken ten or twelve years earlier. Ivy pushed it to the side, noticing a white rectangle on the wall underneath it. The smoke had stained all the walls around it.

"I need you to tell my partner what you told me last night," Ivy said. "About this Ironfist." She heard the telltale sound of a lighter igniting before the woman emerged from the kitchen, a cigarette hanging from her mouth.

"What more is there to tell?"

"Tell us why us being here puts you in danger," Jonathan said.

Andrea perched on the edge of a nearby recliner. "The same reason I didn't want to speak to your partner inside the casino last night. Everybody's got ears these days. Never know who is watching."

"Why would they be watching you?" Ivy asked.

"To make sure I'm not talking to cops," she replied.

Ivy sat on the couch across from her. "You think they might come after you? For your husband's debt?"

Andrea brought a shaky hand up to her lips to drag on the cigarette. "Yeah."

"Tell me everything you know about this Ironfist," Jonathan said.

She shot a pained look at Ivy. "I already told you everything. You tell him."

Jonathan stepped between her and Ivy. "I need to hear it from you."

Andrea's leg bounced up and down. She was jittery, more so than she'd been in the car. Ivy thought she'd just needed a cigarette, but now that she had one, she seemed even *more* wired, which was odd.

She went through the entire story she'd told Ivy, line by line. All the details exactly the same, right down to the letter. Throughout the telling, the woman practically broke down with fear over what might happen to her.

"I mean, what do they expect me to do?" she finally said, practically sobbing. "I only make so much. And with the kids…"

"But just to be clear, they haven't come to collect from you," Jonathan said.

She shook her head. "No. Not yet."

"Okay," he said, standing. He'd taken a seat next to Ivy as they'd both listened. "Thank you for going through it with us."

"Listen," she said, getting back up as they stood to leave. "I changed my mind. Don't mention my or my husband's name. I don't want him to know I've been talking to anyone. Last night, I thought maybe I could get some closure. But I couldn't sleep thinking about it. It's better left alone."

"Are you sure?" Ivy asked.

"Trust me, it's better not to be on his radar if I can help it."

Ivy nodded. "Okay. Thanks for your help." Andrea unlocked the door, but it was shut again before Ivy could barely follow Jonathan over the threshold. As they made their way back to the car, she kept shooting her partner glances. "Well?"

They reached his vehicle, having opted to take the less conspicuous car around town. Jonathan took one glance back at Andrea's house before unlocking the car. "It's a good thing you brought me here, because I'm a hundred percent sure she's lying."

Chapter Seventeen

Ugh, this was driving her *nuts*.

Alice Blair sat at the computer, having spent the better part of twelve hours going through Oakhurst's town records. As part of her clearance with the station, she had access to all the news databases in the world, and yet she hadn't been able to find what she'd been looking for.

Information that might explain what happened to the Baker woman and the two kids under her care.

She'd managed to wriggle her way into the Baker house by tagging along with Detective Bishop, but that hadn't given her much to go on other than a blood stain on the kitchen floor. It wasn't like the kidnapper had left a calling card behind.

But her foray into the house *had* provided her with a nugget of unexpected gold: Ivy herself had once been an orphan who stayed with the missing woman. Alice didn't know if it connected at all, but she was determined to find out.

Ivy was tenacious, that much was obvious. But Alice knew precious little else about the woman, other than she had been recently promoted to detective and put on the Violent Crimes desk. Finding out she had a personal connection to the victim had been…well, a bombshell. And it had been clear from her behavior that Ivy wanted to keep it a secret.

Alice wasn't about to out her to any news organizations, but she did think the connection might go a long way to helping her figure out who took Mrs. Baker. She wasn't sure how, but she had a hunch, deep down, that somehow all of this was related. Which was why she'd spent the past twelve hours poring over record after record, hoping to find something that would lead her to a clue.

Her phone pinged, and Alice picked it up before rolling her eyes.

I'm waiting on an update.

She considered not replying at all but knew Russ would blow a gasket if she didn't keep in touch.

Deep in research. Making progress.

Research faster. Deadline.

Recently, Alice had convinced her boss she would be better *off* the desk than on it. While she enjoyed delivering the evening news to Oakhurst and its surrounding boroughs, sitting behind that desk night after night was *boring*. She'd longed for her field reporter days. She hadn't had as much autonomy then, but with her newfound popularity, she'd gained a bit more leverage over her position in this town. Enough so that she managed to convince Russ she could do both jobs. She could work the desk weeknights, and on the weekends, she would run down her own stories, and work the field.

The only problem was now he was hounding her twice as much.

"Alice!"

God, will the interruptions never stop? How was she supposed to get any work done when people kept pestering her every ten minutes? She got up, walked across the hall, and found her mother sitting up in bed, nightgown askew. "Did you need something?"

"Help me up," her mother said. "I want to go into the living room."

Her mother had been bedridden for the better part of four weeks following her surgery. Not that she'd needed to be. The doctors had said she could be up and walking around in as little as forty-eight hours after the event. But her mother had insisted she knew better and that she needed her rest. It had gone on long enough that Alice was worried she might develop gout just lying there.

So, to find her ready to get up and leave the bedroom was a welcome change. "Here," Alice said, holding out her arm so her mother could grab on to it. The older woman tried pushing herself up, but struggled and didn't make it off the bed. She tried a second time, and with Alice's help, finally managed to get on her feet.

"Not that I'm complaining, but what made you want to get out of bed?"

"It's just time," her mother replied.

Alice knew better than to pursue the subject further. Her mother was the self-appointed expert on all things, and arguing with her was an exercise in futility. Even when she was wrong, she would not admit it. It was a quality Alice had admired when she was younger: never back down, never show weakness. But that philosophy had quickly fallen apart as Alice encountered the "real world." Maybe it worked when you were older because people figured you were senile and not worth arguing with.

Alice gingerly walked her mother down the hallway and into the living room, where she helped her back down on the couch with a grunt. "That's enough for now," she said. "I'll call you when I'm ready to go back."

"I really wish you'd let me get a home health nurse to come in here," Alice said. "They could be with you twenty-four-seven."

"What do I need that for when I have a perfectly good daughter here to help me?" she asked, glaring up at Alice.

"Because I'm gone a lot of the time, Mom. This way if you needed something, or there is an emergency—"

"I'll call Wilfred next door," she replied, giving Alice a dismissive wave. "He brings me anything I need when you're not around. Always happy to help."

Alice didn't miss the passive aggressive insinuation. "He's older than you are," she said. "What if he gets hurt coming over here? Or worse, helping you lift something? You need somebody younger—"

"I *have* somebody younger," she said, looking up at Alice. "But she's never home."

"You know I have a demanding job," Alice replied. "You were the one who told me to live my dream."

Her mother held up one finger. "But not at the expense of family." With that, she grabbed the nearby remote and turned on the TV.

She'd had enough of this argument. It was always the same thing, over and over again. Why wasn't she home more? Why couldn't she drop her entire life to take care of her mother? Why did she have to work at all? It wasn't like she needed money for food or anything. She thought back to her conversation with Jonathan. That had been one of the things they had in common when dating: overbearing mothers intent on running their lives. They'd spent many a Saturday night lamenting their situations over a bottle of wine, though Alice had done most of the imbibing.

Alice sighed. At this rate, her mother would never go back to living on her own. The accident had changed all that, and if she didn't do something, she'd become a permanent fixture in this house.

Which, honestly, wasn't fair to either of them. Alice was rarely at home—though she'd been making more of an effort recently—and her mom needed companionship. She needed not to be alone all day. It was only making things worse. Before the accident she'd had a vibrant social life. But ever since she'd come to live with Alice, that life had died, and a new, isolated one had taken its place. There was no question she would have to have a hard conversation with her mother soon. One she was sure neither of them was looking forward to.

Alice sighed and sat back down at her desk in her bedroom, putting headphones in and trying to get her mind back into the game.

She thought back to the night she and Ivy went through the house. Why hadn't Lieutenant Buckley assigned the case to Ivy, especially when Ivy had insight to the missing woman? She had known that house like the back of her hand.

Somehow, it all came back to Ivy.

Alice did a little more digging into the town's records. Ivy's adoption record was sealed, like everyone else's. If Alice hadn't been in that house, she never would have known about the woman's history. But what circumstances had led Ivy there? What had happened to her family?

She knew from the brief glance she'd gotten at the record, Ivy's original surname had been *Stanford*, not Bishop. If Ivy had been taken to the Baker house, there was a good chance she'd lived nearby before. Rarely were kids moved outside of their hometowns to minimize the disruption in their lives. But Alice figured if you went through something life-changing enough that you had to move into an orphanage, changing towns probably wouldn't matter very much. Still, it helped narrow the search to Oakhurst and the surrounding counties.

She started with all the incarceration records, finding no one in jail with the last name Stanford. That most likely ruled out child abuse or neglect. Alice also searched the obituaries, going back to 2009, when Ivy had been placed with the Bakers. But she didn't find anything on anyone named Stanford. At least no one who seemed to be related. There was a

Gertrude Stanford who had passed the following year, but she had been survived by her family who lived up in Seattle, and there was no mention of Ivy's name anywhere there.

Finally, she searched for Ivy in the school records and found it first in the Mapleton district. Then after 2009, she was removed from the system, having been home-schooled with the Bakers. Her name popped up again in 2010 when she started attending high school, presumably after she'd been adopted.

But Alice found something else interesting. A Daniel Stanford, two years younger than Ivy, at the same school district. But again, after 2009, there was no more mention of him. A search in the local property records revealed a Mike and Jenny Stanford had owned a house over on Dyerle Court.

It was only after she found the name of Ivy's parents did she begin finding the news articles. Articles that long predated her time in Oakhurst. The first mentioned a search for the missing family, taking place in April of 2009. There were additional articles, though the copy grew shorter and shorter until finally, the only mention was a year later when there had been no update to the story.

Ivy's parents and brother had disappeared without a trace.

Alice sat back, crossing her arms. There *had* to be more to it than that. She noticed the cop that had been interviewed for each of the articles was none other than—at the time—Detective Natasha Buckley. Ivy and Jonathan's current boss.

She screwed up her features. That was weird, wasn't it? In addition, Alice had only gotten a brief glance at the adoption record, but she thought she recalled seeing Buckley's name on that as well. That couldn't be right, though…could it? Could Lieutenant Buckley have somehow been involved with Ivy's stay at the orphanage?

There was only one way to find out. Alice needed another look at that record. Fortunately for her, she knew just how to get in unnoticed.

Chapter Eighteen

"Andrea puts on a good show, but she has some classic tells," Jonathan said as they drove.

"Like what?"

"Did you see how nervous she was? I think if I'd popped a balloon in there, she might have had a heart attack."

Ivy had noticed how she couldn't seem to sit still, even while she was smoking. "She was like that last night too. Maybe she's just a high-strung person."

"Maybe. But did you hear any deviation to the story she told you? Any variation at all? Or was it like she was reading it from a book?"

"Wait a second," Ivy said. "You really think she's lying about her husband?"

They pulled up to a stoplight, the first after having left Andrea Dunwitte's house. "No, I think that part is real," he said. "But she's not telling us everything. Which is why I'm pretty sure this plan of posing as people in need of a loan isn't going to work."

"What? Why?" Ivy asked, glancing out the window. A Three Rivers Sheriff's Department vehicle sat in an abandoned fast food restaurant's parking lot across the way. Ivy wasn't sure why, but she found it odd.

"Because I think she's working for Ironfist. Maybe working for is too formal a term. I think she's indebted to him."

"But she told us—"

"She said he'd never come to collect the *money*. But you don't make someone's husband disappear and leave it at that. If she's telling even the smallest bit of truth about this Ironfist, and we have to assume she is, he's a dangerous guy. And guys like that don't just let debts go. My guess is he's squeezing her for information as a way to pay off what her husband owed him. And he's got her so scared she'll do anything to stay out of his clutches. He'll probably be able to terrify her into working for him forever. The question is: what kind of information is he getting from her?"

"She works in the casino security office," Ivy suggested. "But why would a loan shark want someone in there?"

"He could be using her as his eyes and ears, keeping a close watch on the people who give him most of his business. It's always a good idea to keep tabs on the people you're in bed with, especially if you can't count on the law to intervene if something goes wrong. Andrea might be his canary in a coal mine, alerting him to any problems before they come up. And approaching you last night might have been her seeing an opportunity to get out, *if* we could nail Cole Cook. It's a lot more plausible than her helping the case out of the goodness of her own heart."

"She's still taking a risk though. If we can't pin Baker's disappearance on him, she'd be vulnerable." Jonathan made the turn onto the next street, headed back in the direction of the casino. Ivy happened to spot another sheriff's car sitting alongside the road. She craned her neck as they passed to see the deputy inside watching them drive by.

Jonathan nodded. "Which was why I think she was so nervous today. She's had a few hours to think about it. In the morning light, she sees the danger in what she asked last night." He tapped the steering wheel a few times, turning up the crook of his mouth. "Which tells me Cook isn't some low-level offender. He's clever. And he's going to spot two cops a mile away."

Ivy let out a breath, leaning her head back on the headrest. "She might have even gotten worried enough to tell him about me. About us. To insulate herself. Dammit, I should have seen that."

"Don't beat yourself up," he said. "She put on a good show. Maybe she really did want to find out what happened to her husband, and maybe she was doing recon for Cook. All I know is it's too big of a coincidence that you need information about someone in the casino, and she appears to hand you a lead out of nowhere."

"And if he's expecting us, that means going in undercover is out of the question."

Jonathan nodded. "I hate to say I told you so…"

"No," Ivy said. "It's my own fault. I wasn't paying attention. I shouldn't have taken her at face value last night." She pulled out her phone and shot off a quick text to Oliver, letting him know they wouldn't need his services after all. All she got in return was a series of angry emojis. She'd have to make it up to him later.

"That's what you need a partner for," Jonathan said, grinning. "No detective can do it all by themselves. But the question now is, how do we find out what we need to know about Cook?"

Ivy glanced at the rearview mirror, noticing one of the sheriff vehicles had come up behind them. "Um, I think we might have company."

Jonathan shot a look in the rearview, furrowing his brow. "What the hell? I'm not even going the speed limit."

The car behind them turned their lights on.

"Well this is going to be awkward," Ivy said, getting her badge out of her jacket pocket.

"Yeah." He pulled the car over to the curb, shifting it into park and rolling down the window. "Be on your guard."

"For what?" she asked.

They sat in silence as the car pulled up behind them, and the deputy stepped out. He adjusted his hat as another deputy exited passenger side. The driver approached Jonathan first, while the other officer came up to Ivy's window. He tapped on it once and she rolled it down.

"Morning," he said, pointing to the other window. "My partner over there is going to talk to you."

"Morning, folks," the other officer said, leaning down to look in the vehicle. "In town visiting?"

"Investigating," Jonathan said, holding up his badge. Ivy did the same to the deputy on her side.

"Oakhurst, huh?" the one on Jonathan's side asked. His nametag said Billows. "Not down here on vacation, huh?"

"Why did you pull us over?" Jonathan asked, putting his badge back in his jacket.

Billows just chewed on what Ivy assumed was probably tobacco before smiling at them. "You folks have a good day. Safe travels back to Oakhurst." He motioned for his partner to return to the car.

"What in the hell?" Ivy asked as soon as they were out of earshot and the windows were back up.

"I think we just got cased," Jonathan said.

"By the local cops?" Ivy asked.

"Yeah," Jonathan said. "Though I'm not sure they were acting in the capacity of Three Rivers or Coos County." Ivy looked in the rearview again. They were both back in the car, just sitting and watching them. "I get the distinct feeling if we don't drive out of town, we may be run out."

"You really think they were threatening us? They didn't even say anything."

"They didn't have to," he replied. "Think about it. How did they track us down? The only person who knows we're cops in this town is Andrea Dunwitte."

A pit formed in Ivy's stomach. "Do you think we should go back there? Do you think she's okay?"

"We can't go back," Jonathan said, putting the car into gear. "But I understand now why she was so paranoid. They could have been watching her after all."

Ivy recalled the other police vehicles she saw after leaving the Dunwitte house. "If she is working for Cook, and he found out she talked to cops—"

"There's nothing we can do for her now," Jonathan said. "We should go back to the motel, and promptly leave town. We don't want them to tell us twice." He put the car back into drive and pulled out.

"No," Ivy replied. "Not until we find out if he has any connection to Mrs. Baker. He's our only lead."

Jonathan shot her a sympathetic look. "A few years ago I worked this one case in Portland. It was a double murder. Delivery job gone wrong. Come to find out, the driver of the truck had been warned to leave town only a few days before. But he thought he could outsmart or outrun the competition. We don't have operational authority and we don't have anyone watching our backs. Trust me. Staying here is a bad idea. We're in their territory. They just drew a line in the sand, and we're on the wrong side."

TEN MINUTES LATER, THEY WERE BACK AT THE MOTEL, gathering their things. The sheriff's car had followed them about halfway, then turned off on a side street. As they gathered their things, Ivy couldn't help but think leaving was a bad idea. Had they come all this way for nothing?

"Got everything?" Jonathan asked. Ivy didn't respond. She couldn't believe he was tucking tail and running like this.

"Hey," he said, his voice softening. "We're not going to give up. It's a good lead, but we don't have the manpower to do anything about it. Sometimes you just have to learn to let things go."

"And if he has them?" Ivy asked.

"Then we'll come back with evidence and a warrant," Jonathan said.

Ivy let out a long breath. "Fine. Do it your way."

He nodded and they made their way out to their cars. "See you back in Oakhurst," he said before getting into his car.

Ivy did the same, tossing her overnight bag on the passenger seat. She always kept at least one change of clothes in her car, but now she'd have to switch it out for a fresh set. She followed him out of the parking lot, noticing another sheriff's vehicle parked further down the street. Giving up like this was worse than handing in her badge. Cook could have Baker and the kids tied up at this very minute, and they'd never know it. Despite everything she'd been through, it was still the best lead she had.

As they drove over the Bay Bridge, leaving Three Rivers behind, Ivy reached a boiling point. She couldn't just run away like this. Not when lives were on the line. Maybe Jonathan was right, and it was dangerous, but those kids were gone because of *her*. And she had to be the one to set it right.

Before she could stop herself, she jerked the wheel to the left, pulled the parking brake, and did a full one-eighty on the blacktop, pointing back in the direction of Three Rivers. She floored it, glancing back only enough to see Jonathan's brake lights illuminate.

She picked up enough speed that he was out of her rearview in less than thirty seconds. This was more than reckless, this was dangerous, but that wasn't about to stop her. She hadn't spent all this time tracking down Mrs. Baker and the kids just to run away when a couple of cops on the take decided to make an appearance. If the man known as Ironfist thought he could get rid of her that easily, he was sorely mistaken.

As soon as she crossed the bridge back into town, Ivy began searching for Sheriff's vehicles sitting sentry. Surprisingly, all those that had been so plentiful only thirty minutes ago seemed to have disappeared. Good, Cook was satisfied Ivy and Jonathan had left, which meant she was free to track him down. And because she had spent some time yesterday familiarizing herself with the town, she was able to navigate the streets easily, keeping an eye out any sign of the man at the list of businesses Andrea Dunwitte had provided her.

Her desire to return to the woman to make sure she was all right was strong, but if they hadn't been watching her before, then they certainly were now. Ivy only hoped their visit hadn't caused an even bigger problem.

Instead, she focused on the here and now. All she needed was a sign, a direction of some sort. And when she pulled up to the next intersection, and looked across the way at the Neahkahnie restaurant, she smiled.

In its parking lot was the very same car that had pulled them over earlier. If her hunch was correct, the deputies were inside, celebrating a job well-done. And there was no question they would know where to find Cole Cook.

Ivy steeled her nerves. What she was about to do wouldn't be sanctioned by any public police department in the nation.

It was a good thing she wasn't on the clock.

Chapter Nineteen

Ivy ENDED up parking around the back of the building. She didn't want someone inadvertently spotting her car since she was supposed to have left town. Her heart was thundering in her chest as she walked around the building, and her firearm hung heavy under her jacket. If she fired it while not in the course of her duty, she could be charged with a felony. But if everything went to plan, she wouldn't have to fire it at all.

She stayed away from the windows and walked in the front door, which was partitioned off from the main dining room. A short line had formed and was waiting to be seated. Ivy made her way past the line to the cashier's desk where she could get a better look at the different areas in the restaurant. To her right was a counter area with some small booths, all of which were full for Sunday lunch. In front of her was a larger, more expansive dining room with booths along the walls and tables with chairs in the middle. It was also full, but as she looked around, Ivy didn't see the officers that had stopped her and Jonathan.

"Excuse me, ma'am, the line is back there," a hostess said, carrying a few menus under her arm as she approached.

Ivy pulled out her badge. "I'm looking for some colleagues of mine."

The woman's eyes went wide. "Oh, you're with Mr. Cook's group. I'm sorry, I didn't realize. I've only been working here a few weeks."

Ivy tried to contain her surprise at hearing Cook's name, but she wasn't sure she was successful. "That's right. Where…?"

"Oh, right this way, come with me," she said, her voice chipper. She led Ivy through the dining room which connected to another hallway on the far end. A closed bar area faced the dining room itself, but beside it were large meeting rooms, all of which had been set up with tables arranged in different configurations. One of the rooms looked like it was hosting a book club, while another had people praying as their food was being delivered.

The hostess led Ivy to the third room, where the two cops sat at a large eight-person table with a bunch of people in suits Ivy had never seen before. When Ivy stepped in the room, the world stopped.

"Can I get you something to drink?" the hostess asked, oblivious to the room's rise in tension.

"I'm good," Ivy said. "Thanks." She didn't see the hostess excuse herself because she had locked eyes with the man at the head of the table. He was in his fifties, with peppered gray and white hair, and he wore dark glasses which complemented his beard and moustache. Beside him sat two men in suits, as well as another man Ivy could only assume was a politician by the way his smarmy gaze ran her up and down. And there, closest to her at the end of the table, were the two cops that had pulled her over not more than an hour before.

"Who the hell is this?" the man at the head of the table asked.

"Detective Ivy Bishop, Oakhurst Police Department," she said, trying to keep an eye on everyone in the room at once.

The two cops glared at her, their eyes burning with the blazes of a thousand suns.

"You told me she was gone," the man at the head of the table said.

"I'm not so easy to scare off," Ivy replied.

"Where's your partner?" the officer that had been on her side of the car asked.

"Billows," the man at the head of the table ordered.

"Yessir," he replied, seeming to understand the unspoken directive, and approached Ivy.

"Touch me and I guarantee you'll regret it," she said, not taking her eyes off Billows. He must have seen something in her dark brown eyes because he paused.

"You're Cole Cook," Ivy said, turning her attention to the man at the head of the table.

He ran his tongue over his lips. "That's correct."

"Also known as Ironfist," Ivy said. The man she assumed was a politician tugged at his collar, like he really didn't want to be there.

"I'm sorry, Detective. I've never heard that name before," Cook said. He spread his hands so each gripped opposite ends of the table. The two men in suits, who Ivy could only assume were his personal guards looked ready to pounce. And Billows still hadn't sat back down.

She couldn't believe she was doing this, that she'd waltzed into a viper's nest of criminals with nothing but vain hope. It wasn't even in the same ballpark as a longshot, but still, she had to try.

"I'm looking for information on a Jillian Baker," Ivy said. "And two young girls, aged ten and eleven. They've gone… missing."

"And you think I might know something about that," Cook said.

She tilted her head at him. "You have a reputation. Even to someone who doesn't live here."

"Look, I think I should be going," the politician said, standing up.

"Sit down and shut up, Ernie," Cook said sharply. Ernie sat back down. Cook turned back to Ivy. "What kind of reputation is that?"

"One where people who owe you a lot of money disappear," she said.

Cook worked his jaw for a moment, then turned to the suited man beside him. "Do we have a Baker on the books?"

The man pulled out a small black notebook, flipping through it. He communicated with his boss with a small shake of his head.

"Sorry, detective. You're barking up the wrong tree. Never done business with a J. Baker. Now if you don't mind, I'm trying to enjoy my lunch on this fine Sunday." He made a motion to the door.

"That's it?" Ivy asked. "You expect me to believe that?"

Cook sat stunned for a moment before a strange look came over his face. "I don't think you appreciate the position you're in here, little girl."

"Oh, I appreciate it plenty, *little boy*," she replied. "Don't think I don't know how many weapons can be pointed at my head in a moment's notice. And I'm sure you have enough to make anything that happens here today go away and never be mentioned again. But I'm not leaving here until I'm satisfied you didn't have anything to do with their disappearance."

Cook scoffed, not taking his eyes off Ivy. "You've got some balls; I'll give you that." He cleared his throat, taking a drink of water. Every move he made might be some kind of coded hand signal to just shoot her and be done with it. At least if that was the case, Jonathan would figure it out. And maybe he'd still have enough time to save Baker and the kids.

The man known as Ironfist leaned forward, all his attention on Ivy. "What sort of business do you think I'm in? Do you think I like to give money to people who won't pay it back? How does that help me?"

Ernie put his fingers in his ears, avoiding eye contact with everyone.

"You tell me," Ivy said. "You're the one with the reputation."

Cook snarled. "It's bad business to off your clients. Any businessman will tell you that. A dead man can't pay his debts. Does this Baker woman have any family? Anyone to take over her estate when she's gone?"

"No," Ivy replied. "Her husband died two years ago. She doesn't have any other family."

Cook put both his hands up. "Then it wasn't me. I only transact business with people who have…let's call them backup assets."

That sounded like Andrea, and Ivy wanted to mention her name but didn't want to get the woman into any more trouble than she already was.

"A person without anyone to…*mourn* them…well, that just doesn't make sense from my perspective," he said.

"Not even to send a message?" Ivy asked.

"Who's going to get it? She doesn't have anyone," he said. "Except maybe you."

"What?" Ivy asked.

"You're the only person who seems to care about her." He lowered his voice. "And until today, I didn't give a fuck about you, so it wasn't me trying to get your attention. But someone out there obviously is."

"You're saying whoever took her is sending *me* a message?"

He held his hands up again. "I don't really care. Now can I go back to my lunch, or would you like to continue accosting me and my guests?"

Ivy wasn't sure what to do. She hadn't expected Cook to actually tell her the truth. She hadn't even considered he might be right, that someone might be trying to get *Ivy's* attention. But why? Surely there were better ways to do it. And to what end? Why not just contact Ivy directly? What sort of message were they trying to send?

Ivy took one more glance around the room, satisfied it didn't have what she'd come here for. "Enjoy your lunch," she said, catching the eye of Billows again, who still hadn't sat down.

As she walked out, she hoped Cook wasn't the retaliatory type. He'd been more amenable than she'd expected, but that didn't mean he wouldn't shoot her in the back on her way out. Each step she took out of the restaurant was fraught with worry. She didn't take a breath until she was back outside, headed for her car.

If someone wanted her attention, what was she supposed to do about it? That's assuming she could trust what Cook said. Though, the more she thought about it, the more it made sense. Why kill off the people who owed you money, if there was no one to take their place? Andrea Dunwitte's husband went missing presumably because Cook could lean on her for "repayment." Jill Baker didn't have someone like that. Neither did the girls under her care. There was no financial incentive to take any of them.

Which meant—

That same familiar feeling she'd felt in the parking lot of the casino crept up on her. Ivy turned to see the two cops from earlier. She hadn't noticed them following her out of the restaurant. Either they had been really quiet or they'd used an exit she wasn't aware of.

She held her hands up. "I'm going, I'm going."

The lead one—Billows—shook his head. "Oh no. We already gave you that opportunity. You being here reflects badly on us. Which makes us look bad in front of the boss."

"Not even trying to cover up your corruption anymore. Bold," Ivy replied, dropping her hands.

"It's not going to matter to you, because you won't be snitching," the other one said, baring his teeth.

"What are you going to do? Kill me?" she asked. "My partner knows I'm here. People will come looking."

Billows shrugged. "People go missing from around these parts all the time."

Because they were behind the building where Ivy had parked her car, they had some cover from the public-facing streets. Ivy was outnumbered, and she wasn't confident in her ability to take on two assailants at once. Maybe if they weren't trained officers of the "law," but there was no telling what these two could do. Sizing them up, neither looked out of shape or unable to hold their own. Ivy took one last look at her car. There was no way she could get in fast enough and still escape. She didn't have a choice.

She took off running.

Chapter Twenty

HER ARMS AND LEGS PUMPING, Ivy rounded the building, taking off as fast as she could toward the street. She could hear the two cops chasing after her not far behind, and she didn't dare slow down. It was as she'd assumed; they were in shape and wouldn't let up until they caught her. They'd have more trouble out here in the open than they would have in that back alley, but still, she didn't want to get into a fistfight with a couple of cops in the middle of the street.

She had just reached the sidewalk and had prepared to turn so she wouldn't have to cross the street in the middle of traffic when she felt a foot catch her from behind, causing her to tumble headfirst into the concrete. Ivy managed to put her arm up in time to stop from scraping her face on the sidewalk, only to feel a knee plant itself deep into her spine. For a brief second, she thought of the man she'd taken down in the burger parking lot before the air was knocked out of her.

"Get her in cuffs," one of them called out. "We need to get her off the street."

A meaty arm wrapped around her wrist, sending the obligatory shock of electricity through her. Ivy wrenched her arm away and in the same breath managed to twist her entire body with such force that she threw the cop off her back with a guttural growl. Immediately, another two hands came into her field of view, and she swiped at them with all the force she could muster, knocking the man away.

The second officer came back, kicking her in the side just as she thought she'd knocked the other one back, and the blow took so much wind out of her lungs, Ivy wasn't sure she'd ever take a deep breath again. Ivy cried out, as he grappled for her again. She was barely aware that she was laying on her gun, and in a desperate attempt to stop them, she drew it from its holster, only for it to be snatched away.

"Uh-uh," one of them—she thought it was Billows—said. "Naughty girl."

Ivy saw red.

It was like the pain disappeared, replaced by a fiery rage. She reached out and scratched the man across the face, using the full force of her nails. Blood streaks welled immediately, and he cried out, stumbling back and dropping her weapon. Ivy turned to the other one, only for the pain in her side to come roaring back. She was about to say something when she tasted a hint of copper on her tongue. The other man charged her but stopped dead in his tracks.

"Ivy! Get in!"

Ivy turned to see Jonathan, the driver side door of his car open as he pointed his service weapon at the other deputy. She didn't need anyone to tell her twice. She grabbed her weapon from the ground and stumbled around his car, hauling herself into the passenger side. The other cop was screaming as he held his face, but Ivy was just trying to concentrate on breathing.

In. Out.

She closed the door and her eyes at the same time, feeling the car jerk forward as Jonathan sped away from the scene.

"What the hell were you thinking?" he demanded. "They could have killed you!"

"Almost did," she croaked, holding her ribcage. She wasn't sure she didn't have some internal bleeding from that kick.

"Jesus fuck, Ivy, that was the stupidest and most reckless thing you've ever done!"

Ivy smiled despite herself. Jonathan rarely cursed. So it was a treat to hear it when he did. "Thanks for coming back," she croaked.

"Are you okay? What happened?"

She opened her eyes, finding they were already back on the Bay Bridge. "Wait, my car. It's still in the parking lot."

"Sorry, Vee. You're not getting that car back. We can't go back to that town, not without serious backup."

She struggled to move for the wheel. "You don't understand. I can't just leave it. It's my dad's car."

"What?"

"I mean, well, it would have been. It was the car he always wanted."

Jonathan gave her a sympathetic look. "I'm sorry, but by the time we go back they'll have trashed or sold it to a scrap yard just to spite you."

She leaned her head back, tears forming in her eyes. That car was a pain in the ass, but it was *hers*. And it was a reminder of her parents, of what she'd lost. She couldn't just give it up.

"If you're thinking about jumping out of a moving vehicle to go back for it, just know I've put the child locks on," Jonathan said.

She glared at him.

"You deserve it after what you pulled. Do you need a hospital?"

"I'll be okay," she replied.

"We're going to a hospital," he said. "Hold out for an hour or so. I want to get as far away from Three Rivers as possible." She nodded, closing her eyes again. In. Out. It hurt to breathe too deep, so Ivy kept it shallow. "Was it at least worth it? Did you find anything useful? I assume by the look on those thugs that you went after Cook. You wouldn't believe how many places I went looking for you. I thought—"

"It wasn't him," she said.

"What?"

"He didn't take Baker or the kids," she said.

"How do you know?"

She swallowed slowly, then went through the conversation she'd had in the restaurant, along with Cook's rationalization for not taking Baker.

"Then why did he send his thugs after you once you were done?" Jonathan asked.

Ivy shrugged. "Maybe he didn't like me showing up out of the blue like that. Or maybe it was really like they said, they were doing it to curry more favor from him, for screwing up and not getting me out of town earlier."

"You really think they were going to kill you?" he asked.

"Seemed that way."

"I'll have to let the county DA know he might have an enforcement problem down in Three Rivers. It's a pretty little place but is holding some dark secrets."

"Tell me about it," Ivy said, trying to shift in her seat to get comfortable. "Cook did give me one useful piece of information," she finally said. At least she hadn't walked away completely empty handed. If she had, she might not be able to live with the fact she'd probably lost her car and almost her life.

"What was that?"

"He said that if it wasn't a financially motivated disappearance, it was someone trying to send a message." Which meant the real reason for the kidnapping was even more terrifying.

"A message?" Jonathan asked.

Ivy nodded. "Apparently, one directed at me."

～

"Okay, miss Bishop," the doctor said as he walked in with an iPad tucked under his arm. "How are you feeling now?"

"Better," she admitted. She'd been given a round of painkillers not long after she and Jonathan had made it to the hospital. Since then, she'd gone in for X-rays and had been sitting in a waiting room ever since while Jonathan spoke on the phone with a DA down in Coos County. Ivy hadn't realized just how many times physical contact was required in the hospital, having not been in one since she was a teen—an occasion she still couldn't even remember. Thankfully, she managed to keep any actual contact to a minimum.

"I have your results right here." He opened the iPad and selected a series of images. "You have some internal bruising, but we don't see any evidence of bleeding. The copper taste on your tongue was from when you bit the inside of your own cheek."

"Oh," Ivy said. "I didn't realize I did that."

"It happens all the time. Might have been during the confrontation," the doctor said. "The good news is nothing is broken. So, we'll wrap you up and send you on your way, but you'll need to be on light duty for the next four or five days."

"That won't be a problem."

Ivy snapped to the left to see Nat standing in the doorway. Jonathan had stopped his conversation mid-sentence and was staring at their boss with his mouth agape.

"Nat," Ivy croaked, surprised.

"That's right, Nat. *Your boss*," the woman said, coming into the room, her red hair looking even fierier than usual.

"I'll have to call you back," Jonathan said, slipping his phone back into his pocket.

"Yes, well," the doctor said, rocking back on his heels. "I'll get a prescription for the painkillers written up and then we'll get you out of here." He quietly excused himself while Nat and Ivy stared each other down.

Ivy didn't know how Nat had found her here, and right now, she didn't care. It was inevitable the woman would find out what she was doing eventually. Ivy just wished she had something more to show for all the legwork she'd put in.

"Do you want to explain yourselves?" Nat asked.

Ivy tried taking a deep breath, only to wince at the pain in response. "Since you decided to keep me off the Baker case, I took matters into my own hands."

Nat's face turned a shade of red that rivaled her hair. "And you?" she asked Jonathan.

"He had nothing to do with it. I just called him when I needed a ride to the hospital."

She cast her gaze back on Ivy. "That's not what the Three Rivers Sheriff's Office tells me. They said you harassed one of their most upstanding citizens. A man who not only is very generous to their community but is also respected and well-liked."

Ivy snorted derisively. "I wouldn't say asking a few questions constitutes harassment. And upstanding citizen my ass. He's a known criminal; he just happens to have the local cops in his pocket."

Nat gave her a skeptical look. "This is the second time in three days I've received a complaint about you. The first one I could dismiss, but this is serious."

"Why do you think I'm even in here? Two cops under his thumb almost ended up killing me."

"Lieutenant," Jonathan said. "It's true. The whole town seems to at least be aware of this notorious loan shark, Cole Cook, who presents himself as an upstanding citizen but runs a well of organized crime under the surface. Detective Bishop had a hunch he might have something to do with Mrs. Baker's disappearance."

"I thought you had nothing to do with it." Nat glared at Jonathan before turning her attention back to Ivy. "Make any progress on that hypothesis?"

"I think you can cross him off the suspect list," Ivy said under her breath.

"I should suspend you, indefinitely," Nat replied. "Trespassing, unauthorized access to government files, false identification, recklessness, assault—"

"Assault?" Ivy yelled.

"One of the officers in Three Rivers is saying you almost tore his face off."

"Yeah, after he almost broke my ribs and took my service weapon!"

Nat shook her head, dropping her gaze to the floor as she put her hands on her hips. "Ivy, I can't keep doing this. I can't keep dealing with your insubordination. You're too close to all of this. It's become too personal for you. *That's* why I didn't want you on this case. I know you. You're like a dog with a bone. You won't stop…ever."

"Can you blame me?" Ivy yelled, sitting up despite the pain in her side. "I come to you for help, and all I got were non-answers. Do you know *why* I want to find Mrs. Baker so bad? Because she's the only person who can tell me about what happened that night I came to the orphanage. She's the only one who can tell me why I was covered in blood when you found me. Because you'll just keep lying to my face. You've been doing it for fifteen years; I don't see you stopping anytime soon."

Something flashed in Nat's eyes, but it was gone as soon as it had appeared. She held Ivy's gaze a long time, long enough that Ivy thought maybe she might actually say something helpful. "I'm going to recommend to Captain Armstrong that you be removed from the force."

"You can't do that," Jonathan asserted, stepping forward.

"You want to be next?" Nat replied. "I keep getting calls from Portland. Apparently, your mother has some pull with the department up there." He fell silent, his arguments lost in his throat.

Nat turned back to Ivy. "You're going in front of the review board. I'm sorry, Ivy, but you've left me no choice. You obviously can't handle the pressures of the job. Not if you're taking risks like this."

Tears stung Ivy's eyes. How could Nat do this? After everything they'd been through. She'd pushed some boundaries, so what? It didn't mean she deserved to be fired. First her car and now her job? What else could she lose today? The worst part of it was, if Ivy wasn't a cop anymore, she wouldn't be able to keep looking into her own case. Her family would be lost to her forever.

"Don't bother coming into work tomorrow," Nat said as she reached the doorway. "Either of you. I'll be in touch."

As soon as she was gone, Ivy couldn't help it. It was almost instinctive in how quickly it hit her, and she began weeping for the first time in years.

Chapter Twenty-One

ANOTHER DAY, another dollar.

Except, that wasn't exactly true, was it? He wasn't being paid by the hour or even the day here. He'd received half the money from his employer upfront, and the other half would come when the job was done.

The only problem was that the job seemed impossible. He'd already been at this a solid week which had resulted in a net zero return on investment. No information—nothing useful anyway—and nothing new over the past few days. He was getting frustrated. The job wasn't complete until he delivered what the Boss wanted.

He was supposed to be the best. The man who could get results. That's why he'd been hired. That's why he'd agreed to this job. It was nothing he hadn't done before, but this particular nut was proving more difficult than he'd anticipated.

He sighed, pulling out his ring of keys. Seven keys in total, though two of them were for locks on different buildings, one of which was his storage unit. The other was for a jet ski locker out on Fern Ridge Lake. He wished he got out there more often, but he'd been too busy lately, not to mention it was still winter. He'd go back in May; that would be perfect weather.

Key one for the padlock. Key two for the deadbolt. Key three for the handle. He opened the door and descended the stairs, coughing and clearing his throat. He did that every time, just so no one was surprised to see him. He also always wore the same heavy work boots so he'd make a lot of noise. You never knew what people were up to these days. But really, they should hear the door easily living in a place as quiet as this.

As soon as he reached the bottom of the stairs, he turned right, using key number four on the heavy lock. The door swung open with a screech, and he flipped on the light, illuminating the space in heavy fluorescents.

It was sparse down here; it was a basement after all, but it served his purposes. A stench hung in the air, and he wished he had a window to help ventilate the room. But that's what happened when a person didn't wash or shower for a good week.

"Good morning," he said, his voice livelier than he'd expected. Maybe it was because he'd gotten a good night's sleep last night. Or maybe he figured after seven days she might finally be ready to talk. Whatever it was, he was in a good mood for once.

"Got some breakfast for you here before we get started," he said, pulling out a chair and setting the bag he'd brought with him from the kitchen on the only table in the room. It was an old metal folding card table that had seen better days. Half the legs were rusted, and he was sure if he folded it back up, it would snap in two, but it provided for his modest needs down here.

"Not very talkative this morning, huh?" he said, more to himself than to her. "We'll change that. Maybe you'll feel better after a breakfast burrito." He walked over to the utility sink that sat beside some old washer and dryer hookups. The hookups didn't work anymore, but the tap did. He grabbed a dusty glass from a nearby shelf and filled it with cold water.

He turned back to his subject. She was slumped to the side, which was how she slept considering her arms were chained above her head and her feet were shackled to the ground. "Here you go, Mrs. Baker, drink up," he said, offering her the water. But she didn't move. Her matted gray hair covered her entire face, as it sometimes did during their "sessions." Especially the intense ones.

He brushed the hair aside, only to pull back when he saw her eyes were wide open.

"Aw, shit," he said, placing his fingers to the artery in her neck. No pulse. Goddammit. And today was supposed to be a good day. He glanced up to the corner of the room. Had he seen yet? Or was this situation salvageable?

Sighing, he returned to the utility sink and dumped out the glass of water. "Won't be needing this." She must have passed sometime during the night. But she'd been fine during their sessions yesterday. Maybe a little tired, but fine nonetheless. And he'd checked on her last night—still alive then. So what happened between last night and this morning?

One thing was for sure. The Boss wouldn't be happy. He glanced over at the list of questions given to him for the Baker woman to answer. It was a simple list of twelve questions, printed out on a standard piece of paper that had been included with the initial payment. So far, she'd only managed an answer to one of the questions, insisting over and over she didn't know what he was talking about for the rest. It had become tiresome after a while, and he'd taken to harsher and harsher forms of punishment in hopes that it would finally wear her down.

Unfortunately, it only seemed to backfire. She ended up telling him what she thought he wanted to know, but he could tell it was all made up. The Boss had assured him this woman was a master manipulator, someone who would need to be broken again and again before she would finally reveal the truth.

He thought they had made a breakthrough last night. That today would be a turning point. Obviously, he had been wrong. Whatever submission she'd shown last night, maybe it was because she'd known she was close to death and was just trying to run out the clock. That was the only explanation he could come up with, though he doubted it would be good enough for the Boss.

Finally, he realized what that rancid smell was; she'd soiled herself when she'd died. Which only made things messier and would make cleanup longer.

He didn't get paid enough for this. He really didn't. And what would happen now with the rest of his money? There wasn't a contingency for this. He glanced up at the corner of the room again, noting the little red light on the camera.

He also couldn't help but be somewhat apprehensive. There had been no instructions on what to do if she died. Was he supposed to dispose of the body? Dissolve it? Or did the Boss want it for some ungodly reason? Should he wait for contact or just take care of it?

And what about the kids? He'd been feeding and taking care of those brats the entire time, with little to no direction from the Boss. He'd considered just disposing of them, since they were eating him out of house and home and he hadn't been provided extra funds for groceries, but without a direct order, the rule was to maintain the status quo until instructions arrived.

But…he couldn't just leave a dead body in his house. And if he was already going to be disposing of one body, why not three? He already might not be paid for the rest of this job, so why not just get rid of all of them and save himself the trouble?

He left the antechamber, walking back up the stairs so he could grab some cleaning supplies and trash bags. Now wasn't the time to sit idly by and wait to be told what to do. Now was the time to act, and to make sure things were taken care of. After this point, everything was on his dime anyway.

But just as he reached the top of the stairs and a decision of what to do with all three of them, his phone rang, stopping him in his tracks. It was the phone that had been included with the envelope. For emergency use only.

The man hesitated, his finger hovering over the "accept" button.

Chapter Twenty-Two

"Here," Aunt Carol said, handing Ivy a mug of warm tea. She was wrapped up on the couch in a fuzzy blanket, watching the snow fall outside. Jonathan had brought her back to Aunt Carol's after her trip to the hospital, and her adoptive mother had taken over from there. Ivy knew Carol was more than happy to have someone to take care of, and while she would have usually resisted the woman fawning all over her, she'd lost any fight. Nat's decree had left her feeling lost and hollow, and Ivy had begun questioning what she was even doing with her life.

That had been two days ago. And ever since, Ivy had remained mostly on Aunt Carol's couch, barely moving. Barely doing anything. She was lost deep within her own mind, going back and forth on the events of the past few days —and the consequences.

"Ivy, honey?" Ivy looked up, the mug of tea untouched in her hands. "Would you like some lunch? I really think you should eat something."

She wasn't hungry. She wasn't tired. In fact, she wasn't anything at all. It was like she'd been hollowed out of all emotion. And it had made her realize that her job was the single lifeline Ivy had been hanging onto without even realizing. Where were her friends, her loved ones, her hobbies? Other than Aunt Carol, she didn't have any of that. She barely even had the job.

"Ivy?"

"I'm not hungry," she said, setting the mug down on the table beside her. "Thanks." She turned to watch the snow continue to fall. It had started sometime during the night and continued through the day, blanketing the world in a white powder. Ivy liked the snow. It was as if the world was given a blank slate on which to reset. Everything was quiet, the world having shut down. At least that's how it appeared outside her Aunt's window.

Aunt Carol took a seat across from Ivy. "Okay, I've had enough of this," she said, her voice stern. Ivy looked up, surprised by her reaction.

"What?" she asked in a small voice.

"This turmoil you're going through," she replied. "Natasha can't just fire you for this. It's not right."

"I think she can," Ivy said, sighing. "I don't want to talk about it."

"Too bad, because we're talking about it. I've watched you barely move for two days while you try to work out whatever is going on inside your head, and I can't stand by and watch it anymore. As someone who loves you and cares about you, I'm not going to let you keep doing this to yourself. You did what you thought was right. And given the position she put you in, I don't blame you. The fact that she's too stupid or too obtuse to see that is a failing on her part, not yours." She scooted closer, closer than she'd ever been to Ivy, her hands very close to Ivy's blanket. Instinctively, Ivy pulled back. "I want you to understand. What she is doing to you is *not your fault*."

Tears began to well in Ivy's eyes again, but she wiped them away quickly. "You don't understand. What I did...it wasn't sanctioned. It wasn't—"

"I don't care," Carol replied, her voice stern. "Would you have done anything different if you had been assigned the case?"

Ivy thought about it. "No."

"And if you'd been allowed to investigate in the way you saw fit, would she have a leg to stand on?"

"That's just it, though. I took the law into my own hands. I was operating without authorization," Ivy said.

"Because she decided to withhold things from you. Nat knows you, better than almost anyone. Don't you think she knew you might try something like this? If she really had wanted you not to put yourself in this position, don't you think she would have been more open and honest with you?"

"Are you saying she did this on purpose, hoping I would give her a reason to fire me?" Ivy asked, wiping her eyes again.

"I don't know. But it's not like she just met you. She should have known how you would respond to being shut out, especially on a personal case like this. She didn't do you any favors by sidelining you." Carol leaned back, turning to look at the snow. "I just can't figure out what's going on with that girl. She used to be so good to us. And ever since you started working in that new department, it's like…like she's become a stranger."

Ivy considered Carol's words. Had Nat really orchestrated this whole thing? It was almost unfathomable. But by putting Ivy in the position she had, Nat had forced her hand. And Carol was right, Nat knew Ivy better than most. She knew Ivy wouldn't let something small like not being assigned the case stop her. Maybe Nat didn't think Ivy would go as far as to confront a loan shark and his crew without any backup, but she had to have known she wouldn't leave this one alone. Nat had obviously grown distant in the past few months, but Ivy never thought she would have put her in this kind of position on *purpose*.

She reached out for the tea, taking a sip. The warm liquid coated her raw throat and Ivy managed a deep breath, which only caused a slight pain in her side. "I think…I need to talk to my partner."

THE DOORBELL RANG JUST AS IVY HAD FINISHED SHOWERING and slipping into a clean set of clothes. She emerged from her bedroom with her hair still damp. She'd shaken it out as much as she could; it would just have to air dry. "I've got it," she called to Aunt Carol, who was rummaging around in the kitchen.

When she opened the door, Jonathan was standing there, bundled up with a small accumulation of snow on the top of his head. "I said you didn't have to come over." She stepped aside to let him in.

"What else am I going to do? I'm going stir crazy at home."

She conceded the point as he slipped off his shoes. "Oh, you don't have to—"

"Hello there," Aunt Carol said, wiping her hands on her apron as she emerged from the kitchen. She seemed as energetic as a teenager. "I'm Carol, it's so nice to meet you."

Jonathan took her outstretched hand, giving it a firm shake. "Jonathan White. It's a pleasure."

"Welcome to our home," Carol said. "Can I take your coat? I have tea or coffee."

"Okay, you don't need to fawn over him like he's a new puppy," Ivy said. "Here, gimme your coat." Jonathan shrugged out of his black pea coat, and Ivy hung it up in the hall closet. Though when she did, she spotted a bundle wrapped up in the corner that she didn't recall seeing before. Thinking little of it, she returned to the conversation.

"I wanted to thank you for what you did for Ivy," Carol said. "You're a good partner."

"Thank you," Jonathan said, though Ivy spotted some red in his cheeks. "I just didn't want her to go it alone."

Carol leaned in. "Then you've got yourself a challenge," she said, giving him a wink. "Now. Coffee or tea?"

"Coffee, please," he said.

"Why are you wearing a suit?" Ivy asked, leading him into the living room. "You're not at work."

"I dunno," he said. "Sometimes it's hard to stop when you get used to doing something. Most of my closet is suits." Ivy didn't even think she owned a suit, even though Nat had told her on more than one occasion she needed to dress for the job. But in Ivy's opinion, a more casual look helped people trust her more. They saw her more as a kindred spirit rather than a stuffy uptight cop with an agenda, even though that's exactly what she was. Though, that wasn't how she saw Jonathan now that she thought about it. Maybe he was on to something.

"Seriously though, we could have had this conversation over the phone."

"It gave me a chance to test out my skills of driving in bad weather," he said. "Though, they're keeping most of the larger roads clear. I didn't see anyone stuck on the side on my way over."

"Here you are," Carol said, bringing a small tray with a cup and saucer, along with some sugar packets and even a small tin of milk.

"Wow, this is…more than I expected," he said. "Thank you." He took the milk and poured a small amount into the coffee before adding sugar. "Made any progress?"

"Progress?" Ivy asked as Carol returned to the kitchen.

"Yeah, on the case. I assumed that's why you called."

"Oh," Ivy said. That made sense. Jonathan probably hadn't spent the past few days agonizing over the loss of his job because he'd only been put on temporary leave. "No, I need to talk to you about something more…urgent."

"Okay," he said, taking a sip of the coffee.

"Do you think Nat *wanted* this to happen? Me, I mean? Do you think she wanted me to act out enough to give her a reason to dismiss me?"

He set the cup down, folding his hands together as he leaned forward. "You're serious."

"I am. And I'm looking for your professional opinion as a detective. Do you think this has all been a setup?"

He thought about it for a minute. "I guess the real question is, do *you* think that's what she's done?"

"I don't know," Ivy admitted. "Which was why I wanted a second opinion."

"I've worked with the woman in a professional capacity longer than you, but you've known her personally for longer," he said. "I think you'd be more qualified to answer that question than I would."

"Humor me," Ivy said.

He took a deep breath. "In my professional opinion? No, I don't think she'd do that to you. Or anyone on our team. She can be reserved, even cagy. But I don't think she would try to sabotage any of us for her own personal gain. Whatever that may be."

Ivy sat back, deflated. If Nat had set her up, at least it would provide an explanation to her behavior lately.

"That wasn't the answer you were hoping for," he said.

"I just don't know what's going on anymore," Ivy replied. "Every time I think I have a handle on things, the rug gets pulled out from under me. And she's only compounding the problem."

"You know her wife recently got remarried, don't you?" Jonathan asked. "Took full custody of their kid."

Ivy's eyes widened. "What? No, I had no idea. I didn't even realize the divorce was final." That's how out of touch she and Nat had been. There was a time when Ivy knew everything going on in Nat and Samantha's lives. Ivy had even been at Nat's wedding seven years ago. It seemed like a lifetime ago now.

He nodded. "I don't think she's been taking it particularly well. That might explain some of her behavior."

Could Ivy have gotten this whole thing wrong? "You're saying this might not be about me at all? So why keep me, and by extension, you, off this case?"

"I wish I knew," he admitted. "But if there's one thing I do know, it's that other people don't think about us nearly as much as we assume they do."

Had that been it this entire time? Had Nat just been operating from a place of pain, and taking that out on Ivy because she knew Ivy the best? But that meant Ivy's actions were entirely her own fault, and by extension, the loss of her job would be as well. "I think I'm going to need something stronger than coffee," she said, standing.

"Hang on one sec," Jonathan said, reaching into his pocket and pulling out his phone. "This is White." Ivy couldn't hear who was on the other end, but it sounded serious. Jonathan's face went stern. "Yeah. Okay, yeah, got it. Thanks, Frank."

"Frank?" Ivy asked. "Richardson?"

Jonathan nodded, standing. "I asked him to keep me informed if there were any developments on the case, as a favor."

"The Baker case?" Ivy asked, her eyes going wide.

Jonathan made his way to the door. "Better get your shoes on. We need to take a drive."

"Where?"

"Pike's Bluff. They just found a body."

Chapter Twenty-Three

Ivy had to stop a second to catch her breath. Her feet were freezing, she couldn't feel her fingers, and her lungs burned with fire. It didn't help matters that her ribs were still considerably sore and every breath she took drove a dull ache through her midsection.

Ahead of her, Jonathan pushed on, though she'd heard him breathing heavily as well on the way up. She thought she was in better shape than this, but the hike had been longer and more intense than she'd suspected. She needed to get out more, build up her endurance.

"Wait up," she called out, noticing her partner wasn't slowing down.

"We're almost there," he called back.

"I know, I just need a second. You weren't kicked in the ribs three days ago." Ivy recalled that you shouldn't bend over when you were struggling to breathe, that it only made it more difficult for you to recover. She instead straightened her back, pitched her head to the sky, and let the remaining snow fall on her face. It had lightened up in the past few hours, reduced to little more than flurries. The sky was still overcast though, which contributed to the cold. No sun to warm her up as they walked. And since they'd had to trudge through the snow, her boots were beginning to soak through. How had anyone gotten up here in this kind of weather anyway?

Jonathan came back, his hands shoved in his pockets as he bounced up and down, trying to stay warm. "You okay?"

"Yeah, I just need a second," Ivy said, attempting to regulate her breathing. In. Out. She glanced around, taking in the snowy scene. A blanket of white covered the forest floor, coating the evergreens and mossy logs with a powdery white. It didn't snow often around Oakhurst, but Pike's Bluff was at a high enough elevation that it could accumulate when it did.

Of course, Ivy had never hiked Pike's Bluff before, so she didn't quite realize how steep it was. "Are we sure she's up here?"

"I confirmed it with Richardson."

She shook her head. "I just don't see how."

"Maybe he took a lot of breaks," Jonathan said, grinning at her.

Ivy glared at him. "Maybe he didn't carry her at all."

"That's a cheerful thought."

Ivy swallowed one more large gulp of oxygen. "C'mon. Let's get going." Jonathan took point again, leaving Ivy to follow. With every step she took, she swore there was no way this could be right. No way someone could get a body all the way up here. But as they crested the hill, she saw the site for herself.

It had already been taped off with yellow police tape, and Dr. Burns and her CSI team were surveying the site. A couple of other officers stood to the side, watching as they did their work, Frank Richardson among them.

"Helluva hike," Frank said as Jonathan and Ivy approached, extending his hand.

Jonathan took it. "Appreciate the heads up."

"Just don't tell the lieutenant," he replied. "I don't want to get in the same boat as you two." He looked over Jonathan's shoulder. "Bishop."

"Richardson," Ivy said. "Appreciate the call."

"No problem," he replied.

In the middle of the yellow tape was a mound, still covered in snow. But peeking out of the white, Ivy caught glimpses of green and red clothing underneath. She'd hoped there had been a mistake somewhere, that this wasn't the body of Jillian Baker. But she recognized the pattern on that piece of clothing. It had been a dress Mrs. Baker wore all the time when Ivy had been staying with her. It seemed she'd never thrown it away.

"What time did the hikers find her?" Ivy asked.

"About five hours ago," Richardson said. "Of course, she wasn't as concealed as she is now. Snow hadn't accumulated enough by then."

"And no other bodies around?"

"We're waiting on the dogs," Richardson said. "Can't find shit in all this white."

Ivy nodded, making her way over to where Dr. Burns stood close to the body, jotting down notes on an iPad while her people worked the scene, trying to melt the snow with portable heat guns.

"Bishop," Dr. Burns said. "Surprised to see you here. I thought you were on leave."

"I knew her," Ivy replied, coming around to look at the front of Mrs. Baker. She didn't look much different than the woman she'd seen not more than two weeks ago, except her face was pale and sallow, and her skin had lost all its color. She was on her side, about half an inch of snow having accumulated on her. Her eyes were closed, and her dirty gray hair covered part of her face.

So many emotions hit Ivy at once they all managed to cancel each other out. She couldn't do anything other than stand there in stunned silence, staring at the woman she had pinned all her hopes upon. Until today, there had always been the chance she could still be alive somewhere. Now all those doors were closed. "Do you—" Ivy cleared her throat. "Do you have a cause of death?"

"It's damn tricky in this weather," Burns said. "We first need figure out how long she's been out here. I'll have a better idea once we get her back down to Oakhurst. And I'll need to perform an autopsy. Though on first glance I don't see anything obvious such as gunshot wound or blunt force trauma."

"Any chance she could have escaped and made her way here?" Ivy asked.

"Anything is possible, I suppose," Burns said. "It's unlikely a sixty-something-year-old in moderate health could make her way all the way up here in these clothes, but it's not impossible. There is also a chance that perhaps she was dumped even further into the woods and only made it out this far before succumbing to the elements. Because of the snow, we can't get a good look at any footprints in the area, so we're not sure *how* she came to be here."

Pike's Bluff was an area known to avid hikers for its trails, but it was pure wilderness. If Mrs. Baker had been dropped somewhere even deeper in the wilderness and was trying to make her way out, she still had a good hour of hiking to go before reaching civilization. And if she was dumped here already dead, the killer might have thought it was a safe bet but failed to account for the tenacity of Oregon's outdoor enthusiasts.

"We hope to get the site cleared in the next hour, then maybe we can find some evidence," Burns said. "Now that the snow is tapering off, we won't be fighting the elements so much."

"Will you let me know if you find anything?" Ivy asked in a small voice.

Burns nodded, but Ivy kept her eyes locked on Mrs. Baker,

watching all the answers she'd so hoped to find disappear before her eyes. She hunched down in front of Mrs. Baker and pulled on a glove before pushing her hair to the side, revealing a small gash above her left temple. It wouldn't have been enough to kill her, but it was the perfect size to leave a small pool of blood on Mrs. Baker's kitchen floor.

"Nice find," Burns said, hunching down beside her.

"I think it was from the initial attack," Ivy said. "We found some blood on her kitchen floor."

"*We?*" an unfamiliar voice said from the other side of the site. Ivy looked up to see Detective Bruneau and his partner had arrived, both still huffing themselves from the hike.

"Bruneau," Ivy said, standing back up, snapping the glove off.

"What are you doing here, Bishop? You're on suspension. And from what I hear, you're getting fired."

Burns took a step back as Ivy extricated herself from the scene, walking around to face Bruneau. He was a big man, in both directions. He also hadn't shaved in a few days, leaving a haggard gray beard covering most of his face and neck. But his dark eyes were piercing and alert. Ivy had never worked with him before, but he had a reputation for not taking a lot of shit. He also had the reputation for having a temper.

"I knew the woman personally," Ivy said. "I deserved to see her at least one last time."

"How did you even know she was here?" He looked over her shoulder. "White? Is this your doing?"

"Don't worry about *how* I got here," Ivy replied. "You just better hope there aren't two more bodies out there in the snow somewhere. Since it's *your* case."

Bruneau grimaced. "Get the hell out of here, Bishop. Let the people who are supposed to be here do their jobs. From what I hear, you have a knack for interfering, but you're not going to screw this one up."

"You never know," Ivy said, adrenaline surging through

her veins. "I might just put one toe out of line." She lunged at Bruneau, causing him to flinch.

"White, get her the hell out of here before I arrest the both of you!" he yelled.

"C'mon, Ivy," Jonathan said.

"Next time, don't half-ass it," Ivy growled at Bruneau. "You left everything in her house. There could be an important clue in there."

"And how would you know that?" he asked.

Ivy felt Jonathan's presence beside her and decided it was better if she didn't engage in this fight right now. With her luck, it would come to blows, and she was in enough trouble as it was.

"Take care on your way back down," Bruneau said in an overly sarcastic voice as she and Jonathan left the scene.

"Prick," Ivy said as she followed Jonathan back down the mountain.

"Bruneau doesn't work well with others," Jonathan said.

"Yeah, neither do I," she said. "But sure, let's let the guy who knows nothing about the victim work the case. Why not?"

Ahead of them, Ivy caught sight of the canine team making their way up the hill, the handlers being led by two German shepherds who looked like they were having the time of their lives plowing through the snow. She smiled, recalling Oliver's dog. She should give him a call, update him on everything that's been going on. He'd want to know.

As Ivy and Jonathan passed the K9 team, they exchanged pleasantries before heading in opposite directions.

"I guess I should go back and face my fate, huh?" Ivy sighed.

"Sure," Jonathan said. "Or…we could drop by and interview the hikers who found her. You know, just for fun."

Ivy perked up. "What?"

He nodded. "Frank gave me their information while you

were arguing with Bruneau. I think they've got some kind of feud. He hates the man."

"I can't see why." Ivy grinned. "But you, Jonathan White, poster boy for detectives everywhere, you want to help someone who is about to be canned dig herself even deeper?"

Her partner stopped, shooting her a wink. "Why not? What's the lieutenant going to do? Fire you?"

Ivy couldn't help but smile the rest of the way down the mountain.

Chapter Twenty-Four

"Let's just go through it from start to finish, if you don't mind," Ivy said sitting on the kitchen stool with a warm mug of coffee in front of her.

In the kitchen sat Mrs. Matilda Giles, a lean and lanky woman with short blonde hair and a warm complexion. After Ivy and Jonathan had shown up to her home, she had taken to rummaging around in the kitchen to stay busy as she said she'd been so "put off" by the whole experience. Beside her stood her husband Harry Giles, who was as lean as his wife though had something of a mountain man appearance given the amount of flannel he wore in combination with his bushy beard.

Ivy and Jonathan had introduced themselves as detectives with the Oakhurst Police Department, they'd just neglected to say whether they were *specifically* investigating the Baker case.

"Starting from when?" Harry asked. "We were out there early."

"What time?" Ivy asked.

He exchanged a glance with his wife. "Maybe seven thirty. We knew we'd have to fight the snow, so if we wanted to get up to the peak and back down we had to get an early start.

There was no telling how much snow would be on the mountain."

"Turned out to be less than we thought," Matilda said. "We made good time."

"Yeah, until…well, you know."

"You found her at approximately what time?" Ivy asked.

"I'd say it was around nine thirty. Nine forty-five maybe. We figured we'd get to the summit around ten thirty and we were already more than halfway there when we…when we saw her."

"Here," his wife said, handing him a glass of water. "He gets queasy thinking about dead bodies."

"But you don't," Jonathan asked.

"My mother was a nurse. I've seen enough blood for a few lifetimes," she replied. "It doesn't bother me."

"As soon as we found her, we knew we had to come back down. There's no service up there," Harry said, taking a sip of the water.

"So it took us another, what? Twenty, thirty minutes to get a signal?" Margie turned to Ivy. "That's when we called you."

"When you found her, was there a lot of snow on the ground already?" Ivy asked.

Margie nodded. "Yeah, I mean it had been snowing for at least a full day by then. And up there, I'd say there was at least two or three inches on the ground."

"Did you see anything around her? Anything that might indicate how she got there?"

Harry screwed up his features as his wife turned back to the sink. "I think I remember seeing some footprints. But I might have imagined it."

"No, I saw them too," Margie said.

"Footprints in the snow?" Ivy asked. He nodded. "Do you remember if they were on the smaller side? Did they look like they could have belonged to her?"

"I don't really remember," he said. "I was trying not to get sick right there on the trail."

"They were work boot prints," Margie said. "At least, I think they were. And they looked deep. I remember because I noticed them earlier on the trail, and then they veered off into the woods toward the body."

Ivy turned to Jonathan. "Baker had on slippers. The same ones she wore around the house. She wasn't the one wearing those boots up there."

"And you don't remember seeing another pair of footprints?" Jonathan asked.

They both shook their heads.

"Either someone got curious or they were the one who brought her up there," Ivy said.

Jonathan nodded. "It could be either. We still don't know if she got up there under her own power or not."

Margie cleared her throat. "I'll tell you one thing. The reason we didn't go hiking on Monday was because the wind up there would have been terrible. It comes off the water and seems to wrap around those mountains like a fist squeezing the life out of someone. She would have had a hard time getting up there by herself on Monday."

It wasn't ironclad, but at least it was something. And it confirmed there was at least another person involved at some point. Whether that was just a curious onlooker or a person who had something directly to do with Mrs. Baker ending up there, she couldn't yet say.

"After you came down to make the phone call, did you go back up to the site?" Ivy asked.

"No, we waited for the police to arrive and let them know where she was. They told us to go home and wait for someone to contact us."

Ivy nodded. That reminded her, they better get out of there before Bruneau showed up. She stood, the coffee in front of her untouched. "Thanks for all your help. I know it must have been a nasty surprise, but if it weren't for you, she might have remained missing for longer."

Margie wiped her hands on a nearby towel. "I just hope those little girls are okay. We looked around on our way back down but didn't see anything else."

Jonathan stood as well. "Thanks for the hospitality. And the coffee. If we have any further questions, we'll let you know."

Ivy tried to keep a neutral face because, more than likely, they'd be asked all the same questions by Bruneau within the next hour. But it was like Jonathan said, what could Nat do to her now that she hadn't already done? Ivy was going to get to the bottom of this, even if she had to do it as a private citizen or behind bars.

"Not as much as I was hoping for," Jonathan said as they returned to the car.

"No, but it's something at least. Too bad Burns won't be able to get a boot print."

"Not unless it went through the snow into the dirt," Jonathan said. "Which, if someone was carrying a body, wouldn't be out of the question."

Ivy smiled. "I appreciate you trying to cheer me up, but I don't think it's very likely. Do you?"

"You never know," he replied, getting back in. "If I hauled a body all that way and was dead tired, I might not be paying attention to how much evidence I was leaving around the place."

It was a good point, but Ivy knew it was unlikely the CSI team would find much out there. The environment was just too much of an unknown factor. Maybe once the snow melted, there might be something, but that would be a few more days. At this point, it was up to Burns and the autopsy. And Ivy had reached her own dead end. By the time Burns actually got to the autopsy, Ivy would no doubt be out of a job. What was Nat waiting on? She had expected a call to come in first thing this morning, but so far there hadn't been a word. Then again, she wasn't about to poke the bear.

"Want to buy me a final meal?" Ivy asked, shooting another quick text to Oliver, telling him to get Hero ready; she was going to need some animal support after today.

"That's it, huh?" Jonathan said.

"Assuming she doesn't arrest me?" Ivy said. "But I'll keep working on this on my own. And don't worry, you won't need to compromise your position with the department. Oliver can get in and out of the system. One way or another, I'm getting that autopsy report."

"So you're going to fight Bruneau all the way, huh?"

She scoffed. "Maybe not before he was such a dick this morning. But now? Definitely."

"I guess if I have to lose a partner, the least I can do is buy her dinner," Jonathan said, turning the engine over. "What would you prefer?"

"How about Hop Kee?" she asked. "I'm in the mood for Chinese."

"Chinese it is," he replied.

~

"What are you going to do after suspension?" Ivy asked once they'd finished ordering. The restaurant had been in Oakhurst for the better part of five decades and wore it well. Despite the peeling paint and the faded graphical representation of Ancient China along one wall, the restaurant had the feel of a permanent establishment. Like it would be part of the town forever.

"Go back to my other cases, I guess. Assuming I'm not on probation," Jonathan said.

"I guess returning to Portland is out of the question," she said, taking a sip of the Midori Sour she'd ordered. It was incredibly sweet, and she wasn't sure she'd be able to finish it.

"At least for a little while," Jonathan said. "I'll have to face my mother eventually. If I could convince her to leave, I'd bring Marie down here. I think she'd like the smaller-town feel. Less stress."

Ivy scoffed. "Yeah, if bodies quit turning up."

"What about you? Even if you figure out who killed Mrs. Baker and by some miracle find those kids, you're still no closer to knowing what happened to you."

She took another sip of the drink—it was growing on her. "I thought about working with Alice to start an investigation into my past."

Jonathan practically spit out his drink. "What?"

She shrugged. "She's a good reporter. And she knows how to keep a secret. I used to think I could find out what happened on my own, but I made the mistake of trusting Nat. And now that I'm out of a job, I'm going to need some help. I'd ask you, but I don't want you jeopardizing your career. I think Alice would be more than happy to learn about corruption in the Oakhurst Police Department."

"Corruption?" he asked.

She waved him off. "Too strong of a word. But Nat is hiding something, and I'm going to find out what it is if it kills me. Seems we both have people we need to confront, doesn't it?"

"I guess so. But teaming up with Alice? You can't trust her. She'll never be honest with you."

"I don't need her to be honest, I just need her to do her job," Ivy said. "It's either that or leave town and start over somewhere else to try to forget about my past." She took a long sip of the drink. "And if you know anything about me, you know that's not an option."

Jonathan sighed. "If you must. Just…be careful around her."

"She had the opportunity to rat me out when she came to the station, and she didn't do it," Ivy said. "Which tells me she at least has integrity. More than I can say for my soon-to-be ex-boss."

Jonathan raised his water to her cocktail, clinking the plastic cups together. "Well, all my best to you then. Maybe you'll have better luck than I did with her."

Just as Ivy finished her drink, she thought she was feeling the buzz only to realize it was actually her phone, vibrating in her pocket. She checked the time: five fifteen. "Here we go," she said. But it wasn't Nat calling. It was Captain Armstrong. That sent a short pulse of fear down her spine. Nat she could handle, but Armstrong was a different animal.

"This is Bishop."

His voice was gruff and unyielding. "Get down to the station. Right now. If you're not here in fifteen minutes, I'm putting out an APB." He hung up.

Ivy sat, stunned. "Jesus," she muttered.

"What?"

"Armstrong just threatened to arrest me if I'm not back at the station in fifteen minutes."

He crinkled his brow. "Seems a little extreme. Should we get the food to go?"

Ivy slid out of the booth. "We'll just cancel. Whatever is going on, he wasn't playing around."

"Okay," Jonathan replied, pulling out a few bills for the drinks and tossing them on the table. He informed the server they had to leave due to an emergency.

The entire way over to the station Ivy couldn't figure out what could be so urgent. Had Nat finalized her report on Ivy's behavior and Armstrong had determined she *would* be arrested? While Ivy had thought that might be a remote possibility, she didn't think Nat would go that far, despite everything. But Armstrong was far less fond of her. He always had been, ever since she'd been promoted. Ivy thought she might have built some goodwill with the man after bringing in Kieran Woodward, but apparently that had all disappeared.

When they pulled into the station's parking lot, Ivy's heart was hammering. She'd been thinking about this moment for two days and had more or less resigned herself to the fact she would no longer be a detective. But to know that moment was right around the corner made it all that much harder. She wished she could fast-forward past this point in time and just be done with it already.

As they walked into the station, Ivy caught furtive looks from the other officers. It was a far cry from the reception she'd received just a few days ago. She happened to catch Officer Portnoy's eye, but the woman averted her gaze, pretending like she didn't see Ivy. They passed Wright's desk, but the man didn't even look up or acknowledge them.

Was it really *that* bad? And how did everyone already know?

As Ivy and Jonathan climbed the stairs to their department, Nat stood at the top of the stairs, waiting for them. But instead of a scowl, she wore a look of worry, and the deep bags under her eyes told Ivy she hadn't gotten much sleep.

"White, I need to speak with Ivy alone a second," she said.

"Armstrong just called me," Ivy said. "I'm supposed to—"

"Just a second," Nat said.

Jonathan nodded, heading over to his desk while Ivy followed Nat to her office. If they were going to can her, why didn't they just get on with it already? Why drag it out?

Once inside, Nat closed the door behind them. Her hair was pulled back in a loose bun, but strands stuck out at all angles. She really did look worse for wear. "Can't we just get this over with?" Ivy asked. "Here." She held out her badge for Nat.

Nat glanced at it for a moment, before circling her desk. "I need to know right now, is there anything you want to tell me? Anything at all?"

"About?" Ivy asked.

"Your investigation into Baker. Or anything, really."

"You're asking me *now*?" Ivy said, fuming. "I've been asking you for help for the past week and all I've gotten is the cold shoulder. Why would I confide in you now?"

Nat swallowed, hard. "Because this is serious, Ivy. I need to know…are you hiding anything?"

Ivy was stunned almost to the point of silence. "What kind of question is that? Hiding what?"

Nat glanced nervously at the door to her office, seeming to come to a decision. "I had to ask. C'mon, Armstrong is waiting."

"Will you please tell me what's going on?" Ivy asked. "Please. I know we've had our differences lately, but if I ever meant anything to you, just be honest with me."

Nat hesitated a moment. "Armstrong is waiting. I wasn't even supposed to bring you in here." She brushed past Ivy and opened the door, motioning for Ivy to go ahead.

She couldn't believe this. Just when she thought she'd hit rock bottom, this woman seemed to find a way to drag her down deeper. Ivy left her badge on Nat's desk, along with her service weapon. She couldn't even look Nat in the eye as she left, headed for Armstrong's office at the other end of the building.

"Not that way," Nat said. "We need to go down to the morgue."

"The morgue, why?" Ivy asked.

"They're waiting for you."

Ivy caught Jonathan's eye as she and Nat walked past. He moved to get up before Nat shut him down, telling him to stay where he was, that she would deal with him later.

The whole way back down to the morgue Nat was quiet, walking slightly behind Ivy as if she were escorting her. No, as if she were guarding her. Ivy felt like she already had on a pair of cuffs.

Once in the basement, Ivy made her way through the double doors to the morgue. Inside were Captain Armstrong,

Dr. Burns, and one of her assistants, all of them hunched over a small table. They all looked up when Ivy and Nat entered.

"Bishop," Armstrong said.

"Captain," she replied.

"I wanted to give you a chance to explain yourself," he said.

She nodded. "I know. I shouldn't have been investigating the case. It's just that I knew Mrs. Baker, and I thought I might be able to help with—"

"I'm not talking about that," he snapped.

"Then what?"

He grimaced, then nodded to Dr. Burns who gave Ivy a sympathetic look before heading over to the cold storage lockers. She opened one in the middle, pulling out the tray to reveal Mrs. Baker, who had been transported down from the mountain.

"Did you already do the autopsy?" Ivy asked.

"Not exactly," Burns said. Baker was naked, though covered with a sheet from her neck all the way down to her ankles.

"I don't understand," Ivy said. "What's going on?"

"Show her," Armstrong said.

Burns pulled back the sheet, exposing Mrs. Baker all the way down to her midsection. And there, in the middle of her chest, had been carved the words: *Ivy Stanford.*

Chapter Twenty-Five

"Care to explain?" Armstrong asked.

Ivy found she couldn't form any words. What was her name doing carved into Mrs. Baker's body? And not the name she chose for herself after she turned eighteen, but her *given* name, her *family* name. A name only a few people truly knew.

"Lieutenant Buckley has confirmed for us that Stanford was your previous surname," Armstrong said. "I want to know what it's doing on my victim."

"I—I don't know," Ivy admitted. She couldn't quit staring at the severe and ragged lines of her name. The flesh had even been torn in some areas. "Was she…I mean did it happen while she—"

"I'm afraid so," Dr. Burns said. "You can see evidence of healing around some of the wounds. She was still alive when this was done to her."

"Or when she did it to herself," Armstrong said.

Ivy's head snapped up. "What?"

Armstrong nodded to Burns again. The doctor sighed. "I haven't been able to do a full investigation, but from the slanted angle of the incisions, there is a possibility Baker did this to herself."

"But…why would anyone—"

"You're the detective," Armstrong said. "If you were dying and only had a sharp object nearby, what's the last thing you'd want to communicate?"

No. That was ludicrous.

"This is ridiculous," Nat said before Ivy could even finish processing the captain's insinuation. "You're saying Ivy kidnapped Mrs. Baker and those kids, then tortured her and dropped her in the woods to die?"

"We don't know what happened," he replied. "All I know is it's not a good look to have your name carved on a victim that's been missing for a week. Personally, I would like to hear Detective Bishop's explanation." He turned to her.

"I…don't have one," she replied. She had no idea why Mrs. Baker, or anyone for that matter, would carve her name on her body. It didn't make sense. "You're *sure* this was done while she was still alive?"

Burns nodded. "No question."

"Captain," Nat said. "Ivy didn't kidnap anyone."

"She knew the victim. Had visited her earlier in the week before she disappeared," he said, his dark eyes narrowed at Ivy. But that wasn't what surprised Ivy the most. It was the fact Nat was *defending* her.

"She also took an oath to serve and protect," Nat said. "Is there any other evidence that puts Ivy anywhere within a hundred miles of this body before today? Any fingerprints? Any forensics?"

"You know the teams aren't finished yet," Armstrong said. "It'll be a few days at least."

"Then how about we wait until deciding to unilaterally convict her?" Nat shouted. Ivy couldn't believe it; the woman was going to bat for her. "It's a bad call, Damian, and you know it."

Armstrong huffed. "I don't like my detectives being in the middle of cases. Until we figure all this out, I want her monitored." He turned to her. "Bishop, you're under house arrest. You leave, and I'll put you behind bars."

"That's overkill," Nat said. "And illegal."

"I seem to recall you were on the verge of firing her yourself not more than twenty-four hours ago," Armstrong said.

"That was different," Nat said. "That was—it doesn't matter. Ivy isn't a flight risk."

"I know she's not. Because she's going to stay in her house until we determine who killed this woman." He said it as though it was a certainty, but Ivy felt lightheaded. She couldn't think straight, it was all too much.

"I still think—"

"Look, it's either I know she's in her home, or we detain her here." Armstrong turned to Ivy. "Your call."

Ivy found she had to steady herself against the cold freezers. "No, I'll...go home." What choice did she have? Armstrong was on the rampage, ready to arrest her then and there. At least if she was at home she would have time to think, to figure out who could have done this. There weren't that many people who knew her real name, which should narrow the field considerably. But if she was confined to her house, there was only so much she could do.

"*Bishop.*"

She looked up to see Armstrong staring her down. "I said follow the Lieutenant. You need to be outfitted with a monitor."

"A monitor?" she asked, still dazed from the whole experience.

"For your ankle," Armstrong said.

"This is insane," Nat said. "She hasn't been arrested."

"And this will make sure she doesn't need to," he said without a moment's hesitation. "Right?"

Right. Like a common criminal.

Nat continued to apologize the whole way back up the stairs as they made their way to tech services. She seemed angrier about this than Ivy was. Ivy was sure she'd be livid later, but right now, she was just shocked. Shocked from seeing Mrs. Baker like that, shocked from the accusations, and shocked that Cole Cook had been right. Someone definitely wanted her attention.

The question was who?

IVY SAT ON HER BED, TRYING TO TAKE HER MIND OFF THINGS BY diving into one of her favorite books, but the words just wouldn't coalesce on the page. She found herself re-reading the same passages over and over again before she finally just shut the book out of frustration. As she tried to turn over on the bed, the small device that had been affixed around her ankle made contact with the bedframe and Ivy cursed, looking down at the stupid thing. The little red light on the side burned continuously, like it was mocking her. Nat had helped her get it fitted before bringing her back to her apartment and setting up the perimeter that she was not to cross. If she took one step outside of the apartment, the unit would go off, alerting everyone in the department.

Throughout the drive, Nat continued to be strangely apologetic, promising they would get everything worked out. She'd even assured Ivy she wouldn't be fired; she had just been blowing off steam when she learned Ivy had gone behind her back. She was planning to talk to Armstrong again, get him to see reason. The woman was like Doctor Jekyll and Mr. Hyde. Ivy never knew which version she'd get.

As soon as she was left alone in her apartment, everything hit her. All of her anger, fury and rage exploded as she wrenched open the cabinets and yanked all the dishes out and onto the floor, for no other reason than the fact it felt good. It was a good thing Ivy had plastic plates in her cabinets, otherwise the neighbors might have called the police right back.

It wasn't that she was mad at being called a criminal—okay, yes, she was. But she was more upset that someone had used her name to implicate her in all of this. She found herself at the center of an investigation that had already been deeply personal to her. And there was literally nothing she could do about it. She just had to sit here and hope things worked themselves out.

Given her luck, she'd probably be in jail next week.

A knock came at her door just as Ivy had decided she wasn't making any progress on the book and had tossed it to the side.

She opened it to find Oliver on the other side, Hero at his feet on a red leash. The pup barked once as soon as he saw Ivy.

"Hey," Ivy said. "What are you doing here?"

"Heard on the grapevine you were incarcerated," Oliver replied. "We came to help."

"You sure you're not too mad about all the wasted documentation?" Ivy asked. Hero barked again, bringing a smile to her face.

"It was only an hour's worth of work," he admitted. "It wasn't that hard."

She stood aside to let them in. Hero led the way, eager to explore the unfamiliar apartment. "Forget to call the cleaners?" Oliver asked as he let Hero off the leash. He immediately went to exploring all the plasticware all over the floor before moving on to the living room. "Just my frustration. What grapevine?"

"Oh, you know," Oliver said. "Just my constant monitoring of police chatter. Gotta stay on top of things."

Ivy narrowed her gaze. "You broke into the system again, didn't you?"

He shrugged. "Got a good look at the case they're building against you. So far, it's pretty flimsy."

Ivy groaned. "There's already a case open against me?"

"Case number 74656 if I'm not mistaken," he replied.

Ivy had foolishly held out hope that Armstrong was just blowing a lot of hot wind, much in the same way Nat had, but it seemed like he was serious. "Who's the case officer?"

"Haven't assigned one yet. But if you want my bet, he'll probably give it to Bruneau."

"Wouldn't that just be the icing on the cake?" Ivy asked, heading into the kitchen. "Want a water…or something?"

"Water is good," Oliver said.

Ivy pulled out a couple of bottles from the fridge, only to find Hero sitting at her feet, looking up at her expectantly.

"Oh, I forgot to tell you. He's food motivated," Oliver said.

Ivy reached down and stroked Hero's head. "I see. Unfortunately, I don't have much to eat here." She handed Oliver a bottle as she opened the other, pouring it into a shallow bowl for Hero. "I've been staying with Aunt Carol the past few days. I thought maybe I could go back through all her records. See if I could find anything helpful."

"And did you?" he asked.

"No. There's nothing to find. Only two people knew anything about what happened that night, and one of them is now dead. While the other one…" Ivy sighed. "I just can't explain her. One second she's cold, then she's hot. Then she's cold again. And I can't trust a single word out of her mouth."

Oliver took a sip of his water, sliding onto one of the stools in the kitchen. "I wish I could remember something about that night. But I didn't even know you'd arrived until the following morning. And I don't remember either of the Bakers saying a word." He paused. "Maybe it would be worth talking to Woodward again?"

Ivy shook her head. "I feel like I got as much out of him about that night as I'm going to get. He swore he didn't remember anything else. Plus, I'm not exactly in a position to talk to him again."

"I mean, you could," Oliver said, looking at the door. "Just a few steps out that door and they'll lock you up with him."

"Funny," Ivy said. "No, he was transferred to county. Armstrong would keep me in Oakhurst's jail until he's satisfied I didn't do this or he makes something up to convict me."

"You think he'd really do that?" Oliver asked.

She nodded. "He wasn't above skirting the law when we were going after Woodward. If he gets enough pressure from the public and the mayor, I think he'll *find* a solution."

"Crooked cops," Oliver said, shaking his head. "That's why I love my business. Everything is neutral. You just gotta follow the money."

She glared at him. "I don't think it's that simple."

"I just can't figure out how someone even *knew* about your name to do that," Oliver said. "I mean, how many people were even aware Bishop wasn't your real last name?"

"It *is* my real last name, now," Ivy said. "But to answer your question, I don't know. You know, so does Aunt Carol. And Nat. And I guess the person down at the state records department who approved the name change seven years ago. And obviously Mrs. Baker knew. But I don't believe she did that to herself. Even if she was being coerced…she wasn't a masochistic kind of person. Remember how she'd get woozy at even the sight of blood?"

"Yeah," he chuckled. "And that time we covered my forehead with ketchup to try and make her faint?"

"You were a good sport about it," Ivy said.

He nodded. "Those were good times. Glad to see I'm not on the suspect list this time. But just in case, I brought proof I've been home with Hero for the past three days, working. I've had food delivered and everything."

Ivy gave him a sly grin. "I know better than to make the same mistake twice." She made her way into the living room, taking a seat on the couch. "I just don't know what to do. It's all gone to hell."

"Well, you're not just going to sit around here and mope, are you?" he asked.

"What choice do I have?"

Oliver got down on one knee, inspecting the unit around her ankle. "I can disable it. They'll never even know."

She pulled her leg away, apprehensive. "Oh, no. Armstrong is already itching for a reason to put me away."

"And you're just going to sit here and let other people decide your fate?"

He was right, that wasn't like her in the slightest. "Okay," she said, curious. "Where exactly would I go? It's not like I can go look at the autopsy results from Burns."

"No, but I can," he replied. "And who knows, maybe they'll lead to something."

She shook her head. "No, I need to find those two little girls. I can't be worried about my own problems right now."

"Your altruism is sickening," Oliver said, making a gagging face. "Listen, you find whoever kidnapped Mrs. Baker, you find the girls. The goals are one in the same."

"I suppose," she said, thinking it over. If Armstrong or anyone from the precinct learned she was out of her apartment, no amount of goodwill would change the fact she'd escaped house arrest. Even if she wasn't found to be connected to Mrs. Baker's murder, it wouldn't be good. And then her career really would be over.

But…maybe Oliver had a point and didn't even realize it. Plus, no one was as motivated or as invested as she was to see this thing to the end. It didn't matter how good of a cop Bruneau was, he'd never put himself on the line to find out what happened. He didn't have a reason to.

"I think I have an idea," she said. "But if we're going to do this. We're going to need some help."

Chapter Twenty-Six

"Oh, this can't be good," Jonathan said, standing in Ivy's doorway. She'd sent him a cryptic text as to not alert anyone who might be monitoring his cell phone messages. Not that she was paranoid enough to think anyone might be doing that, but Oliver had insisted.

"What?" she asked, standing just on the threshold.

"*Watch-im!*"

Hero scampered past Ivy's feet, running out into the hall like he was on a mission. She almost went out after him, only to remember her ankle monitor. Fortunately, Jonathan reached down and scooped the small dog up with the skill of someone who'd done it a hundred times, bringing him back into the apartment and setting him down.

"Yours, I assume?" he asked Oliver.

"That's Hero," Oliver said. "Thanks for grabbing him. He's still getting used to new places. I don't think he likes being cooped up in my house. My yard isn't exactly dog friendly yet."

"No problem," Jonathan said, turning back to Ivy who had secured the door again. "What's he doing here?"

"Moral support," she replied. "And we need your help."

"*We?*" Jonathan asked. Ivy couldn't help but notice he said it in much the same way Oliver had when he thought she had been going through Mrs. Baker's house with Jonathan. "I thought your text meant you needed me to bring you food or something."

"I'm not hungry," she said.

Oliver perked up. "I could eat." Jonathan did his best to ignore him. "Hey, how were you so quick to grab Hero? Is that part of your reflex training?" Oliver's words were tainted with sarcasm, but Jonathan ignored them. Hero had been circling Jonathan ever since he'd brought him back into the apartment.

"My sister has a pug. Same size. You get used to carrying them around."

Oliver seemed to soften. "Yeah. Thanks again. I'm still getting used to this whole pet ownership thing."

"Just out of curiosity," Jonathan said while petting Hero, who stopped circling to enjoy the attention. "What made you decide to get a dog out of the blue?"

Oliver seemed to hesitate, something Ivy found odd. He was usually so quick and confident. "You know, just felt the need."

"Felt the need?" Jonathan pressed. "Ever owned a dog before?"

"No," Oliver admitted.

"Make life changing decisions on a whim often?"

"What's with the third degree here?" He looked around the taller man. "Ivy, tell him to back off."

"Sorry," Jonathan said, though he didn't sound sorry. "Sometimes I just flip into detective mode." He seemed to reset himself, turning to Ivy. "Speaking of dogs, the K9 units didn't find anything else on the bluff. No scents or trails of the girls. They could still be alive."

"That's a relief," Ivy said.

"I could have told you that," Oliver muttered.

"Nat put you on the case?" Ivy asked.

Jonathan neared the seats in the kitchen. "I wish. No, I had to do some digging. She's got me doing desk work, though no more talk of probation. I think she's wound up too tightly about you. Everyone at the station is talking about it."

"Anything helpful?" she asked, hating the hope in her voice.

"Mostly gossip. But our boss has already been in one shouting match with Armstrong. Loud enough for the entire building to hear." He gave Ivy a hopeful look. "She is adamant in her defense of you."

"See, this is what I'm talking about," Ivy said, turning to Oliver.

"It *is* strange," Jonathan said. "After how angry she was at the hospital."

"Wait, you didn't say anything about a hospital," Oliver stood, alarmed.

"It was nothing, I'm fine," Ivy replied.

Jonathan turned to Oliver. "She kicked two guy's asses in the middle of the street down in Three Rivers."

"Really? Wow." But his tone didn't indicate he was impressed. It was more trepidatious.

"What?" Ivy asked.

"Nothing," Oliver said too fast. "Shall we get down to it?"

Jonathan perched on one of the nearby kitchen stools. "I'd like to hear this as well, considering I don't know why I'm here."

"We need you to run interference," Ivy said.

"Interference for what?"

Ivy exchanged a look with Oliver. "I need to talk to Kieran Woodward again."

"Woodward, why? You told me he didn't know anything else about what happened to you that night."

Ivy shook her head. "Not about that. He knew my last name. Even if he didn't remember it right away, he knew it."

"But he couldn't have done this, he's been in custody for the last week," Jonathan said.

"I know, but think about it. We've had a serial killer, an abduction, and a related homicide all in under a month, all connected to the Bakers."

"You're saying Woodward knows something about the kidnappings?"

"She's saying he knows who does," Oliver said, rubbing Hero's ears. The dog had finally had his fill of Ivy's apartment and, finding no food on Jonathan, had returned to Oliver.

"But there's no way Armstrong, Nat, or anyone else will authorize me to talk to him. Not while I've got this thing on." She held up her ankle for effect.

"You're not thinking of trying to sneak in there, are you?" Jonathan asked. "There are cameras everywhere, you'd be stopped before you made it halfway—"

"Sneak in? No," Ivy said with more than a sparkle in her eye.

"Wait, you want to get incarcerated *on purpose*?"

She gave him a solemn nod.

"How? You can't get into county, at least not for a few days. Hell, I'd probably have to bring you in myself unless I want Armstrong's hammer."

Ivy chuckled. "You're cute when you curse. No, Oliver is going to deactivate my bracelet long enough for me to drive out to the sheriff department's jurisdiction. At that point he'll turn it back on, and they'll be forced to bring me in."

"Where you come in is running interference on Oakhurst PD," Oliver said. "Ivy needs as much time with Woodward as she can get, but your boss is going to want to get her back into town right away."

Jonathan scoffed and stood. "Are you crazy? You'd be giving up everything…for what? An off chance he *might* know something? Just let me interview him."

"You know that won't work," Ivy said, leaning back on the

couch. "He barely talked to me. And unless I missed something, the psychiatrists haven't been able to get anything out of him either."

"But what if he really doesn't know anything?" Jonathan asks. "Or he doesn't cooperate?"

"No one said it wasn't a risk," Ivy replied.

"It's a big risk. Too big. You'll have a record, it will stain your entire career. Why not just let Bruneau work the case? You obviously didn't kill Baker. I'm sure you'll be exonerated in no time."

Ivy leaned forward. "The kids," she said. Jonathan sighed. "They're my responsibility. If I'd reported Baker when I should have, none of this would have happened. They'd be safe with another family right now."

"You don't know that. The kids could have been the original target, which would explain why we haven't found them yet. Baker could have been collateral damage. Plus, I was there that day too. I have just as much responsibility for not reporting her as you do."

"Which is why you're going to help us," Oliver replied. "You just need to stall your boss and anyone else who might come for her as long as possible."

"And how am I supposed to do that?" Jonathan snapped. A small section of hair had come loose from his usually coiffed scalp, falling over his forehead. He pushed it back into place with a scowl.

"Be creative," Oliver said. Jonathan scoffed derisively. "Hey, I don't like it any more than you do. But all three of us need to work together or this has no chance."

"It has no chance as is," Jonathan said. "It's going to take at least an hour to process Ivy once she's in custody. And that's if it's a slow day. And how are you even going to talk to Woodward anyway? It's not like they're just going to let you choose your cell."

"Leave that part to me," Oliver said. "Don't worry. I'll make sure they're cozy neighbors."

"This is insane," Jonathan said.

"I know," Ivy replied. "But if we don't do it, and those girls' bodies turn up on Pike's Bluff, I'm not going to be able to live with that. I've already failed Mrs. Baker. I can't fail them too."

Jonathan's eyes turned up. "*You* didn't fail her. It wasn't even your case."

"Yes, it was," she replied. "It was always my case."

"Dammit," Jonathan said, causing Ivy to smirk again. "But I'm going on the record now to say I fully disagree with this plan."

"Noted," Ivy said, heading for the door. "Shall we get started?"

~

THIS HAS TO WORK. IT HAS TO.

Ivy sat in the passenger seat of Oliver's car, staring at the train depot across the street. Her ankle monitor had been off for over three hours, and no one had come looking for them yet. She figured Oliver really was as good as he claimed to be, otherwise she would have been swarmed by beat cops the minute they'd pulled out of the apartment complex.

"You ready?" Oliver asked.

"No," she replied. Even though she'd been the one to come up with the plan, now that they were close to execution, she wasn't sure she could go through with it. If she was wrong, and Kieran didn't know anything or she couldn't get him to talk, it would all be over. Even if it did work and she managed to get something out of him, she wasn't walking away from this unscathed.

She might even end up spending some real time behind

bars, though she was confident she could plead that down with a good attorney. But no matter what, she'd kiss her career goodbye. Everything she'd worked for, everything she'd sacrificed…all of it had been worth it to get closer to finding out what happened to her family. Ever since she could remember, even before the Black Pistons, she had thought about becoming a police officer, even if it had mostly been due to Nat's influence in her life. And now she was about to throw that all away.

"Ivy," Oliver said. "Clock's ticking."

Hero barked from the backseat, and Ivy winced. She was stalling, and she knew it. "Okay," she replied. "Wait until I'm about halfway to the station, then turn it back on."

"Got it," he said. "Do you need anything else?"

She shook her head. "Just get out of here as quickly as you can. I don't want you getting caught up in this."

"I *am* caught up in this," he reminded her. "But I know what you mean. If I don't make it back home before you're pinched, I can keep an eye on you remotely."

"Including everything that happens after?" she asked.

"As much as we can control." He hesitated. "Hey, just in case I don't get the chance to ask again…was it something about me?"

"Huh?" she asked, her concentration broken.

"The other day, when you said you'd started experimenting with physical contact. You said you weren't ready when I tried…but then your partner said you beat the crap out of two guys down in Three Rivers. I just…is there something wrong with me?"

"It's not you," she said. "Well, actually it is." She turned to him. "It's just easier with strangers. Touching people I'm close to feels more complicated." She pursed her lips. "So I guess it is you, but not exclusively you, if that makes sense."

"It's impressive," he said, "that you're making the leap. There was a time when I thought you'd never do that again."

"I can't live like that forever, and if there's anything

Kieran taught me, it's that I'm more capable than I give myself credit for a lot of the time."

"That's the truth," Oliver said.

Though it probably hadn't been his intention, Oliver's question reminded Ivy of her courage. She had done worse and survived. She would survive this as well, no matter which way it went. She took one more deep breath. "Okay. Wish me luck."

"You don't need it," he said. "I know you've got this."

"Thanks," she replied. "For everything." He nodded. As soon as she stepped out of the car a blast of wind hit her, knocking her back. Undeterred, Ivy made her way in the direction of the train station. She was about halfway across the street when she felt the device strapped around her ankle buzz and emit a loud alarm.

Instead of continuing to the train station, she busted out into a sprint, headed down the street that ran parallel to the train tracks. She had to make it look like she was trying to get away, but she couldn't do such a good job they wouldn't be able to catch up with her.

Her phone immediately began vibrating in her pocket. Ivy didn't bother pulling it out. No doubt it was Nat, trying to talk sense into Ivy. But she was already thinking clearer than ever.

Finally, Ivy had to stop running as the cold air burned her lungs. She didn't dare get off the road, but she remained on the side in the ditch, bundled up and walking in the direction of the next closest town, a good twenty miles away.

Before she could even think about the chill seeping into her clothes and her shoes, she saw the first set of flashing lights appear on the horizon.

Chapter Twenty-Seven

Ivy heard the telltale click of the camera, but there was no flash.

"Turn to the right."

She complied, hearing the camera click again.

"Step this way."

They brought her into a room adjacent to where she'd just had her mugshots taken, and they began the process of fingerprinting her. The Douglas County deputy who arrested her had only asked her for identification and she'd complied, saying nothing and refusing to answer any questions. Of the eight deputies she'd encountered since being arrested, half had seemed sympathetic, and the other half only shook their heads at Ivy like she was the stupidest woman in the world.

She'd first been brought into the sheriff's office where Sheriff Connors tried to get her to explain how she got from the middle of Oakhurst all the way out to Elkmont train station without the monitor going off, also informing her that he'd been in contact with both Armstrong and Buckley, and someone from the Oakhurst PD would be along to collect her shortly. In the meantime, she'd be remanded in the county lockup.

Ivy had remained stone-faced, not offering any emotion he might pick up on or use against her. He'd asked her if she wanted to speak to a lawyer while she waited, but her silence had only bought her more derision from the man. Eventually he'd become so frustrated that he relented and sent her through processing.

"I don't get it," the woman fingerprinting Ivy said. "I heard about you, breaking that big case down in Oakhurst. First serial killer in the town's history, wasn't it? How does someone go from that to this?"

Ivy could think of a few ways, but decided it was better to remain silent for her cover. She still had a job to do, and any discussion might cut short her already limited time here.

As soon as she was fingerprinted and searched again to make sure she didn't have any weapons or dangerous objects, including her shoelaces, she was assigned a cell and escorted back into the lockup.

Only about twenty of the fifty or so cells were occupied, though Ivy caught a glimpse of Kieran Woodward as soon as they entered the cell block. The man didn't even look up as Ivy passed; he seemed like he'd been drugged with something. More than likely a tactic to prevent him from harming himself. Which would only make her job harder.

"D-16…check that for me T," the woman asked into her radio as she and Ivy passed Woodward's cell, which was D-15. The cells were cinder block on three sides, with only a caged opening on the front. It would be difficult to interact with Woodward, but not impossible.

"Those are the orders," the voice said through the radio.

The deputy escorting Ivy screwed up her face. "Well, I'm going to move you one over. We got plenty of room here, you don't need to be locked up beside *him*." She guided Ivy down to D-17.

"No, that's fine," Ivy said, her heart suddenly in her throat. If she wasn't in the cell right next to Woodward, she'd have a harder time getting him to talk. "I wouldn't want you to get in trouble."

"Pssh," the deputy replied. "Connors is always trying to cut corners…either that or this is petty revenge on his part. We all know you captured Woodward. Putting you right next to him would be cruel." She turned to her radio again. "Open D-17."

"But—" Ivy began as the door rattled open.

"Here," she said, ushering Ivy inside. "I'm sorry we even have to do this. If it were up to me, you could wait in one of the offices." She turned back to her radio. "*Close seventeen.*"

There was nothing Ivy could do. She couldn't argue without it becoming suspicious, which might cause them to pull her from the cell block entirely and start a round of questioning. At least, that's what she would do if someone in her custody was acting so out of character. She'd been amazed Connors or someone else hadn't already taken her into an interrogation room. But she'd been betting they didn't want to deal with her and would rather just leave it up to Oakhurst.

"If you need anything, just yell," the deputy said after the cell closed. "You shouldn't be here too long. Again, I'm sorry." She gave Ivy a sympathetic look before turning and heading back out.

Ivy felt bad for deceiving the woman, but she had a bigger problem. Woodward seemed completely out of it. It would have been enough of a challenge to get his attention when she was right beside him. Now he was a good ten feet away, barely visible down the hallway. She'd have to shout if she even wanted to be heard. She couldn't believe she'd made it this far only to be stymied by something as common as physical distance. The irony wasn't lost on her.

"Hey," she called out. "Kieran. It's Ivy." There was no response. "Ivy *Stanford*. Remember me? From the cliff?"

Still nothing. This wasn't going to work. Ivy looked around her cell for something…*anything* she could use to get his attention. But there was nothing in the cell other than a bed suspended from the wall and a toilet.

Ivy's eyes widened. She pulled open the toilet paper dispenser, yanking it from the holder. She then proceeded to unwind the entire roll, leaving nothing but the cardboard center. She put the cardboard to her mouth and stuck it out the bars of the cell, pointed at Woodward's. Her hope that it would direct more of her voice in his direction in the cavernous cell block.

"*Hey, Woodward!*"

She heard him stir in the other cell, the shuffling of blankets and sheets. "Who…who said that?" His voice was almost hoarse, like he hadn't spoken in a few days.

"Remember me?" she asked. "The girl who saved your life?"

He mumbled something unintelligible then, "Where are you?" His words were slightly slurred, confirming Ivy's drug suspicions. It was a miracle she'd managed to get his attention at all. But it gave her an idea. If he was under the influence, she might be able to use that to her advantage. It was a risk, but she didn't know how much time she had. A risk might be exactly what she needed right now.

"I'm in your mind," she replied. "Because you have something I need."

She wished she could see his face, gauge his reaction. He was silent for a moment, and Ivy assumed her gamble had fallen flat. "Why can't you just leave me alone?" he asked, his voice pitching higher. "What do you want from me?"

Ivy smiled. Perhaps not so flat after all. "Information, Kieran. And you're going to give it to me," she said. "It's the only way I'll leave. And that's what you really want, isn't it?"

"Yes, *please*," he said. "Just go away."

"Who told you to kill those people, Kieran? Who told you to cut off their heads and dispose of their bodies?"

"N-no one, I did that. It was me," he said, though she detected a tremble in his voice.

"Who told you it was okay?" she asked. He didn't respond. "Who, Kieran? I'm not going to leave you alone until you tell me."

"*I don't know*," he replied, and Ivy to perked up. *So there* was *someone else.*

"Did you tell him about Mrs. Baker?" Ivy asked. "Did you tell him to kidnap her?"

"No," he cried out, his voice wavering and pathetic.

"She's dead, Kieran," Ivy said. "He killed her."

"No!" he yelled again. "No, no, no, no—"

Time to push him to the limit. "Tell me who he is, Kieran, and all this goes away. It all stops. I just need a name. Who told you it was okay to kill those people? Who else knew about Mrs. Baker?"

"Shepard!" he yelled out, loud enough for anyone in the lockup to hear. "John Shepard!"

Just as he yelled out, Ivy heard the door to the lockup open. "What in the hell is going on in here?" the deputy called out.

Woodward was practically screaming while Ivy had retreated to the back of her cell, shoving the toilet paper under her mattress. She could picture him, holding both sides of his head, maybe even clawing at himself to try and get her voice out of there.

For someone who killed over a dozen people, she thought it was a fitting punishment. At least, more fitting than any the state could dole out. If Kieran Woodward went crazy inside his cell, she could live with that.

"Woodward, *shut up!*" the deputy yelled, slamming what sounded like a club against the bars of the cell. The sound echoed through the whole block, causing some of the other inmates further down to yell out. Woodward let out another high-pitched scream. Ivy pressed herself up against the bars of her cell to see two more deputies enter, though she couldn't tell what they were doing. The first deputy called for Woodward's cell to be opened. After that, all Ivy could hear was the sounds of someone struggling and grunting, along with muffled orders coming from one deputy to another. She had no idea what they were doing to Woodward, and she didn't really care. Last she checked, the DA hadn't even set a court date for his arraignment as they were waiting on results from the psychological tests. No matter what, Woodward would never be getting out. It was just a matter of where he'd end up once it was all said and done.

All that mattered was she had a name. How that name related to Mrs. Baker and the disappearance of the children, she didn't know. Was Shepard pulling the strings, or was he responsible for the kidnappings? Or was he involved in some other way? She couldn't be sure, but what mattered was she finally had something solid.

"Bishop!"

Ivy glanced up to see the deputy had returned to the front of her cell. Beads of sweat had broken out over her forehead, and she was breathing heavily.

"Everything okay?" Ivy asked.

"Let's go, your ride is here."

Chapter Twenty-Eight

"I can't believe you would do this," Nat said, escorting Ivy out of the Douglas County Sheriff's Office to her car. "After everything you worked for, just to throw it all away like this." She shook her head, opening the passenger side door for Ivy. "Do I need to put you in the back? Are you going to be a threat to me?"

"No more than you are to me," Ivy replied, glaring at the other woman.

"I stood up for you. And this is how you repay me."

Ivy barked a laugh. "Stood up for me? You haven't been on my side since the day you hired me. You know I should have been the one working this case from the beginning. Maybe I wouldn't have had to take such drastic measures if I'd been allowed to *do the job you hired me for*."

"Get in," Nat said, glaring at Ivy.

Ivy's hands were locked in handcuffs in front of her, but she had no trouble maneuvering herself into the passenger seat. Nat closed the door and rounded the car. Why had she been the one to come pick Ivy up? They'd planned for Jonathan to make the trip, so she could at least relay any intel she found. Now this would delay things even further.

Nat got in and pulled out of the parking lot, headed for the highway back to Oakhurst. "Even if you had been working this case, it wouldn't have stopped your name from showing up carved into our victim. You should have stayed at home and let me handle this. Now it's out of my control."

"You know me better than that," Ivy said.

"I *thought* I did," she replied. "I thought you were smart enough to know when to sit down and shut up. But clearly I was wrong. What I want to know is how you got all the way out here without that bracelet going off."

Ivy remained silent. She wasn't about to implicate Oliver.

"It's going to come out one way or another. But fine, keep quiet. I've arranged for you to meet with the public defender when we get back to Oakhurst. You can work on a strategy with them. I'll do what I can, but Armstrong won't go easy on you. You know how much he doesn't like being made the fool. In fact, we're both in hot water, because I'm the one who convinced him you could be trusted not to leave your apartment while we ironed all this out."

Ivy said nothing, though she hadn't considered what would happen to Nat in all of this. Probably because she was still mad at the woman she'd once looked up to like a big sister. Much like Woodward, Ivy didn't care what happened to Nat anymore. She'd been betrayed so many times she no longer felt any remorse.

But that wasn't exactly true. Even though Nat had betrayed Ivy over and over again, Ivy still couldn't help but feel some sense of loyalty to the woman. And she couldn't explain why. Maybe it was because Nat had been the first person by her side after her family disappeared. Or maybe it was because she'd always wanted a big sister, and Nat had filled that void when Ivy had needed her the most. Whatever the reason, Ivy couldn't write the woman off. Not completely.

"I didn't mean to get you into hot water," Ivy said. "I had a good reason for what I did."

"I'd love to hear it," Nat replied, keeping her eyes straight ahead. "Because right now things aren't looking good for any of us. Including your *partner*, who I'm inclined to believe knew about this little stunt of yours."

Ivy turned to Nat, alarmed.

"Would you believe just as we got word about your charade, the fire alarm was pulled? It was chaos for a good hour. Strangely, Detective White, who had been there minutes earlier, could not be accounted for."

Ivy suppressed a smile, looking back out at the approaching horizon. Maybe not the most creative diversion, but an effective one. Jonathan had given her the time she'd needed.

"But I'm sure we'll find the truth when we have time to go over all the station cameras."

Ivy's good humor disappeared. Another casualty of her actions. This was why she preferred to do things alone. That way no one else risked anything for her, no one else could be hurt. Now Jonathan was in the crosshairs too. And if Nat somehow found out Oliver was involved…he'd go to prison for sure. There was only one option left. And it meant putting her faith in someone who had shown Ivy she couldn't be trusted. But first, Ivy needed reassurance.

Ivy took a deep breath. "I need something from you."

It was Nat's turn to laugh. "I think you've gotten all you're going to get from me."

Ivy ignored her. "I need you to be the woman who saved me that night. Just for a few minutes. I need you to be the same person who watched my back, who made sure I was safe all those years. I need you…to be honest."

Nat went eerily still. Ivy took that to mean she knew what Ivy was about to ask. "You watched my interview with Kieran Woodward."

"Yes," Nat said, her voice having gone soft.

"He said the night you brought me to Mrs. Baker's house,

you told her that I was found covered in blood. And that Mrs. Baker needed to watch me for anything…unusual." It was like all the air had been sucked out of the car. Even the engine seemed to have gone quiet. "Whose blood was it? And why did you tell her that?"

Nat went to open her mouth, and Ivy could already see the excuses coming.

"And *don't* you dare lie to me again. Don't tell me we can't trust the word of a serial killer because I know the profile. Kieran Woodward has the emotional range of a five-year-old. He's as unlikely to lie as he is to lead a normal, healthy life. Tell me the truth."

Nat sighed. "The truth…is I don't know whose blood it was. I thought it was *your* blood at first. But when we cleaned you off, you didn't have a scratch on you. You witnessed something, Ivy, but I don't know what. I asked Mrs. Baker to keep an eye on you in the event you remembered something. I was afraid that if it all came back at once, you…you might have a psychological break."

Ivy turned to her. "Why not just tell me that from the beginning?"

"I wanted to," Nat said. "But in speaking with specialists, especially child psychiatrists, I was advised not to mention it. They said you not remembering was your mind protecting you from something that could potentially permanently damage you. There's a reason you don't remember, Ivy."

"But all this time," she said. "Am I never meant to know?"

"That's not up to me." She turned to look at Ivy, and for the first time in years, Ivy saw the same woman she'd seen as a child looking back at her. "You're an adult now. These are questions you have to answer for yourself."

"You mean I should start seeing a therapist," Ivy said.

"It probably wouldn't be a bad first step," Nat replied. "I've been seeing one since my marriage fell apart. It's not an easy solution by any means, but it has helped."

"Why isn't any of this in the case file?" Ivy asked. "*My* case file?"

"I scrubbed the file because I knew you'd look as soon as you became a police officer," Nat replied. "And to be honest, you had a lot of other issues. Including having a difficult time doing your job."

"What?" Ivy asked. "No, I wasn't."

"You think I didn't notice that every time you brought an offender in, your partner was the one escorting them? Or that you never shook hands with anyone in the station?"

"Dammit." Ivy was dumbfounded. Here she thought she'd had everyone fooled.

"I knew you well enough to know it wasn't normal behavior. And I kept an eye on you. The minute it began affecting your performance, I was pulling you from the force. But it never did. Somehow, even with your…phobia, you managed to become an effective officer. Even garnered yourself a promotion."

"Why didn't you ever say anything?"

Nat scoffed. "How would you have reacted if I had? You and I haven't been on the best of terms lately. Do you really think that conversation would have been helpful?"

Ivy blinked a few times. "No, I suppose not."

"But then you saved Woodward, and since then, things have been changing. You've been more confident, and cockier. But you've proven that you could handle the mental stress of it. Me grabbing you in the office the other day…I was testing your limits. Seeing how much you could take. Which makes me believe you could have handled this information. So for not telling you sooner, I'm sorry."

Ivy wasn't sure how to feel. Nat was saying everything she'd been wanting from the woman for months. It was like all their old wounds had finally started to close and heal. Seems all it had taken for Nat to open up was for Ivy to take a trip to prison.

Ivy cleared her throat. "Recently, I've learned I'm stronger than I think I am."

"That's very true," Nat replied. "But I don't think any amount of strength is going to get you out of this one."

"Maybe that's true," Ivy said. "But as long as we're being honest, I have something I need to tell you."

Nat creased her forehead, glancing over at Ivy.

"I have a lead. And if you want to save those two little girls, I'm going to need you to trust me."

Chapter Twenty-Nine

Nat yanked the steering wheel to the right, pulling into an abandoned parking lot that had once belonged to a church. The building's roof had begun to cave in, and litter was strewn all over the lot, including broken glass.

Regardless, Nat skidded the car to a stop and turned to glare at Ivy.

"Say that again."

"I said, Kieran named someone who might have been targeting Mrs. Baker or the girls. A man named John Shepard."

"He actually spoke?"

Ivy pulled back. "Well, I didn't make it up. Check the county feeds if you don't believe me."

"And you think he's telling the truth?"

"I told you; Woodward doesn't lie. Especially not under pressure. He's practically comatose, like he's under hypnosis."

"You're telling me a man whom no professional has been able to get to say one word just happened to give you crucial case information?"

Ivy nodded, unable to comprehend how Nat wasn't

putting this together. "Duh. I'm the only one he'll talk to. You *know* that."

"We just figured after your last conversation during your… interrogation, he wouldn't be willing to speak to you again."

"Did you ever test that theory?" Ivy asked. Nat remained silent. "He talks to me because he *knows* me. He remembers me from when we were at Mrs. Baker's home together."

"And you really think he knows something about their kidnapping?"

"I think it's highly unlikely to have a serial killer and a kidnapper-slash-murderer in the same sleepy town in the same week and for them not to be connected. It would be strange for him *not* to know something. I don't guess Bruneau ever explored that option."

Nat took a deep breath, sitting back. "So you breaking your house arrest was all just a ploy to get to Woodward? To get him to talk?"

Ivy nodded.

"What if he hadn't said anything? Or I'd come to pick you up before you had a chance to speak with him?"

"Listen, we're on the clock. I would love to spar about this all day long, but there are two little girls out there in danger. We have a name; we need to go after him."

"I'll call it in," Nat said. "Figure out how to track this John Shepard down. But I still have to bring you back in. You broke the law."

"We don't have time for this," Ivy said. "Wherever Shepard is, he's got those girls. And you, Jonathan, Armstrong, everyone in the department needs to be out there looking for him, right now."

Nat pursed her lips, then pulled out her phone. "Hey Wilson. Yeah, it's me. I need a DMV search. Last name Shepard, first name John. Start with the state of Oregon." She continued to watch Ivy as she listened on the other end. "Yeah, okay. Let's go with the younger one first." She nodded, even though only Ivy could see her. "Text that to me, will you? Yeah, thanks." She hung up.

"Well?"

"Two John Shepards registered in Oregon, one right here in Oakhurst, the other in Portland. The one in Portland is in his eighties, but I'm going to get the Portland PD on it immediately."

"And the one here?" Ivy asked.

"I'll call Bruneau," Nat said, preparing to dial again.

"That's fine, if you want him to screw it up," Ivy said. Nat hesitated. "He left a ton of evidence behind in the Baker house. Hadn't even started going through all the documentation. He probably took one look at the wall of papers, said 'fuck it,' and grabbed the computer, figuring the job was done."

Nat dropped the phone to her lap. "What do you suggest instead?"

"*We* go investigate Shepard. Right now."

Nat laughed, though this time it seemed genuine. "Are you *trying* to get me fired? I have to bring you in. You're facing *charges*."

"Look, we both know I didn't have anything to do with Mrs. Baker's death. But someone else out there knows me. I *deserve* to know the truth, which means I should be the one to track down Shepard. You know I can do it. And you owe me. For all the lies."

Nat winced, and in that moment, it made her look old beyond her years. Ivy hadn't known about her divorce, but it was clear to her now the stress had taken a toll on the woman. She could see it in the lines around her eyes, which hadn't been as prevalent before. Or the wisps of gray hair that had infiltrated Nat's normally crimson mane.

"It's a bad idea," Nat said. "How can I trust—"

"Are you serious right now?" Ivy demanded. "I have put my entire life on the line for this case. Do you think I'm just going to run away when you uncuff me? You're going to have a hard time *keeping* me in jail if you don't let me find this guy."

Nat seemed to think about it. "Fine. We will go to his residence and knock on the door. But that's it. After that, we head back to the station and you can argue this with Armstrong. I'll let you and him work out your future. After that, I'm done."

"Fine," Ivy said.

"Fine." Nat pulled out of the abandoned lot, then plugging the information from the text into her GPS. "The house isn't far from here. Oh, and I'm calling backup."

"But—"

"That's the deal. Take it or leave it," Nat said.

Ivy sat quietly as they drove down the deserted highway. Following the GPS, it looked like Shepard's house was on the outskirts of town and in the middle of privately owned property. The perfect place to hold someone hostage. As they drove, the woods seemed to grow denser and denser around them, turning into a canopy that blocked out the gray sky. Ahead, Ivy caught sight of a black and white that had parked on the side of the road.

"We'll confer with them before heading up," Nat said.

"Ahem," Ivy offered up her wrists, which were still bound with the handcuffs. "I don't think it's going to be great for morale if he sees me in these."

Nat dug the key out of her pocket and tossed it to Ivy. She managed to unlock and stow the cuffs under the seat just before they pulled up to the patrol officer standing outside of his car. Nat rolled down the window.

"Ma'ams," Officer Ashdown said. "Got another unit right behind you. Two minutes out."

"Good," Nat said. "We'll park in the tree line, about a hundred feet from the house. Approach from all directions. And we may have hostages in there, so everyone needs to be on their guard."

He nodded, pulling a shotgun out of his backseat. "We'll be ready, ma'am."

Nat pulled ahead along the winding road that had turned into a driveway. Just before she came around the curve, she parked on the side of the road, killing the engine.

"I need a gun," Ivy said.

Nat blew out a long breath. "This is *not* a good idea." She reached over and unlocked the glove box, which fell open revealing a .357 magnum.

"Overcompensate much?" Ivy asked.

"It's what I have. Take it or leave it." She showed Ivy a picture of Shepard from his most recent driver's license photo on her phone. "Get a good look."

Ivy memorized the face of John Shepard before taking the weapon and getting out. He wasn't bad looking by any means, but his eyes told a different story, even in a DMV photo. This was not a man they wanted to fuck around with. Their encounter needed to be quick and clean. Nat got out, holding a small radio that had been tuned to their action channel. "You and I will approach from the front as soon as I get word everyone else is in position."

Ivy nodded, that anxious feeling having crept back into her gut. She hadn't actually thought she'd be able to convince Nat to bring her here. And there was always the chance she'd misjudged Woodward, and he'd been lying this entire time. But he hadn't been lying about the blood, Nat had confirmed that much. Which meant there was a good chance the house before them contained the answers she needed. And, she hoped, the girls. Once they were safe, they could iron the rest of this mess out.

"Beta and Gamma in position," the voice said over the radio.

"All units, move in. Keep it slow and quiet." Nat nodded to Ivy as they made their way up the driveway, sticking close to the trees. Ivy pulled her weapon out as soon as the house came into view. It was a ranch that had been built into the side of a hill, so part of the basement was exposed to make it a second level. The driveway ran up to and beside the house, but there was no car present and no garage. The home was covered in old wood shingles and looked like it had been there for a while. As far as Ivy could tell, there weren't any lights on in the house.

Nat motioned for Ivy to head around to the side of the basement. Meanwhile, Nat climbed the steps to the front door. Ivy made her way to the door on the side of the house. It had a small window at the top and was situated beside another window built into the concrete. Ivy spun when she heard a noise, only to realize it was another officer approaching from the south. She nodded at him as she tried the door, but it was locked. The light blue paint of the door was cracked and old, and it looked like some wood-boring insects might have chipped away at the edges over the years. Ivy was willing to bet it could be compromised if she kicked hard enough. They didn't have a warrant, but this investigation had all gone to shit anyway.

Stand back she mouthed to the other officer, whose eyes went wide. Ivy stepped back and kicked the door as hard as she could. It cracked but didn't give. Scrambling, she kicked it again, producing a terrible ripping sound as the door broke into the home.

"This is the Oakhurst police!" Ivy yelled. "Everyone put your hands up where we can see them, we have you surrounded!" The officer ran to the opposite side of the door frame as Ivy peered inside quickly, assessing the situation. The basement was mostly dark, and she didn't see any shapes inside.

"We are coming in and we're armed!" Ivy yelled again. "Get down on the ground with your face down and your hands extended to both sides."

She checked the corner again but saw nothing. That didn't

mean someone couldn't be sitting in the dark, just waiting for a good shot. But there was no response inside.

"What the hell are you doing?" Nat hissed, running down the hill to Ivy and the other officer.

"They might be in there," Ivy said. "Cover me, I'm going in."

"No—" Nat said, but Ivy didn't listen. She rounded the corner, looking for some cover and finding it behind an old row of cabinets that looked like they might have once been a kitchen of sorts.

A light came on from the doorway and Ivy realized either Nat or the officer must have had a flashlight. It covered all corners of the room, revealing no one else inside. Ivy relaxed her shoulders just as the fluorescent lights above them came on. She looked over to see Nat had found a switch near the door.

The room was about what she'd expected. Concrete floor, cinder block walls with periodic windows along the tops. A wood-paneled wall ran across the back of the room, with another door inset into it. In the middle of the room was a kind of table that had been tilted up, like a platform. As Ivy drew closer, she realized straps had been nailed in to the top and bottom of the table, allowing someone to be suspended on it. A closer examination revealed what looked like dried body fluids on the table.

"She was here," Ivy said. "He had her."

"He could still be here," Nat said, motioning to the officer behind her. He made his way in, followed by two more as they began checking the rooms beyond. Ivy heard them call out "clear" periodically while she and Nat continued to look around the basement. Finally, Officer Ashdown returned, his shotgun strapped around his back.

"House is clear, ma'am. No one else here."

Nat nodded, and she and Ivy put their weapons away. "Set

up a perimeter and keep the area clear. I'll call it in to Bruneau."

He nodded and was off again.

"Well, looks like your gamble paid off," Nat said. "I'd say from the looks of this we have the right guy."

But Ivy wasn't really listening. She had been distracted by a small table with an overturned chair beside it. On the table was a sheet of paper, splattered with drops of blood. And written at the top of the paper was the question: *What does Ivy Stanford know?*

Chapter Thirty

"What the hell?" Ivy asked, staring at the paper. It looked to have been handwritten and unfolded. She reached out to grab it.

"No!" Nat said, taking her arm and pulling it away.

Ivy blinked a few times, coming to her senses. This was a crime scene. The paper was evidence. She couldn't just potentially taint a piece of evidence, no matter how much she wanted to.

Nat still had a hold of her arm, but something was different this time. That usual deep pressure and strike of electricity wasn't there, which was strange.

Nat seemed to realize what she was doing, and let go, stepping back from Ivy. She couldn't quite put it to words, only feelings. It was as though she'd lost ahold of something, as if she'd been swimming with a trinket in her hand and had let it go, watching it sink deeper into the ocean. As she looked up, Ivy realized she was breathing harder than normal.

"I'm…sorry," Nat said. "I shouldn't have done that. I just didn't want you contaminating the scene."

"No," Ivy replied. What the hell had that *been*? "You were right." She turned back to the paper, glad to have something else to focus on other than her anxieties. "It has my name on it."

Nat looked at the paper. "And blood."

"What was going on here?" Ivy asked. "What does this have to do with *me*?"

"I don't know," Nat said. "But I'm calling Bruneau and telling him to bring the CSI team in." She pulled out her phone and began dialing. "Armstrong is going to have an aneurism."

It didn't really matter to Ivy what Armstrong thought about this. She needed to know why her name was on that paper. Her *old* name. Just like what had been carved into Mrs. Baker's chest. The rest of the paper was blank, but it looked like there could be tick marks below the question. Places for answers to go, perhaps.

Ivy scanned the rest of the basement. At the far side was a small pot sink with some paper towels hanging from an old plastic dispenser above it. She reached over and grabbed a paper towel, tearing it off and returned to the table as Nat spoke into her phone.

Carefully, Ivy used the towel to lift the piece of paper by the edge, being careful not to smudge anything. On the other side of the paper were more questions, though these were typed while the script on the other side had been handwritten. One said, *What does she know about her family?* while the other said *Has she ever mentioned a kidnapping?* The rest of the questions were more banal in nature, such as *Who are her friends?* and *What does she do in her free time?*

Ivy allowed the paper to rest, though she couldn't quite believe what she was seeing. What did all this mean? Had her family been kidnapped? And if so, by who? Did this Shepard have something to do with it?

She needed to find him, *immediately*.

Ivy scanned the rest of the room, looking for anything that might prove useful. There were some bloody rags in the aforementioned pot sink, which would have to be tested. The smell of something rotten hung in the air as well. Ivy glanced up to the corners of the room to find one what looked like wires sticking out of the wall. Curious, she went in for a closer look. It appeared as though something had been removed from the cinder block. A couple of wires hung loose and there were two holes where screws used to be. What could have been there? A camera or speaker, more than likely.

As Nat continued issuing directions over the phone, Ivy scanned the rest of the basement, heading through the door into the other rooms and finding stairs to the upper floor. On the other side of the stairs were two more rooms, both with heavy doors that had been broken in by the officers. Ivy peered in both, which seemed identical.

Not only that, they seemed *familiar*. Having just come from a jail cell, she knew a prison when she saw one. A bed, a toilet and not much else in each room. Was this where he'd kept them when he wasn't working them over on the table? The girls in one room and Mrs. Baker in the other? Ivy had to admit, it didn't look good for the two girls. CSI would have to test all the blood to find out how much of it belonged to Mrs. Baker and how much didn't.

"Burns and her team are on their way over," Nat said, finding Ivy in one of the rooms. "Damn. This isn't encouraging."

"No," Ivy said softly.

"C'mon," Nat said. "Ashdown and the others can keep an eye on things here. We need to get you back. Try to explain all of this to Armstrong. Maybe if we're lucky we can avoid formal charges."

"You have to promise to keep me in the loop," Ivy said as they lingered in the open doorway. "You can't leave me in the dark, not anymore."

"I'll do everything I can," Nat said. "But you're part of this investigation now. We'll have to follow procedure. I shouldn't have brought you this far. I just hope you realize I'm on your side, here."

Ivy's phone buzzed in her pocket at the same time she heard a crackle over the radio of one of the nearby officers. Ivy glanced at her phone; it was a text message from Jonathan in all caps.

FOUND HIM. LIC SPOTTED @ BUS STATION.

Suddenly, her heart threatened to pound right out of her chest. Someone must have spotted him from the APB Nat issued. And the bus station wasn't far from here.

She glanced at Nat who was distracted by her own phone, probably reading a similar message. The alert would have gone out to all active-duty officers or anyone who might be close. But there was no way Nat would allow Ivy to confront the man, or even be on site.

Still, Ivy knew what she had to do.

Her gaze met Nat's just as the woman looked up from her phone. The look that passed between them could have said a thousand words, and yet lasted less than half a second before Ivy took off running.

"Ivy!" Nat yelled, hot on her heels.

But Ivy was fast. And despite the pain in her side, she pushed through it, determined to get to Nat's car first. Her boss always had a bad habit of leaving her keys inside the car; her car was such a **POS** no one would bother to steal it.

Still, Ivy could almost feel the heat of Nat's breath on the back of her neck as she ran. The car was directly ahead of them, and the path was clear.

"Bishop, don't do it!" Nat yelled again, more authoritative this time. But Ivy wouldn't be deterred. She was going to find this John Shepard and learn what he knew. No one wanted to stop him more than Ivy did. At least for Mrs. Baker's sake. And those girls.

Ivy reached the car, slamming into the side, and yanking the driver's side door open and closed again just as Nat reached her. Thankfully, Ivy was able to lock the doors before Nat could open them again, but that didn't stop her boss from pounding on the window, yelling obscenities at Ivy. Ivy dropped the visor, found the keys, and started the car as Nat's protests became more urgent.

"You are going to be fired!" Nat yelled through the window. "It's all over if you do this."

"I have to confront him," Ivy said. "Don't worry. I'll bring him in."

"No, you won't," Nat yelled over the roar of the engine. "I'll have you arrested on sight!"

"Do what you have to do," Ivy replied, then threw the car into reverse and spun the wheels, causing Nat to step back. Ivy jerked the wheel around and in no time was speeding down Shepard's long driveway.

She put on her seatbelt as she reached the main highway and drove fifteen miles over the speed limit to reach the bus station. It was funny; she had gone to the train station and Shepard had gone to the bus. Imagine if they'd been at the same place at the same time. Without the information from Woodward, he would have passed her by and she wouldn't have given him another thought.

Thanks to her knowledge of the back roads of Oakhurst, she managed to reach the bus station in under ten minutes. She didn't see any other police cars in the main parking lot, but that didn't mean Bruneau or some of the other detectives weren't already there. Still, she parked haphazardly in a no-parking zone and jumped out, headed for the buses. She pulled out her phone again, calling Jonathan.

"Ivy," he said. "Where are you?"

"I need details on Shepard, what was the report?" Ivy asked.

"His car was spotted at the bus station, but that's all we've got right now. There are two units on the way. Where *are* you?"

"I'm at the station," Ivy said, running across the street to the buses, scanning the crowds for anyone who matched Shepard's description.

"*I'm* at the station," Jonathan replied.

Ivy turned to her right to see her partner about thirty feet away near the ticket counter, his long coat flowing behind him like a cape with a phone up to his ear. She smiled.

"What happened with Nat? I thought she was bringing you back?" Jonathan asked into the phone. "Hello?"

"Hey," Ivy said, approaching as she slipped her phone back into her pocket. He turned, startled, almost like he couldn't believe she was there. "I'll explain everything later. But we have to hurry. I don't want to lose him. If we can corner him here, we can end this."

"You're not on duty," Jonathan said, looking down at her waistband. "Where did you get a gun?"

"Don't worry about it. Let's just find him. I'll deal with the consequences of everything else later."

"If you say so," he replied, looking unsure.

"Split up, but keep an open line," Ivy said, holding up her phone. "He may already be on a bus."

Jonathan nodded, and they headed off in opposite directions. Ivy knew she was under the clock here. Nat would be right on her heels with one of the other officers, not to mention anyone else from the department who would show up hunting Shepard. She had to set this right, if for no other reason than to atone for allowing this to happen in the first place.

She scanned the crowds, not realizing just how many people used the bus station on a regular basis. Most of the chairs in the waiting area were full, half the people asleep, reading or listening to their headphones. A couple of people milled about, headed to the restrooms and back. A few homeless people were making the rounds, asking for handouts, while others slept on the floors. Bus announcements were being called out every few minutes, but Ivy didn't see Shepard anywhere among the crowd.

Why would he come here? Was he just trying for a clean getaway? Was he looking for a new start somewhere else? Did he even know they were on to him? Probably not, in Ivy's estimation. So he wouldn't be hurrying along. He'd be taking his time, thinking he was doing everything necessary to disappear. He'd probably wiped his car of all fingerprints and ditched any kind of identification on his person. Otherwise, why else be here? Why not stay at his house?

Ivy kept thinking about those loose wires in the corner of the basement. What could have been there?

Then she saw them. Two small bodies, standing side by side with their backs to Ivy as they prepared to board a bus headed for Salt Lake City. Beside them stood a man who, from the back, was a dead ringer for Shepard.

The girls, Ivy thought. They were still alive. But if she didn't handle this correctly, that might not be the case for much longer. If she could just sneak up behind them and take Shepard down without much fuss, they would be safe. It would have all been worth it.

I've got him, bus to Salt Lake she texted to Jonathan, then slipped her phone back in her pocket.

She approached carefully; her gaze locked on Shepard's back. She was only fifteen feet from him. Fifteen feet and it would all be over.

"Excuse me, got a buck or two?" a man asked, coming up beside her.

"Leave me alone," Ivy said, not breaking her attention.

"C'mon, just a buck," the guy said, more insistent this time. "I ain't askin' for much." He reached his hand out, blocking Ivy's way.

"I don't have any change," Ivy reiterated, increasingly

frustrated and trying to keep her attention on Shepard. "Try someone else." She reached out to knock the man's hand away, but on doing so, her jacket opened up just enough so that her weapon tucked into her belt became visible.

"Gun! She's got a gun!" the homeless man yelled.

Chaos erupted around them as people began screaming and running. Shepard turned, locked eyes with Ivy and grabbed one of the little girls like a shield. The other girl, Jessa, grabbed onto Shepard and began yanking on him, trying to get him to let go.

The crowd parted as people ran in all directions, but Ivy already had her gun out and trained on Shepard.

"It's over, Shepard. Oakhurst Police. Let the girl go."

"Not gonna happen," he growled, producing a gun of his own and putting it to Taylor's head. Silent tears flowed down her cheeks, but otherwise, to Ivy, she looked unharmed.

"Lettergo!" Jessa yelled, but Shepard kicked her away, and she stumbled to the side.

"You've got nowhere to go, Shepard!" Ivy glanced to her right to see Jonathan had taken up a position close by, his weapon also trained on Shepard.

"Yes, I do," he replied. "I'm taking this bus, unless you want her brains splattered all over the side of it."

"This is the Oakhurst Police Department," Ivy heard from behind her. "Let go of your hostage and you won't be harmed." She didn't need to turn around to recognize it as Nat's voice; she'd finally caught up with her. In fact, there were probably at least five officers who had their weapons trained on Shepard at the moment. The only problem was no one could guarantee a clear shot with Taylor in the way.

Ivy could see Shepard's panic on his face. He'd been boxed in, which only made him more dangerous. She had no doubt he would kill the little girl if he didn't see another way out.

She lowered her weapon, placing it on the ground and

holding up her hands. "Okay," she said. "Let's just take this calmly." She shot a glance at Jessa on the ground next to them. Her eyes were like fire, but she was too scared to get up and run. All her attention was on her sister. He technically had two hostages. But that was it. Everyone else had cleared the area. And as far as Ivy could see, there was no bus driver, but there could already be people on the bus.

"I'm not going in," Shepard said. "Understand me?"

Ivy nodded. "I believe you. Just don't hurt anyone. We can figure a way out of this, okay?" She turned her attention to Taylor, who was openly crying. "It's going to be okay. Do you remember me? I was at your house last week."

The little girl sniffed a few times, then nodded.

"Wait, *you're* Stanford?" Shepard asked.

Ivy ignored him, focusing her attention on the girl. "You know, sometimes even when we're scared, we can still be brave. Can you be brave for me?"

"Look, you're gonna let me on this bus, let it leave, and not follow me. I'm not letting her go until I know I'm not being followed," Shepard said.

But Ivy was barely listening. She had Taylor's attention. Her tears had slowed, and her eyes were locked on Ivy's. "You're stronger than you think you are," Ivy said. "You can do anything."

Taylor's eyes widened, and for a moment Ivy thought she might have pushed too far, that Shepard was ready to end it all. But the little girl seemed to find some steel within herself, opened her mouth, and bit down on Shepard's hand as hard as she could. Blood gushed from Shepard's wound as he yelled out and dropped the girl the same time.

Ivy rushed him, and Jonathan did the same. He took the two girls into his arms as Ivy grabbed Shepard's hand with the gun, wrenched it so he dropped the weapon before he could squeeze the trigger, then had him on his back in under three seconds. He grunted under the pain.

"John Shepard, you are under arrest for the murder of Jillian Baker and the kidnapping of Jessica and Taylor Hampton."

Officers swarmed them, getting Shepard under control from Ivy. Once she was sure they had him, she stepped back, allowing them to get him into custody. The man was fighting like hell, but with four officers pinning him down, he wasn't going anywhere.

Ivy took a deep breath and turned to Jonathan, who was checking to make sure the girls were okay. "That was very brave," Ivy said to Taylor. "Where did you learn to do that?"

"From watching my favorite show," the girl replied, wiping her eyes. "A woman was a hostage but bit the guy and got away. I just…didn't think I could do it until you said something."

Ivy couldn't help but beam. "Are you okay? Both of you?" They nodded. "Okay. My partner here is going to make sure you're taken care of. You're safe now."

"Can we see the inside of your police building?" Taylor asked.

"I'm sure we can work something out," Ivy chuckled, standing back up. But when she turned, she found herself staring right into the fiery eyes of her boss. And despite her heroics, Ivy knew there was no avoiding the consequences of her actions.

She had run out of time.

Chapter Thirty-One

Ivy sat in the chair, staring at her boss's boss across the desk. Armstrong was a big man, whether he was standing or sitting. It almost didn't seem to matter. And his facial expression never changed, locked into a permanent frown. He'd been staring at Ivy for a good two minutes, but she'd just stared right back. There was no question she had crossed the line. In fact, the line was so far behind her now it was invisible. The line was a distant memory. But she didn't care. She'd saved Taylor and Jessa. She'd stopped Shepard, and now they had Mrs. Baker's killer in custody. All she needed now was answers.

But she wasn't sure how she'd ever get them from the inside of a jail cell.

Nat stood off to the side. She hadn't said a word to Ivy ever since the bus station, even when Ivy had returned her weapon or offered to put herself back into cuffs for the ride back to the station. But the disappointment on Nat's face was worse than when Ivy had known Nat was lying to her. At least then Ivy knew she was doing good work. Now…there was no telling where this would go.

"I should fire you," Armstrong finally said. "I should fire

and arrest you. And throw your insubordinate ass in jail for five years for what you pulled."

Ivy knew better than to speak up. Armstrong continued. "In fact, I don't think anyone would blame me if I did. You are a rogue officer. You don't follow the chain of command; you don't listen to your superior officer, and you take the law into your own hands. Everything the book says, you do the opposite."

Ivy couldn't disagree. She'd violated statute after statute. All in the pursuit of the truth.

"And yet," Armstrong said, finally breaking eye contact and looking at the paper on his desk. "You apprehended the suspect and stopped him from harming two more hostages."

"*And* she figured out who the suspect was," Nat said. "Without her, we never would have known about John Shepard."

"Lieutenant, do me a favor and shut up," Armstrong said.

Ivy couldn't help but feel a small swell of pride at Nat's endorsement. It was like a giant wall of ice between them had melted. Nat was still on her side, and she was being honest with Ivy. She might be upset at her for going after Shepard, but Ivy no longer felt like Nat was shutting her out completely.

"The mayor wants to give you a commendation," Armstrong said. "For first apprehending Woodward, and now Shepard. He feels like the city owes you a debt of gratitude." Ivy swore the captain twitched as he spat the words.

She couldn't quite believe what she was hearing. They wanted to give *her* a commendation?

"Of course, Mayor Garland doesn't know you weren't officially operating under the law. He thinks this was your case, that we assigned it to you after the Baker woman went missing." Armstrong leaned forward. "He also doesn't know your name was carved into her chest."

"I think we can all agree that Ivy had nothing to do with that," Nat said. "I spoke to Burns, she had her people compare the pattern to Shepard's handwriting, and there are enough indications for a match." Armstrong shot her a look, causing Nat to stare at her feet.

"You're suspended," Armstrong said. "Indefinitely. Until I can figure out what to do with you."

"That's outrageous," Nat said before Ivy could even think of a response. She approached the desk, getting up in Armstrong's face. "The only reason she was under house arrest was because *you* thought she was a suspect. Clearly, she wasn't."

"Then she should have stayed there and let us do our jobs," Armstrong said.

"If she had, we would have lost Shepard and those girls forever," Nat replied. "Ivy risked her career and her life to find him and bring him to justice. And you're going to *suspend* her?"

"I should lock her up," Armstrong said, glaring at Ivy.

"And how well do you think that would go over with the court of public opinion? Or the mayor?"

Armstrong huffed. "It doesn't change the fact she broke the law."

"Then put her on desk duty. But do you really want the bad press that comes with a suspension?"

Armstrong glared at Nat, then turned back to Ivy. "One more step out of line, and you're done. And I want to see your ass in this office every morning at eight a.m. sharp. Until all of this calms down."

"Thank you, sir," Ivy said, but she couldn't help herself. "I was only searching for the truth."

"Get out of my sight," he replied. Ivy didn't need to be told twice. She and Nat left the office together.

She couldn't believe she wasn't being led away in handcuffs, much less still had a job. "Thank you for defending me in there," she said as Nat headed for the interrogation rooms.

"I told you, I'm on your side. But you're damn lucky," she

replied. "He was well within his rights to bring down the hammer. The public pressure is the only thing that saved your ass."

"That, and the fact I led you to the guy." Ivy smiled, knowing it would only annoy Nat. "Speaking of which, now that my job is no longer in question, when do I get to interrogate the creep?"

Nat barked a genuine laugh. "You think you're getting in there? No way. Even if you *were* in good standing, you're personally connected to this case." She narrowed her eyes. "Which was part of the reason I didn't want you working it in the first place."

"Fair enough," Ivy said. "Still, I would have been able to help. I might have figured out the Woodward connection earlier. Maybe even saved Mrs. Baker."

"Maybe," Nat replied. "But this is still Bruneau's case. *He'll* do the interrogation."

"Can I at least watch?"

Nat glared at her, then turned and headed back to her office. Ivy took that as a yes.

She headed down to the interrogation rooms, hoping they hadn't already finished processing Shepard. She didn't want to miss a thing and was buoyed by the fact she still had a job.

"Hey," Jonathan said, heading in her direction. "What happened with Armstrong?"

"Desk duty," she replied. "For the foreseeable future."

His eyebrows shot up. "You're kidding."

"I know. I'm headed down to watch the interrogation. Wanna watch? Maybe Shepard will be willing to talk."

"Doubt it," Jonathan said. "He's not like Woodward. He's a professional. Bruneau is in there with him now, but he's not getting anywhere."

"Seriously? Shit," Ivy said, rushing to the interrogation rooms with Jonathan not far behind. The door to room three was closed, indicating officers were inside. Ivy made her way over to an adjacent room where the conversation was being recorded. Officer Portnoy looked up from the bank of monitors when Ivy entered. Three different cameras had been set up in the room, and right now, all three cameras were on John Shepard.

"Bishop, what are you doing here?" Portnoy asked.

"Just curious," Ivy said. "Mind if I take a seat?" Jonathan entered right behind her.

"Sure, just…stay out of the way. They're trying to figure out if he's been involved in any other incidents."

"And he hasn't lawyered up?" Ivy asked.

"Not yet. Knock on wood." She lightly rapped on the table holding the equipment. She then flipped a switch on one of the nearby monitors and the room was filled with the conversation a few rooms over.

"—saying that you knew nothing about Jillian Baker before you kidnapped her?" That was Bruneau's voice, which matched what they were seeing on the monitors.

"I told you, it was just a job," Shepard said, taking a drag from a cigarette. He'd been chained to the wall by one arm, but his other was free. Ivy couldn't see, but she figured his feet were probably locked down too. He sat at a short table against the wall, while Bruneau and his partner sat in chairs across from him, just out of the man's reach.

"But you can't tell us who hired you." Ivy's eyes widened. *Someone had* hired *him?*

"Do you think I'd be sitting here on my ass if I could?" Shepard spat. "I would have flipped on the guy a dozen times already. You think I want to take the fall for this?"

"But you did kill Mrs. Baker, didn't you?" Bruneau asked.

"As I've already explained, she died in her sleep. She wasn't supposed to die."

"Why not?" Bruneau asked.

"Because *he* didn't want her to!" Shepard was getting frustrated. He put his cigarette out on the table, leaning back as he rubbed his forehead with his free hand. Ivy couldn't believe this. Who was he talking about? A *third* party, other than him and Woodward?

"And you know nothing about this man who hired you? Nothing at all."

"Look. As I've said, he contacted me by mail, then by phone, always using a voice modifier. I can't even say it *was* a man. He had me install a camera so he could watch my progress—"

"Which you pulled from the wall," Bruneau said.

"Yeah, once the old lady died, I freaked out a little, okay? Thought about dumping the kids."

"Why didn't you?"

Shepard hesitated. Ivy was on the edge of her seat.

"John, we can sit here all day if you want to. But the fact is you're on the hook for murder and kidnapping. You're not getting out of this. But cooperating now will go a long way to making your future life in prison easier."

"He knew she was dead," Shepard finally said. "Saw it on the camera. Told me to take the kids, get out of town. Dispose of the body. And when I reached Salt Lake City, there would be an extra fifty thousand waiting for me there."

Bruneau let out a low whistle. "That's a lot of extra dough."

"Otherwise, I would have gotten rid of those two brats days ago," Shepard said. "Always whining about something. *I'm hungry. I'm cold,*" he mocked.

"Okay," Bruneau said, flipping the page on his notepad. "Let's talk about Ivy Stanford." Ivy shot a glance at Jonathan.

Shepard made a derisive noise. "I never want to hear that name again."

"Where did you first hear it?"

"Where do you think? It was in the letter he sent. He had me question the old woman over and over again. Really put her through the paces, you know?"

Bruneau shot a quick glance to the nearest camera. "And you didn't have any trouble torturing a defenseless old woman?"

"The guy told me she was a big gambler, owed a lot of people money. He hired me to put her through the wringer. But like I said, she wasn't supposed to die."

Bruneau reached over and picked up an evidence bag. Ivy recognized the sheet of paper from Shepard's basement. The one with her name on it. "And this?"

"He wanted answers," Shepard said.

"About?"

"I dunno, man. It was all on this Ivy woman. He wanted to know what the old woman knew about her. It honestly didn't make much sense to me. But every morning, I would go down there and we'd start with the questions. *What does Ivy know? What does she suspect? What does she remember? Where is her family?* None of the normal stuff. With jobs like this, I usually ask about places people keep hidden money, or rich relatives, or some way to recoup the losses. But he didn't seem to care about that."

"Did you ever ask him about it?" Bruneau asked.

Shepard laughed. "You don't get it, man. It wasn't exactly two-way communication. He sent a message; I did the job. That's it."

"What about the carving on the woman's chest?" Bruneau's partner asked.

Shepard just shook his head. "Another task I was asked to complete. Don't ask me why, man. I'm not the idea guy, here."

"And you've never met Ivy before," Bruneau said.

"I think she was the bitch who drove her knee into my back," Shepard said, rubbing his back with his free hand. Ivy couldn't help but smile. "But before that, no."

"Did your contact ever try to speak with you in person? Any contact other than the phone or by mail?"

Shepard huffed. "He was adamant about not leaving a

trace. No emails, always used a burner phone. Or said he did. I'm sure you'll check. But he didn't strike me as careless. He doesn't want to be found."

"Or you're just making him up to take the blame off yourself," Bruneau said.

"And what would be the point of me kidnapping an old woman and a couple of kids if I wasn't getting paid for it?"

"I can think of a few reasons," Bruneau's partner said.

"Hey, fuck you," Shepard replied. "That's not my deal. I sure as shit wouldn't have gone to all that trouble for nothing. Check my bank account, notice any large deposits? You think I made those on my own?"

Bruneau stood, gathering his things. "One way or another, we'll find out."

"Hey, you said if I cooperated, it'd make things easier, right?" Shepard asked. "Right?"

Bruneau and his partner left the room, and Shepard flopped back against his chair, defeated.

"They'll take a few more runs at him," Portnoy said, flipping the audio back off. "Don't worry, they won't give up that easy."

"Thanks," Ivy said, but her mind was whirling with all the possibilities. If Shepard was telling the truth, who could have hired him? Not Kieran Woodward, that much was for certain. Who else knew enough about Ivy to know her real name?

She motioned for Jonathan to follow her back out into the hallway. "I need to speak to Kieran again."

"You think Sheriff Connors is going to let you anywhere near his department again?"

"I have to know if Shepard is telling the truth. Kieran is the only one who can confirm his story. If there really is someone else behind the scenes..." She trailed off. Whoever this person was, it seemed like they knew exactly what happened to her family. She still didn't understand why Mrs. Baker was involved, though. Why take her and torture her?

Shepard didn't seem to know. But if Kieran knew Shepard, maybe he knew the identity of this other mystery person.

Jonathan's face fell. "I didn't want to tell you this until later, but I saw an update come through on Woodward. He's fully comatose. What happened in there between you two?"

"Fully comatose?" Ivy asked.

Jonathan nodded. "They have him on life support, keeping his body from shutting itself down. But he's not awake. It's like his brain just…switched off."

"*Dammit,*" she said. She must have pushed him too far. She'd need to take a closer look at the reports to make sure. "So what am I supposed to do?"

"Hope Shepard remembers something? Or that Bruneau's CSI team comes up with something at his house? Something that traces back to this mastermind." He took a deep breath. "Maybe it's a good thing you'll be on desk duty for a while."

She turned to him. "Why is that?"

"Because it seems someone out there is hunting for you."

Chapter Thirty-Two

"THE GOOD NEWS IS, both girls seem fine physically," Nat said, reading off the report on her computer. "Whatever Shepard did to Baker, it didn't extend to the girls. It looks like they were nothing more than collateral damage…hostages in the event he needed them. Baker was the real target."

Ivy sat across from her, having spent the past two days on desk duty. She'd already grown bored with the assignment but had to admit it was better than being fired. Armstrong and Nat had *amended* the case record to show Ivy had been working the case all along, something which had infuriated Bruneau. She'd also received the commendation from the mayor, which had culminated in a handshake Ivy'd endured, but had found not as bad as she'd anticipated. She figured all of it had been to prevent another scandal on Armstrong's watch and save face with the mayor. "What about their adoption status?" she asked. "What will happen to them?"

"Social services will work to find another home, though it might not be here in Oakhurst. With all the press surrounding this case, a couple of crazies are sure to come out of the woodwork, looking for an easy meal ticket. Moving them to another part of the state might be the safest thing for them."

"But they'll be kept together?" Ivy asked.

"As far as I know, yes. After what they've endured, the state doesn't want to inflict any more trauma on them. Speaking of which." She reached into her desk and pulled out another file. "Initial reports from the psychiatrist we have working with them hasn't provided much information. They didn't hear or see much. From their reports, they were kept in one of the basement rooms and fed intermittently. They could hear Mrs. Baker screaming, but other than that, they didn't see or hear anything else useful. Certainly nothing about this mystery person."

Ivy shook her head. "I hate they had to endure that. It's going to be with them the rest of their lives."

"More than likely, yes. Also Burns's team came back with very little. It was as Shepard said, all the communication was one way. We're still working to trace any phone calls made to his cell and pull anything we can from the physical evidence, but it's not looking good. Whoever this mystery person is, they know what they're doing."

"Why target Mrs. Baker, though?" Ivy asked. "What do they think she knew? If someone were coming after me, wouldn't they go after Aunt Carol instead? Or someone I've actually spoken to in the past ten years?"

"Who knows why criminals do what they do," Nat said. "We still can't verify there even *is* a third person. Shepard could be making it all up. This third person story could all be nothing more than Shepard attempting to shift the blame away from himself. Maybe he gets his rocks off by torturing old ladies. He's not the most appealing of people."

"That still doesn't explain why he had my name, or why he carved it into her chest."

"Who knows what happened in that basement?" Nat said. "Maybe Mrs. Baker called out your name, or even tried threatening him, knowing you were a cop. And maybe he didn't like that. Maybe he carved your name to both torture and humiliate her at the same time. The point is, we have him now, and until some actual evidence shows up that can corroborate his 'story' about some separate, shadowy architect, I'm satisfied in believing he was behind it and that he helped set Kieran Woodward on our town."

Ivy had to admit, Shepard's story about a mysterious third party was flimsy, and if this case hadn't involved her personally, she probably wouldn't have put any stock in it at all.

Something about all this still felt off, but Nat was right. Until there was evidence to back it up, there was little they could do.

"There's another matter," Nat said, causing Ivy to look back up. "Your car."

"I'm sure it's in a hundred different parts, all being shipped out of Three Rivers by now," Ivy said.

"More than likely. But I managed to procure you a replacement."

Ivy perked up. This was unexpected.

Nat tossed a pair of keys across the desk. "It's not a Corvette, but it's better than nothing. You can't keep taking the bus even if you are just on desk duty for now."

"Wait a second," Ivy said. "Does Armstrong know about this?"

"Does he need to?" Nat asked.

Ivy couldn't help but grin. Not at the fact that Nat had procured a car for her, but because for the first time in months, maybe even years, she finally felt like she and Nat were back on the same page. A page that had been sorely blank for a long time. "Thanks. You didn't have to do that."

"I know. But I figured I owed you. You were right, I should have trusted you enough to put you on the case. Maybe if I had, all of this could have been avoided." She smiled at Ivy. "But I won't be making that mistake again."

Ivy took the keys. They were simple, without modern key fobs. That was promising.

"I'll let you know if there's any update on Shepard. Until then, keep on the desk until Armstrong calms down. You know how he is. In a few days, something else will distract him and he'll move on."

Ivy couldn't quite believe it. Maybe she should just let it all go and move on. Woodward was out of the picture; Shepard was off the streets. She'd done her job and it had almost cost her everything. Maybe it was time to take a rest, stop pushing so hard. After all, a lot had changed in a small amount of time. Ivy still needed time to adjust.

Ivy ignored the suspicious feeling in her gut that wouldn't go away. She stood. "Thanks again."

"You're welcome, Detective," Nat said. "And if it's not too premature, welcome back."

Ivy left the office feeling better than she had in months. When she saw Jonathan shooting her worried glances, she reassured him everything was fine and even managed to convince him to come outside to see her new ride.

"C'mon, it *has* to be a police auction car," Jonathan said as they descended the stairs.

"Doesn't mean it can't be nice. The Corvette was an auction car."

"I wouldn't have called that car nice," he replied.

She gave him a quick sneer. "Very funny." As they reached the parking lot, the sun had come out, warming up the air.

"Okay, which one is it?" he asked.

Ivy scanned the parking lot. It was mostly patrol cars and the vehicles of people who worked there. It wasn't like she could press a button on the keys and find out. But then her eyes landed on one car that looked out of place, considering it was about twenty years older than anything else in the lot.

"Oh man," Ivy said, walking up to it. "A silver 1984 Nissan Fairlady Z." And it looked to be in pretty good condition.

"*That* thing?" Jonathan asked. "It looks like a piece of junk."

"Yeah," she replied, fitting the key in the door and unlocking it. "It's perfect." She shot him a glance. "Wanna take it for a spin?"

"With you at the wheel? No thanks," he laughed.

"Aw, c'mon ya big baby."

Jonathan pulled his lips between his teeth before blowing out a long breath. "Okay, fine. But try to keep it under a hundred."

"You know me," Ivy said, slipping into the driver's seat and gripping the wheel. "No promises."

Epilogue

NAT SAT AT HER DESK, drumming her fingers on the wood. It
was half past seven, but Wright and some of the others were
still somewhere in the office. She usually didn't stay this late,
but all this business with Shepard had everyone working over-
time. Despite the fact she wasn't alone, Nat decided she
needed to risk it.

She stood, going over to her door and locking it from the
inside. Then she returned to one of the many cabinets in her
room, pulled out a set of keys, and opened the top drawer.
She pushed all of the files aside, revealing a false bottom. Nat
pushed on the back of the lid and the top popped up, uncovering stacks and stacks of pages. She reached in, yanking them
all out at once. She needed to go back over everything she'd
collected, everything from the past fifteen years. She didn't
have a lot of time on her hands. There was no telling when
something might happen with Ivy that could endanger
everything.

Nat took the stack to her desk and began flipping through
the top few pages, transcripts of her conversations with Mrs.
Baker, right up until the night she'd been kidnapped. She had
been in regular contact with the woman ever since Ivy had

come to see her, but Baker had insisted nothing seemed out of the ordinary with Ivy. Still, Nat hadn't quite believed her. Baker had always seemed to have a good bead on Ivy, and even though they hadn't seen each other in years, Nat felt like Baker hadn't been telling her the truth about her encounter with Ivy when she came to investigate Woodward a few weeks ago. Even more infuriatingly, Baker seemed determined to lie to her about it.

But now, it seemed there was nothing else she could do. The woman was dead. And Nat would just have to move on.

How she didn't break under Shepard's torture, Nat didn't know.

Then again, maybe she did. Maybe she told Shepard everything she knew. But if that was the case, why was Shepard keeping quiet? She'd gone over all of Bruneau's interview tapes; he seemed adamant that he didn't know a thing about Ivy. Surely by now he would have made a deal? After all, wasn't that the kind of person he purported himself to be?

A knock on Nat's door startled her so much she jumped. She quickly gathered all the documents back up and slipped it all back into the cabinet, shutting and locking it.

"Wright, is that you?" she asked, pocketing the keys.

"Not exactly," came a sultry voice from the other side. Nat screwed up her face before unlocking the door to reveal Alice Blair standing on the other side, a snide smile on her face. "Evening, Lieutenant."

"What are you doing here?" Nat asked. "How did you even get in the precinct?"

"Oh, I have my ways. Aren't you going to invite me in?" Nat stepped aside to allow Alice into her office. "My. Quite the packrat I see."

"Just what the hell do you want, Blair?" Nat asked. "I'm busy here."

"I had a couple of questions," Alice said, perching her

rear against Nat's desk and crossing her arms. "About Detective Bishop."

Nat glared at her before closing the door again. "I don't have time to make a statement to the press. Detective Bishop is back on active duty."

"And the rumors floating around saying she was a suspect?"

"Completely false," Nat said, rounding the desk and taking a seat.

Alice scoffed, her gaze following Nat. "You're not a bad liar, but at least now I know your tells. So when I ask you the real question, I'll know if you're being honest or not."

"And what's the real question?" Nat asked.

Alice only smiled. "What really happened to Ivy's family? And why did you cover it up?"

To Be Continued...

Want to read more about Ivy?

IN THE QUIET COMMUNITY OF OAKHURST, THE BRUTAL MURDER of a beloved local priest sends shockwaves through the town. Detective Ivy Bishop, coming off two of the toughest cases of her career, is thrust into an investigation that seems straightforward but quickly unravels into something far more sinister.

As Ivy delves into the priest's life, she uncovers hidden connections to an underground crime network operating right under the town's nose. The deeper she digs, the more she realizes that the priest's death is just the tip of the iceberg. The investigation twists and turns, revealing secrets that Oakhurst's elite would kill to keep buried.

Each clue leads Ivy closer to the heart of something far darker than the shadows of an empty church, exposing a web of corruption, betrayal, and greed that extends to the highest echelons of society. As she navigates this treacherous terrain, Ivy finds herself confronting the darkest aspects of humanity.

With stakes higher than ever, Ivy must untangle the intricate conspiracy before it claims more lives, including her own.

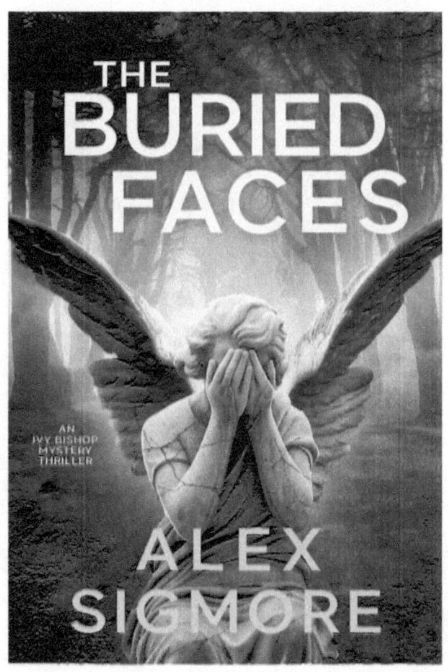

To get your copy of THE BURIED FACES, CLICK HERE or scan the code below with your phone.

FREE book offer!
Where did it all begin for Ivy?

I HOPE YOU ENJOYED *THE GIRL WITHOUT A CLUE*. IF YOU'D like to learn more about Ivy's backstory and how she became a detective, including how she originally met Jonathan, then you're in luck! *Bishop's Edge* introduces Ivy and tells the story of the case that both put her career on the line *and* catapulted her into the VC Unit.

Interested? CLICK HERE to get your free copy now!

Not Available Anywhere Else!

You'll also be the first to know when each new book in Ivy's series becomes available!

CLICK HERE or scan the code below to download for FREE!

A Note from Alex

Dear reader,

I can't tell you how exciting it is following along with Ivy's adventures. We're only two books in and there have been some major revelations! One of my goals with this series was to make it similar to *Emily Slate's* series without being a direct copy and I am so pleased with how it's turning out. Ivy has a complicated past and is such a fun character.

As always, thank you for joining me on this journey. Whether you're new here, or have been following along from book one of my debut series, I want to thank you from the bottom of my heart for continuing to support me. As I've always said, *you* are the reason I write!

Because I'm still a relatively new writer with a growing following, I ask that if you enjoyed this book, please leave a review or recommend to your friends. Writing is my passion and I want to continue to bring you many more Ivy Bishop books in the future!

Thank you for being a loyal reader,
Alex

The Ivy Bishop Mystery Thriller Series

Free Prequel - Bishop's Edge (Ivy Bishop Bonus Story)

Her Dark Secret - (Ivy Bishop Series Book One)

The Girl Without a Clue - (Ivy Bishop Series Book Two)

The Buried Faces - (Ivy Bishop Series Book Three)

Her Hidden Lies - (Ivy Bishop Series Book Four)

One Dark Night - (Ivy Bishop Series Book Five)

The Emily Slate FBI Mystery Series

Free Prequel - Her Last Shot (Emily Slate Bonus Story)

His Perfect Crime - (Emily Slate Series Book One)

The Collection Girls - (Emily Slate Series Book Two)

Smoke and Ashes - (Emily Slate Series Book Three)

Her Final Words - (Emily Slate Series Book Four)

Can't Miss Her - (Emily Slate Series Book Five)

The Lost Daughter - (Emily Slate Series Book Six)

The Secret Seven - (Emily Slate Series Book Seven)

A Liar's Grave - (Emily Slate Series Book Eight)

Oh What Fun - (Emily Slate Series Holiday Special)

The Girl in the Wall - (Emily Slate Series Book Nine)

His Final Act - (Emily Slate Series Book Ten)

The Vanishing Eyes - (Emily Slate Series Book Eleven)

Edge of the Woods - (Emily Slate Series Book Twelve)

Ties That Bind - (Emily Slate Series Book Thirteen)

The Missing Bones - (Emily Slate Series Book Fourteen)

Blood in the Sand - (Emily Slate Series Book Fifteen)

The Passage - (Emily Slate Series Book Sixteen)

Fire in the Sky - (Emily Slate Series Book Seventeen)

The Killing Jar - (Emily Slate Series Book Eighteen)

The Oak Creek Mystery Series

The Darkest Game

Never Strike Twice

Standalone Psychological Thrillers

The Forgotten Wife